THE AMERICAN MAIN

Volume Three of *The Continental Divide*

Alanson Rand

ROSE ISLAND

Acknowledgments

Special thanks to Joey Clark, Debbie Witt, and Cathy Rathbun for pointing out when I was making no sense.

Copyright 2016, 2021 Alanson Rand
Cover art and design copyright 2016 Timothy Stead
Editor: Timothy Stead

ISBN (print edition): 978-1-946843-05-0

Also by Alanson Rand:

<u>The Continental Divide</u>
Waking in Ruins
Anarchista
The American Main
Wednesday's Children
Eighteen Hells
The Year of Endings

<u>A Drive with Auntie (coming 2021)</u>
East to Eden
The Shores of Distant Time

KEY FIGURES IN THE REVOLUTION OF 2043

Victoria Lang MD, a former director of Chalys Pharmaceuticals
Ada Lang, her daughter
Mae Esteban, MD, the former Surgeon General of the United States

Krista Warner, author of *The Rake*
Arista Molle, a television journalist
Jackson Falling Knife Ripley, a former stained-glass artist
Elise Ripley, his wife

Rear Admiral Adam Harris, Commander, Submarine Force, US Pacific Fleet
Captain Juliette Bricker, Commander, USS *Patrick Henry*
Commander Ennis Quinn, Executive Officer, USS *Patrick Henry*
Lt. Commander Tala Ripley, Strategic Warfare Officer, USS *Patrick Henry*

William Gibbon, President of the United States
Gabriel Cheyn, Vice President of the United States
Marcus Grimes, Gabriel Cheyn's Chief of Staff
Noah Hayborn, Speaker of the House

National Security Forces
Bob Downs, Watcher
Raphael Vinola, Deputy Watcher
Philip Cochon, Day Chief – Intelligence
Ari Stein, Night Chief – Intelligence
Hideki Buta, Day Chief – Acquisition
Ryan Beckmann, Night Chief – Acquisition
Sara Hogue, Day Chief – Tactical Operations
Tom Riddick, Night Chief – Tactical Operations
Peter Mochyn, Day Chief – Cybermeasures

A SUDDEN STOP

Day 37
Thursday morning, September 24, 2043
West Atherton, Indiana

Krista and Ada sat side by side in the dry grass a safe distance from the burning Hugo. "Told you it had airbags," Ada said.

"You shouldn't blame yourself. You were doing fine till you ran into it. I didn't see the feckin thing at all."

"It was as big as a…well, big as a tree, for god's sake." She pounded her fists on her knees. "I told you this would happen. You can't trust me behind the wheel."

"This is pea-soup fug, Ada. That's why you didn't see the tree, and that's all there is to it. Stop talking yourself into being a crappy driver. And it would help if you stopped holding the feckin wheel like a life ring from the *Titanic*."

"I couldn't drive a nail into a bucket of water," Ada grumbled. *"That's all there is to it."*

"Oh, stop bashing yourself. That's my job." Krista looked at the Hugo thirty feet away. Ada had hit the tree at full speed: The windshield now touched the tree trunk, headlights peeked around both sides, and blue flames licked out from under the buckled hood.

The flames reached the gas tank and the little car exploded, shaking the grass and showering them with dead leaves. The airbags blossomed into pink balls of fire, releasing a cloud of sparkling greenish motes that floated into the bare branches above.

"Ooh," Krista said.

"Ahh," Ada said, flicking leaves off her legs. "So. Alternatives?"

"We'll steal another car, that's all. If there isn't one around here, we'll walk to the next town and find one."

"Yeah, except I can't walk far in these freakin boots."

"I guess they're uncomfortable?"

"God, yes. They're made for standing around in, not walking. I'll be sore all over if I try to walk five or ten miles in these things."

"So take them off and walk in your socks," Krista said.

"I can't." Ada scowled and pounded her knees again. "I left my socks in the motel room. I'm an idiot."

"You're not an idiot. I left my panties back there, and believe me, I'm feeling it."

"No bra, no panties, and you say you're not a slut."

"Hey, I'm not the one who snogged Deputy Galahan. You practically sucked the tonsils out of his throat, for chrissakes!"

Ada smiled and leaned back in the grass. "He doesn't have tonsils, kid."

"Kid!"

"Deputy Galahan." Ada sighed and gazed softly into the dark fug. She rolled her hips trying to make herself comfortable, and then she crossed her legs, snorted, and uncrossed them again. "Ahh, crap. I'll be buffin the muffin about that for the rest of my life. I'm so horny, I'll have to read a dozen British romances to get my sex drive back to normal."

"I still can't believe you jumped him like that."

"What can I say? I just wasn't feeling manxious." She stood and brushed the dirt from her jeans. "I'll try walking to the next town, but I can't boost another car without tools."

Krista snapped her fingers. "Oh, about that. I meant to tell you. Roger has a woodshop out in the garage. It's a tool candyland. You should take a look."

"Yeah? That's good. Maybe he has –" She cocked her head and listened to a distant sound. "Do you hear a drone?"

"Coming from up north. We'd better get inside fast."

They ran through the front door, locked it, and then turned off the living room lights and stood in the kitchen, far from the windows. A few minutes later, the drone passed overhead.

"They're looking for us again, just like in Columbus," Krista said after the thrumming faded. "They're not giving up."

"Nope. They won't stop till they get us." Ada turned on the kitchen lights and mixed two glasses of the baby food drink. "We only have three cans of this stuff left."

"I'm getting sick of it anyway," Krista said. She downed the glass in one gulp. "But it's better than starving to death."

"And it tasted so good last night." Ada grimaced as she emptied her glass, and then she set it on the counter and picked up her tablet. "4:24 AM. If we have to walk, it'll be tough staying out of the drone's sights even if we time them. There's nothing but empty fields out there. We'll have to run like hell after they pass over and hope we can hide when they come back." She rinsed her glass and walked to the garage door. "Unless we can find another car. Since I wrecked the Hugo, it's my job to get us another one. I'll see if Roger left anything behind I can use." The door clicked shut behind her.

Krista poured another shake into her glass and sipped; the taste was terrible and getting worse with each gulp. She finished the drink and walked into the garage, where Ada was checking out the tools on the pegboard walls.

"This is great! Roger has everything!" She laid a handful of pliers on a large wooden table, and then she plucked a sharp, wood-handled tool from the wall and slid it into her boot. "Hey, this fits perfectly in here!"

"What's that?"

"It's like an ice pick or an awl." She slid it in and out a few times. "Basic equipment for a *femme fatale!*"

"I'm sorry I even brought that up. You're going to get carried away, I know it." Krista walked around the garage and pawed through the items on the shelves. "Tools will come in handy if we can find a car, but we'll never find one if we don't make ourselves invisible to the drone's radar rays."

"Radar *waves*. Radar units emit an electromagnetic wave, not a particle."

"Whatever," Krista said.

"Oh, don't give me that 'whatever' stuff. You're so superstitious cuz you don't understand how the universe works. People fear what they don't understand. That's why you're afraid of everything."

"Everybody's shooting at me. Understanding how a gun works won't make it harmless, for chrissakes," Krista said, looking into a box she'd pulled down from a shelf. "I've got plenty of reasons to be afraid of the world right now."

"Whatever."

"God, you're annoying." She pulled out a thin silver blanket and held it up. "Would these reflect the radar waves?"

Ada rubbed a corner of it between her fingers. "This could be useful. It's a survival blanket with an aluminum film. If a drone comes over, we can open that up and climb under it. Are there any more?"

She pulled out another and dropped it on the table. "Ask and ye shall receive, kiddo."

Ada pulled a small zippered pouch from another shelf, opened it, and smiled. "I always wanted a real lock pick set! I asked The Commander to get me one for Christmas, but she said I was dangerous enough without it."

"Yeah? Well, right now you need to get as dangerous as you can. Merry Christmas!"

THE ROAD TO REVENGE

Day 37
Thursday evening, September 24, 2043
West Atherton, Indiana

They finished packing their bags just before sunset. Jamming in the last two cans of baby food was difficult, but they managed with a little effort and abundant swearing.

Ada wrapped her feet in soft towels she found in the shop, slipped on her boots, and then unzipped the straps on her bookbag to turn it into a backpack. She put it on and slung the shotgun over her shoulder, and Krista picked up her pack and the briefcase. They checked their gear and their tablets, and with the silver blankets wrapped around their necks, they headed for the door.

BY THE TIME THE DRONE RETURNED, they were walking alongside the road leading north. They ran into a grassy ditch and crawled under the blankets, and neither felt a tingle from the passing drone's radar.

The fug was even thicker tonight; in the moist bottomlands by the river, it became almost sentient, determined to climb into every orifice and pore. Krista couldn't see Ada, just an arm's length away, and she reached out and took her hand. They listened for engines, fearing they'd be surprised by a car running without lights or a predator lurking in the fug.

However, the road was silent. The only sounds they heard were the weak croaking of tree frogs by the river and the chirping of an unseen insect in the grass. Every so often, Ada clapped and startled them into silence.

"Keep an eye out for driveways," Krista said. "I wouldn't be counting on finding many, but we should check for cars or food if we see one. How long till we hit the next town?"

"Seven miles from when we got on the road. I'd say ninety-one minutes at this rate."

They became quiet again, as conversation prevented them from hearing cars and drones, and both listened intently to the world around them.

AN HOUR LATER, they found two stacks of wooden pallets beside the road, and they spread their blankets over the gap between them and sat inside. They drank another baby-food shake and rubbed their feet.

"I'm not used to walking this much," Krista said, rubbing her big toe. "And I'm wearing sneakers. Your feet must really hurt."

"It's not my feet that hurt. It's my shins." Ada massaged the front of her leg and winced. "I'm getting outta shape. God, even a Hugo would be welcome right now."

They sat in their makeshift tent and smoked while listening for approaching threats. When they finished, they started pulling down the blankets, but then Krista froze and laid her hand on Ada's shoulder.

"Get down," she hissed. Tires crunched across the gravel pavement, and they crawled behind the pallets and flattened their bodies into the stubble of harvested cornstalks. The sound grew closer, and then the cornstalks rustled as someone started walking toward the pallets.

"Cancha hold it five minutes?" a man asked from near the road. "Sundown don't like us out in the air widdat virus around."

"Just a minute." The light of a struck match set the fug aglow for a second, and then a splashing sound came from the other side of the pallets.

"Make it quick. C'mon, we can piss at da fort," the distant voice said.

"But Sundown don't like me smokin, and I'm gettin a smoke in before I get locked up in there agin," a deep voice said a few feet away. "No smokin, no drinkin. Fuck, some days I'd just rather suck in some virus and get it over with than listen to that ole man preach on."

"Yeah, you change your mind, you saw da way Nicole went, man. Dat was ugly."

The nearer voice groaned. "Ever'thin she did was ugly, no surprise she died ugly too. The Rock, it ate up her face, man. Think Sundown woulda took better care of his own niece." The splattering sound stopped and then started again. "Yo, nobody out here anyway, and you just catch it from folk. I'm okay."

"You done yet?"

"Finishin my smoke. Cool yer jets, Low Man."

"Just don't want Sundown gettin pissed we took so long wit da water. Dude watches ever'thin we do. C'mon, man, let's go." The footsteps headed away, and then a door slammed and the unseen vehicle roared up the road.

Krista waited, afraid that a trap awaited them, but then she heard the drone's wail again. They threw the blankets over the pallets and scurried beneath them. After the drone passed over, they stayed inside a few more minutes to be safe.

Ada lit a cigarette, the flame quivering in her shaking hands, and passed the lighter to Krista. They sat in the close, quiet dark for a minute.

"We've got to avoid them," Krista said. "They sounded rough."

"Yeah, and they're only five minutes up the road in some fort. We'll have to pass them sometime. We'll need to be quiet."

"A fort. It shouldn't be so hard to find one of them and walk around it." Krista laid her head back against the pallet. "I hate to ask this, but should we have just shot them and taken their truck?"

"They didn't do anything to us. That'd be murder. Besides that, we only have one shell left in the shotgun, and there were two of them."

Krista puffed out her cheeks and crushed her cigarette into the dirt, and then they pulled down their blankets and shouldered their gear. As they headed north again, the river pulled away to the west and a stand of trees lined the road.

They stood in a regular pattern like rows of soldiers, and the sweet-sour smell of rotting apples blew over them. The orchard hadn't been harvested; like its caretakers, it had been neglected and left to rot. Ada, starving as usual, climbed into a few trees but found only four apples that were still edible. Krista carved away the worm-eaten parts, determined not to find half a worm in her apple, but only a few mouthfuls remained when she was done.

They walked alongside the road listening for the sounds of a fort or a car, but the land was silent as death, and even the bugs weren't chirping. After a few more minutes, Ada walked into a wooden post, squawked, and rubbed her nose. She staggered back a few steps and read the quivering sign:

WELCOME TO ~~NORTH ATHERTON~~ REVENGE
POPULATION ~~81~~ 7

"This looks ominous," Ada said.
"This looks *frightening*," Krista said. "I'm getting a Black Dog feeling."
"Black Dog?"
"It's an eldritch feeling, like predation, evil, and despair all rolled into one. Something out there wants to waste us. We've got to be extra careful."

Ada grunted and squinted into the fug, but she could see nothing beyond the sign. "We oughta walk through this orchard and stay off the road for a while. You're right, there's no way to know what we're getting into."

Krista nodded, and they walked into the rows of trees and turned north. They needed to stoop to get under the low branches, and the going was slow, but the orchard seemed empty of lurking predators. After a few more minutes, they crossed through a final row, and a gravel embankment rose above them.

"Train tracks," Ada whispered, looking right and left down a dirt road that paralleled the embankment. "It looks clear." They scrambled up the slope of loose stone and found a pair of bright silver rails at the top. Ada laid her hand on one and shook her head. "No trains coming right now, but these get used regularly. Maybe we should wait for a train to come and hitch a ride. These tracks head west."

Krista peered down the tracks. "The river's thataway. The tracks would go over a bridge."

Ada kicked a piece of gravel with her toe and scowled. "Right. Cops might be watching it."

Krista squinted into the fug beyond the embankment and saw faint smudges in the distance. "I think I see lights ahead. Why don't we walk

The Road to Revenge

around the outside of town and see if we can find a car? If the place is as empty as the sign says, we should be safe."

They slid down the other side of the embankment and into more rows of apple trees. They were older on this side of the tracks and the branches were higher, so they made good time crossing through the litter of decaying apples and dry leaves. As in the other orchard, the long-dead harvesters hadn't taken the fruit, and it rotted overhead and underfoot.

The orchard seemed to have no end in the thick atmosphere, and each new row of trees that materialized from the fug was another depressing surprise. After a few more minutes, though, a bright spot grew in the fug ahead and their spirits lifted.

They ducked under their blankets as a drone zoomed over and then crept toward the light. The orchard opened into a clearing beyond the next row, and the light was in the middle of it.

"That's got to be a building," Krista said, peeking around a tree trunk. "The light looks like it's coming from behind something. Let's leave our stuff here and take a look."

"I'll take Mickey with us just in case," Ada said, and Krista shot her a nervous glance. "Don't worry. I'll stay next to you."

"That's why I'm worried. My ears are still ringing from the last time you fired that thing," Krista said. Ada held up the shotgun and let her watch as she flipped on the safety.

They crept from the shelter of the trees into a field of rutted dirt strewn with trash and rusted machinery. As they approached the light, the dark silhouette of a building took shape; the light emanated from somewhere beyond the building and spun a fuzzy halo around it. After a few more steps, they spotted the outline of a truck parked in the building's shadows. Ada tiptoed to the driver's side and opened the door. "This is boostable. I just need a few minutes," she whispered.

Krista nodded and crept to the front of the building; the light shone from the top of an old wooden building and over a broad concrete porch. A metal door stood in the center, flanked by narrow windows with faint light streaming from inside. She sidled along the wall to peek into them.

As she edged closer, she heard voices. She stopped, listened for a moment, and then crept back to the truck. Ada crouched near the front, and Krista motioned that they should return to the orchard. They weaved through the obstacle course in the field and rested against a tree trunk.

"All right, that place is on the road we were avoiding, so after we steal it, we've got a way out," Krista said. "The problem is that I heard people inside. Men, at least two of them."

"The engine's still warm, so it's been run recently. They might be the two we heard out in the fields." Ada frowned and looked at the shotgun. "And they were talking about someone else, so there's at least three in there."

"Right," Krista said, rubbing the bridge of her nose. "We should pass by this place. I get the feeling there's something really wrong here, that I do. This is a Black Dog horrorshow, kiddo."

"No, I think we can pull this off as long as we do it right," Ada said. "We'll put our stuff in the pickup, and I'll wire the ignition. You'll take the gun and shoot anyone who comes out. When I get the thing running, you come back and drive, and I'll jump into the back with the gun and cover our escape."

"You make that sound simple," Krista said, "and it's the simplest plans that get banjaxed beyond belief. And I'm not so sure I could shoot anyone even if I knew how to use a gun."

The Road to Revenge

"It's a twelve-gauge shotgun. You don't need to aim. They'll all drop the first time they hear the thing boom, anyway."

"Still, I don't know about this."

Ada sighed and grabbed her bookbag. "Yeah, you're right. This is a bad idea. Let's move on and find another car." Krista picked up her backpack and the briefcase, and they walked to the end of the clearing and into the orchard. Once there, they crossed the rows and continued north.

As they walked away from the light, the orchard fell into dark, fuggy shadow, and Ada raised her hands to avoid walking face-first into a tree. Seconds later, she felt an arm in front of her. "Look, I know it's hard to see, but could you watch where you're going?" she hissed.

"What did you say?" Krista's voice came from far away, and then Ada saw what she'd walked into. She stifled a shriek and staggered back until she bumped into a tree, and then she slid down into a crouch, shivering and staring at the thing dangling from the tree branch.

Krista stumbled through the leaves toward her voice. "Ada?" she whispered. "Are you okay? What happened?" She heard a noise ahead and moved toward it, and then her face bumped into something soft and rank. She took a step back and looked up, and in the faint light from the building, she saw the face of a man with a black tongue and bulging eyes leering at her from above. A rough rope looped over a high branch bit into his neck. The word 'UNCLEAN' was printed on a cardboard sign pinned to his shirt, and a pack of cigarettes was stuffed in his mouth.

She gasped and drew a breath to power a full scream, and then she bit down hard on a finger and backed away from the thing. Her foot rolled over an apple, and she lost her balance and fell to the ground in a heap.

"Ada?" she croaked, and an answering groan came from ahead. Krista crawled toward the sound, making a wide circle around the hanging man, and soon found her shaking at the base of the tree.

"Are you okay?" Krista asked, and Ada clutched Krista's chest.

"I walked into it," she whispered. "I *touched* it."

"So did I," Krista said, glancing at the dangling figure. "Omigod, that's gross."

"Someone hanged him. This is a bad place, and the people in there are bad people."

Krista held her tight and rubbed her back. "I know. We've got to get out of this funhouse. Something horrific lives here, something that snacks on life or something."

Ada nodded and shivered, and they sat for a few minutes until they could think clearly. "I can't walk another step into this orchard, not with these things hanging around. Let's steal the truck and blow the hell outta here. And if anyone comes out of that shack, shoot the bastard."

"I don't have a problem with that now," Krista said. "Whoever's in that building isn't innocent anymore. This was just a lynching. I'm not sure when being 'unclean' became a capital offense, unless someone in there's making up their own rules."

"I'll bet they're Aluminati. Arkies hate anything dirty – dirty thoughts, dirty habits, dirty talk, it's all the same to them, but the Aluminati are even worse," Ada said, looking up at Krista. "They'll kill you just for being dirty. They're really out there, deep-space, like wearing tin-foil hats and everything. They have serious OCD about cleanliness."

"I guess I don't care about why they hanged this guy as much as whether they hang me. We need to work this out so we don't end up in their hands."

The drone sounded again in the north, and they unfolded their blankets. After it passed, they discussed Ada's plan.

"We have to be quiet and surprise them," Ada said. "They won't be able to chase us if we jump the thing quick and burn rubber. They might not even have guns. Maybe that's why they hanged that guy instead of shooting him."

"Let's hope so," Krista said. "Let's hope they didn't do it just to be cruel."

They dithered for a few more minutes until it was obvious they were stalling, and then they crawled into the clearing. After weaving through the debris to the truck, they dropped their gear on the passenger seat.

Ada flipped the shotgun's safety off and handed it to Krista, and then she shimmied under the dashboard.

ADA PULLED A BUNDLE OF WIRES from behind the dash. She turned on her flashlight, covering most of the beam with her body, and searched for the correct wires to cross.

She'd just found the battery wire and was looking for the ignition when she heard a creak from the back of the building. Footsteps approached, and she curled up in the footwell and closed the door quietly. The footsteps stopped and splashing began. The man whistled tunelessly as he attended to his toilet, and then the footsteps clopped to the back of the building and the unseen door.

A train horn honked nearby. Hoping the racket would mask the sound of her movements or the sound of a starting truck, she opened the door, dangled her legs out, and reached under the dash again.

Then strong hands grabbed her legs. She tried to scream, but they clamped over her mouth and lifted her out of the truck.

KRISTA STOOD BY THE FIRST WINDOW and listened for the truck's starter. A train horn blared, and she struggled to hear what was going on inside. She crept forward and peeked through the window but saw nothing.

Ada had said it should take three minutes to start the truck, and it had been longer than that. She didn't want to leave the front door uncovered, though, so she backed toward the steps while keeping the shotgun aimed at the entrance. "Ada!" she hissed. "How long is this gonna take?" Ada didn't answer, and she hissed again and glanced over her shoulder.

The door to the truck was closed. She ran to it and looked inside, and then she searched the yard around it, but she found nothing. Ada was gone.

GAZING UPON HEAVEN

The man kicked open the back door and dragged Ada into a large, dimly lit room with yellowed walls and no ceiling. A sign over the front door said N. ATHERTON GRANGE NO. 722. Sleeping bags were piled on both sides of the door, and dirty faces peeked from them. "The fuck, Girly Boy? We was sleepin…the hell is this?"

The man behind her growled, "Found this tryin to steal our truck." It was the same voice she'd heard out in the field. Another man, as thin and small as a malnourished boy, flicked a light switch and more bulbs lit near the ceiling.

The men stood slowly, blinking in the bright light and running their fingers through greasy hair. A fleshy man in a stained T-shirt waddled from behind a stack of boxes with MEAL, READY TO EAT, INDIVIDUAL printed on the side.

"Look what we caught, Chunk," the boy-man said, and the fat man smiled.

"Good job, Low Man. Go get Sundown. He's in da back room." Chunk leered at Ada. "He gonna wanna see this."

One man who'd been sleeping walked over, pulling up his pants. He was short but had the physique of someone who worked out ten times a day, with arms as thick as Ada's thigh. "Could use me one a these, Girly Boy," he said with a gap-toothed smile, and the arm around her chest pulled her away.

"Back off, Hackle," Girly Boy said. "This is Sundown's props."

Over by the crate, Chunk nodded. "You don't wanna be crossing Sundown on this. You just go sit down and wait your damn turn like ever'body else." Hackle stomped to the door like an angry fireplug and sat on his sleeping bag cross-legged. He picked up a small red rubber ball and tossed it from hand to hand as he stared at her breasts.

Chunk reached into a box, pulled out a coarse rope, and reached for her wrists. She tried to wriggle away, but Girly Boy's arm tightened and pulled her off the floor. Chunk started tying her hands, but she thrashed so much that he couldn't tie her wrists closer than a foot together. After a few minutes of trying to tighten her bonds, he gave up. "This'll be good 'nuff," he said. "Gonna have to take this off anyway, once she goes down on her back."

She struggled against the arm holding her, but it tightened around her chest again, clamping her so hard that she could only draw shallow breaths. Her heart thudded, and with each beat, panic swelled higher. She tried to remember her mother's advice on how to stop these spirals, but she couldn't and panicked even more, knowing there'd be no patch to soothe her, no Krista to cry on, no way out – it was one girl against six men, and those were odds even she couldn't beat. She drew as much air into her constricted chest as she could and shrieked, and then a stinking hand covered her mouth.

From behind her, a door creaked and footsteps approached. "Peace, Girly Boy," a smooth voice said, and the arm dropped from her chest. She rubbed her ribs and turned to see who had spoken.

"I am called Sundown," said a tall, thin man in a long nightshirt that covered his knees. His eyelids drooped, and his face was wrinkled and spotted, as were his veined hands. He was hairless above the jawline, but a wiry gray beard dangled beneath it that brushed his chest. His cold blue eyes roved over her, up and down and into every fold and nook, and she shivered.

He stepped forward and sniffed her hair. Hackle handed him a flashlight and grabbed her arms, and Sundown pulled open her mouth and ran his fingers over her clenched teeth. "It partakes of lungweed," he said as if describing the anatomy of an insect, "but no matter. It will be unclean no more in our house." He pulled up the sleeves of her blouse and smiled when he saw the vaccination target on her arm. "It is good," he said. "What are you called?" he asked, and Ada clamped her teeth together again. His expression softened, and he rested a bony hand on her shoulder.

"Hands off, you fascist fuckstick!"

"It is all right, child. You have been named, have you not?"

"Bertha," she spat.

Sundown smiled. "The Old German name for a bright girl. Hmm…Bertha…a berth." He smiled even wider, revealing a row of stubby yellow teeth. "A berth for the ship sailing the sheets of night. Yes, a fitting name." The smile faded from his face and leaned forward until his nose was almost touching hers. "Are you a virgin, child?"

She spat in his eye. "You vile piece of shit!"

Sundown wiped the spittle away and smiled again, but this time it was empty of warmth. "Did you know that the letters in 'vile' also spell 'live'? They are mirrors of the same reality – to be vile is to live, and to live, one must simultaneously be vile. I find that fascinating." He turned to the line of men behind him.

"Brothers!" he bellowed in a pulpit voice. "Many of you have doubted our destiny although you have not voiced this. Yet I know these doubts, for once I felt them when I was unclean, when I built my church on the Rock of Base-M. To be summoned to God's mission challenges belief: Have I really been called? Have I really been chosen? These doubts erode our faith and certainty, but that makes us human." He raised his hands to the ceiling and looked up. "But it is transcending these doubts that makes us divine!"

He lowered his arms and pointed at each man in turn, who bowed their heads. "When Nicole passed this week, I saw in your eyes and your hearts that you doubted our mission. You doubted we could sustain the strength of our seed in this time of the Chrysalis, and thus you doubted the Chrysalis itself. And so I prayed to Jesus and his son The Profit Joseph to deliver unto us a sign and strengthen your resolve, so when we emerge from the Chrysalis, we can repopulate this battered Eden in our image and fulfill the destiny set for us by the Lord God himself!"

He paced in front of them with his hands behind his back. "I alone prayed for the return of our sustenance – and my prayers were answered! He gives us this day our daily bread!" he cried, and he pointed at Ada. "A virgin pure and vaccinated! We will suffer the disappointment of Nicole no more!"

He pushed her backward, and she stumbled and fell, knocking her head against the wood floor. A buzzing sound reverberated in her skull. "You shall *lay* on your back and *gaze* upon heaven!" Sundown cried, raising his arms and wiggling his hands like they'd gone numb. The men cheered and surged forward, but Sundown gave a brief shout of warning and stopped them. One by one, they fell to their knees.

"My brothers, it will be a virgin for only one. Be at peace, for it is I who will choose as leader of the Chrysalis." The men grumbled but stayed on their knees. "Thus it shall be: Girly Boy found it, so shall he tame it."

A thin voice piped up next to Ada. "Sundown, I was –"

Sundown patted the man's shoulder. "Low Man, perhaps you misunderstand the meaning of your proud name." He motioned the men into a circle. "Brothers, before we receive this sacrament, we must pray and raise our thanks on high for this blessing."

The men gathered around him except for Low Man, who stood by her feet, and Hackle, who knelt by her side and leaned toward her. "Get used to the view, darlin, cuz that's all you're gonna be seein. Long as you can take it, that is. We wore out Nicole in two weeks." He turned to where the men congregated and closed his eyes, and after a few seconds, he began to mouth the same prayer they were chanting.

She looked for a way out, but the front door was bolted and the back door was thirty feet away. She'd get caught long before she reached it.

However, Hackle was deep in prayer, and Low Man still had his back turned to her; she could take Low Man hostage and bargain her way out if she killed Hackle first. But her chances of succeeding were minuscule, and she'd probably die if she tried.

She looked at the kneeling men and realized that living scared her more than dying. She slid her hands down to her boot, pulled out the awl, and turned it over in her hand. The blade was only three inches long, but it would kill Hackle if she jabbed it under his third rib and nicked the pulmonary artery. He was muscular but also small, so the blade might reach his artery.

She felt the sharp tip with her finger and also felt the end of her life; she blinked a few times, stunned to realize she was breathing her last breaths. *Life blows. It's been a fifteen-year shitshow, and of course it all ends with me getting fucked to death,* she thought as she turned the awl with the blade sticking out of her fist. *I'm not gonna be some Prayboy Bunny. If I've gotta die, it's gonna be fast.*

Soundlessly, she pulled her feet beneath her – and then she lunged at Hackle, pulling her knife hand forward and up with all her strength. The awl plunged into his back next to the spine, and he arched backward. She tried to pull it out, but his muscles had locked the blade in place.

She jumped behind Low Man and looped the rope connecting her wrists around his neck, pulling back hard. He grunted and tried to twist away, but she jammed a knee into his back and yanked the rope. His hands fluttered, reaching for his neck, and he stomped his foot on the floor. The men in the circle turned.

Hopping on one foot, she pulled Low Man by the neck until her back touched the wall. She started edging to the door, but Girly Boy blocked her way.

"Back off or I'll strangle him!" she yelled, and she pulled the rope tighter. Low Man gurgled and strained, but his movements slowed and weakened the more she pulled.

Sundown approached her, his cold eyes sparkling with amusement. "Kill him. We are seven and have food for only seven. If you want to eat, he must die."

"I'll do it! Lemme go and you can have him back!"

"I intended to hang him tomorrow," he said with a wave of his hand. "Free your passions, Bertha. Enhance your life by taking Low Man's."

"Take it," the men behind him chanted. *"Take it, take it, take it…"*

Ada edged to her right, but Girly Boy refused to move. "You guys are fuckin nuts."

"No, Bertha," Sundown said. "We are survivors."

Ada sensed Girly Boy's movement in her peripheral vision. Something black whirled at her, and at the last moment, she saw Girly Boy's boot connect with Low Man's nose. His head snapped back and hit hers, thumping her head against the hard wall. Her brain buzzed again, and then her hands lost their grip and she slid down the wall.

KRISTA CREPT ALONGSIDE THE BUILDING. Ada wasn't hiding in the clearing and hadn't run back to the orchard; the only way she could vanish so fast was if she'd gone inside. She hadn't used the front door, so there had to be another entrance in back.

She sidled to the end of the wall and listened, but it was quiet around the corner. Praying not to trip over the trash littering the yard, she raised the shotgun and slid along the back wall, feeling with her right hand. After

Gazing upon Heaven

a minute, she touched a doorknob and wrapped her fingers around it – and then froze.

She didn't know what had happened; Ada might have been invited inside or might have been captured. However, if she was a prisoner, she couldn't just bust into the place. There were at least three people in there, and she only had one shell in the gun.

With the shotgun ready at her shoulder, she scurried back to the front porch and edged up to the window. She heard the faint sound of many voices inside and peeked around the edge of the window with one eye. A cluster of six men stood in the middle of the room, and they appeared agitated.

One man moved and she saw Ada's boot, and then she heard her shriek. Krista grabbed the door handle, but it wouldn't turn. She ran off the porch, and she was halfway to the back door when she realized that confronting six men with a nearly empty shotgun was suicide. With a snort, she ran to the pickup truck and opened the passenger door. She searched their bags for something to use as a weapon, but she found nothing.

She stumbled back into the clearing, and then she sank to her knees and cried as reality hit her: Her best friend had been captured by thugs, and she couldn't save her. All she could do was listen to Ada's screams until they stopped.

The picture of a pink hat lying in the dust flicked into her mind, and she winced; unless she found some way to change the odds, she'd fail Ada just like she'd failed Spring. But she couldn't think of anything.

What's my clever Kobayashi Maru? she thought. *Lure them out and bash them one by one? Shoot one guy and hope that keeps the others back? Or just admit defeat and give up? I'm not some hardass, and I can only fake it so far.*

She sat in the dirt and glared at the shadowy silhouette of the building. "I'm nothing," she whispered to herself. "I'm not what I'm pretending to be, and I never will be." She waited for Figment to object, but it was silent. She sat motionless, another piece of junk in a forgotten junkyard.

BOB DOWNS HIT TWELVE MILES AN HOUR on the treadmill and sweated away the toxins and impurities he'd absorbed after watching the unclean world for twelve hours. Endorphins flooded his bloodstream and set off fireworks in his brain. However frustrating the Watch Room was, life was sweet when he ran.

He reached into the tray for his water bottle, and as he did, he noticed that the screen of his tablet had just turned on. Puzzled, he tapped the treadmill's stop button and peered at the screen. "Tala Ripley? Who on Earth is that?" He wiped his face and tapped the tablet. "Hello?"

"Downs?"

"Who's this?"

"Krista Warner."

He leaned against the mirrored gym wall. "I hope you've called to accept my amnesty offer."

After a pause, she said, "That I have."

He smiled at the Bob Downs in the mirror, and then he noticed the number on his tablet and ran to a wall monitor. After tapping in his access code, he navigated to the Tactical Operations screen. "Let's work this out, then. I assume you have a few minutes to iron out the details?"

"I don't, so I'll tell you how this has got to go. I'll be in Chicago tomorrow morning. I'll call you with a location, and you'll send an unarmed driver there who'll take me to O'Hare Airport. Once the plane's in the air, I'll call you with the location of my tablet. Agreed?"

Downs looked at the TacOps monitor and frowned – the Watch Room hadn't responded yet, and he needed to buy them time. "Agreed. In return, we won't seize your trust's assets, and we'll cease our pursuit. However, we'll notify the media that you've fled the country."

"I understand. I'm giving up, and I'm not trying to hide that. I'll tell everyone that the chase wore me down till I couldn't go on anymore."

The computers were slow tonight, and he was tempted to run into the Watch Room himself and crack heads to get this done. "Should I tell the driver to expect only one passenger?"

"I'll be traveling alone."

"What happened to the Lang girl?" Downs asked.

"I left her at an Activist safe house. She was slowing me down."

"And what about the package she was carrying?"

"Why is that important?"

"It isn't. It only has small sentimental value to me. It's a picture of my dear departed mother, that's all."

Krista laughed. "You have sentiments, boyo? Gimme a break. That's a human thing."

"Let's not start this again, Miss Warner. Where's her package?"

"It isn't part of the deal. You get my tablet, and that's all."

"Understood." He tapped the monitor again as if it would speed the process. The Watch Room had to be asleep tonight, and he made a mental note to bring the subject up with Raphael. "Now that this is over, I must admit – against my better judgment – that I respect the run you've had. No one's ever eluded us as long as you."

"Go fuck yourself, Downs. Don't talk about respect like we were noble adversaries."

"For once, I'm pleased to hear your profanities. It's said that cursing is the dialect of the defeated, the *patois* of the powerless, and as such, your coarse language confirms your capitulation. It's a most enjoyable sound."

"I never used to swear, but since I met you, I've been cussin up a storm. It's all due to your splendid influence. Before I met you, I never hated anybody. Before I met you, I never wished a prolonged and painful death on anyone."

"Be grateful we're not in my office, Warner."

"How scary. Listen, just make the arrangements and stay by your damn phone tomorrow morning, ya follow?"

"And you keep your phone with you at all times. I'll need to coordinate the arrangements with you. Do we have a deal?"

"We have a deal."

PULLING THE SILVER THREAD

Day 37
Thursday night, September 24, 2043
St. Elizabeth's Hospital for the Indigent, Washington, DC

As hooligans in Indiana prepared to ravage her daughter, Victoria Lang was getting drunk and glaring at the flaking plaster wall of her cell.

The Tommy Connors interrogation hadn't gone well. Not only hadn't he known where Ada was, the man's arteries had burst like firehoses when she cut his throat. It had taken more than an hour to wipe his blood off her shoes.

The murders had been pointless; the Chalys executives would have told her where Ada was once they felt the blade on their throats. The Federals didn't know either– even though the NTC interrogator had said Ada was in their custody, they'd asked Victoria questions that the girl would have readily answered. Ada's inability to keep a secret was something of a legend, so she knew that the Federals had been lying.

Now all she had was three more murders on her record, zero answers, and below-zero optimism. She'd hoped one of her victims would reveal something, anything, that said the silver thread connecting her to Ada still existed. On most nights when she sat alone with her memories, she couldn't feel it at all, and that was then she climbed deep into the bottle to forget.

She sniffed the vapors rising from her glass, which smelled so much better than the reek of mold and rat feces permeating the Cages. "Yes, I'm going insane. I'm adapting to a stressful environment by becoming a homicidal sociopath. There it is, Tori. Own it."

When she'd read that Mae Esteban had retired from public life to return to St. Elizabeth's, her spirits had lifted because she needed the company of an old friend more than ever. Mae only came for one night's

Pulling the Silver Thread

duty, though. She attended a rally in central Anacostia the following evening, and she was running the town by the time it was over. All the orderlies in the staff cafeteria could talk about was how she was rallying the marginalized and neglected of Southeast DC, who were demanding to know why they weren't getting the vaccine.

That she ended up in charge was no surprise. Mae had the charisma, vision, and passion of a natural leader, and wherever she went or whatever she did, she rose to the top. That thought just intensified her depression, though. Mae was making a difference up there, while she was twenty feet belowground sleeping with the rats. She sipped her whiskey and looked at the decay eating the cell walls, a perfect metaphor for her life.

The time had come to take a chance. Tomorrow, she'd go to the surface and find Mae despite the risk of capture. She'd drag her friend to the nearest bar and tell her every secret and every worry –

A calling hit her so hard that she doubled over and whimpered. Her soul twisted as it had on that day she signed Ada's future away, but this was more intense: She felt dread, mortal fear, an ending.

Ada was alive, but her child was dying. The realization knocked the wind from her chest and she labored to breathe, but each breath felt like her last. Ada was dying, and she was too.

"Oh, my god, no, no, no," she whispered. "My baby's dying…oh, my god, no…"

A FALL OF EMBERS

Day 37
Thursday night, September 24, 2043
Revenge, Indiana

Ada lay spread-eagled on something soft, her hands over her head, and rough rope fibers bit into her wrists and ankles. She heard voices in the distance, but she couldn't understand them because the person lying beside her was making a loud noise like they were trying to breathe through a whistle. She opened her eyes, and what she saw was fuzzy. As her vision cleared, the brown wood rafters of the old grange roof took shape.

Her neck was stiff, but she could move her head slowly. She turned to the right and saw Girly Boy, who sat cross-legged on the floor next to her. "You ready for work? Cuz I am." Moments later, the gray face of Sundown appeared beside him.

"Bertha." He smiled the menacing, joyless grin again and sat on the floor opposite Girly Boy. "You have a strong spirit. Such a thing of life. In fact, one may say the spirit is life itself, and as such, it should be celebrated. However, this is not your function in our Chrysalis. Spirit and life are what we must reap from you so we may strengthen and fulfill God's mission." He took a package from Chunk while Girly Boy watched with rapt interest. "Have you read the Book of the Archangel, Bertha?"

She shook her head and pulled at the ropes; her arms and legs were tied tightly and couldn't move more than an inch either way.

"In the Book, one passage has become the guidepost of my life. At crucial turnings, this guidepost gives me direction. As a Base-M addict living in the gutter and doing anything for my next Rock, this passage saved me and lifted me into the world of the clean and the saved."

He leaned closer, and the sour reek of his breath washed over her. "The Book says the corn of the field grows tall, and its fruit grows heavy and ripe as it awaits the reaping of man; man, as the steward of the land, must reap what he needs, or the field will not flourish the next year. This message set me on the path to the light, Bertha, and filled my life with the abundance of mortal joy."

He peered into a box he was holding, frowned, and whispered to Chunk, who scurried away. "This is the truth of the Lord, and it is oftentimes forgotten in our heathen culture even though it has always been so. It is man's responsibility, as steward of the field, to sow and reap in accordance with God's will. Nicole defied God's will – her fruit grew ripe, yet she refused to be reaped. She spat in the eye of God, one might say. Fortunately, men have been given the tools of reaping, and I used one to make Nicole whole and natural in the eyes of the Lord. Ever after, she yielded her bounty freely."

Chunk returned and the rattling sound resumed; Sundown grunted after a moment and turned back to her holding a light-blue crystal the size of a pea. "Base-M made her whole, as it will you. With one Rock, I confer upon you the gift of death, Bertha, for the Rock will grasp you for the rest of your short life. But in that five years you will live a hundred, and when your death comes, you will not cringe as much of humankind does – you will rush forward and embrace it. This is my gift to you."

Girly Boy leaned forward. "You'll look like you're a hundred when you're twenty, and you'll be glad to die, is what he's sayin. And you'll fuck anythin for the Rock every minute till then."

Sundown shot him a stern glare. "Did I not say that?"

"I was translatin, old man," Girly Boy said. "Yer hard to follow."

Sundown reached forward and grabbed her mouth, but she clenched her teeth tight and thrashed back and forth. "This is a solemn moment, child," Sundown said as he struggled with her. Girly Boy reached over her head, grasped her jaw in his hands, and pulled her teeth apart. Sundown dropped the blue crystal on her tongue. "It is done," Sundown said, and the other men in the room sang a ragged chorus of *Rock of Ages*.

Girly Boy kept her mouth clamped shut. "Let it dissolve. Don't swallow it or you'll puke."

A tangy sweetness exploded in her mouth as the crystal melted. She tried to spit it out, but Girly Boy's grip on her jaw was too tight; she whipped her head from side to side, but he still held on.

The Rock was melting fast, and she needed to get it out of her mouth. She rolled it to the back of her tongue and took a slow breath through her nose, and when her lungs were full, she snorted the crystal to the top of her throat. It tickled and threatened to fall back into her mouth, so she snorted again and blew it into her nostril. Even there, it continued to dissolve, and a saccharine sourness invaded her sinuses.

She forced the tip of her tongue between her teeth and bit down hard. The sharp pain made her nose run, and within seconds, the crystal was blanketed by a flood of mucus. Tears ran down her cheeks.

"Don't get so emotional, Bertha babe," Girly Boy said. "We got enough Rock left over from Nicole to keep you flyin. Enjoy the magic rug ride." He opened her mouth and shined the flashlight inside. "Yeah, yer done now. I'm gonna go take a piss, and then we can get down to the ins and outs of yer new job." He stood, smoothed his long ponytail and straightened his trench coat, and then sauntered to the back door.

She watched him leave and tried to get her bearings. Sundown and Chunk were talking on the other side of the room. To her left, Low Man lay on his back on a sleeping bag; his eyes were closed, and the strained whistling came from his throat. Beyond him, Hackle lay on the floor and gawped at the ceiling the way dead men do. By the front door, two other men had already climbed into their sleeping bags.

She pulled the ropes, but they felt as if they were anchored to something. Looking over her head, she saw that they were tied with a cluster of knots to large eyebolts in the wall.

Her head spun, and the room suddenly brightened and glowed with color. The rafters changed hues; they became a deep and vibrant brown, shimmering in the light, the grain of the wood standing high and proud. It was interesting, the grain – no, it was fascinating, it was infinitely complex and mesmerizing as it whorled and turned in on itself, revealing fundamental truths as the grain snaked endlessly…

Ada clamped down on her tongue and blew out hard through her nose. A wet nugget landed on her cheek and rolled onto the floor.

…And the wood was so happy. It was playful, funny wood, and it was exciting to watch it frolic and dance its forbidden dance in the flickering light. A terrifying hollowness swelled between her legs, and she slowly became wet; she loved wood now, she *wanted* wood now. She never knew it was so erotic, that it was a massive turn-on…

She bit down hard on her tongue again, and the pain banished the hallucination. Closing her eyes to the temptation of the rafters, she prayed for Deputy Galahan to bust down the door and rescue her before Girly Boy came back, before he gave her another Rock, before she stopped caring forever. She turned to see the back door and prayed for him to burst through it and release her from this hell.

I can't do anything for myself anymore. I can't fight and I can't die, and all my life I'll be a fuckpuppet for anyone with a Rock...I wish I could die, I don't want to live like this...Please, Deputy Galahan...

She heard a thud outside the door. It slammed against the wall, spraying the room with wood splinters from the shattered latch, and Girly Boy backed in from the darkness with his hands raised.

Then Krista walked into the light with a shotgun aimed at his nose.

"Everybody freeze or your friend here gets a twelve-gauge haircut!"

Sundown jumped at Krista, and she whirled and pulled the trigger. The gun boomed and shredded his shin and ankle. He hit the floor face-first as Chunk grabbed his leg where he'd been hit by a piece of shot. Girly Boy lunged, but she spun back and poked the big smoking barrel in his face. "Luck ain't a lady tonight, chump. Now grab some air, or I'll fill ya fulla daylight."

Girly Boy raised his hands again, and she yelled, "The resta ya, up against this wall to my right. Now!" They wandered to the wall, and the two men by the front door crawled naked from their sleeping bags. Krista noticed that Low Man and Hackle weren't moving and yelled to them. "You two over there! Get up and get going too!"

"They're probably dead. Little bitch wasted 'em," Girly Boy said, and then he shrugged. "They were assholes anyway."

"Good. Saves me some lead. Now, you're gonna untie the girl, ya follow?"

Ada looked up with wide, pleading eyes and Krista nodded back, unsmiling. Girly Boy knelt near her head and fussed with the knots on her hands. While he was busy, Krista slipped something pink into his trench coat pocket. Ada looked at her, puzzled, but Krista shook her head. "Hurry it up!" she yelled at Girly Boy.

"The knots is all knotted, lady."

"Don't tell me your problems, fuckwit. Just move it!"

"Whatcha gonna do? Kill me cuz the knots is too tight? I'm doing the best I can."

She leaned forward and spoke into his ear. "Oh, you're just beggin for a gunpowder enema, boyo."

"The fuck? Like you –"

She shoved the barrel into his rectum. Girly Boy gulped, and the ropes fell from Ada's hands seconds later. She sat up and rubbed her wrists.

Krista nudged him in the back with the barrel. "You go over there against the wall with the others, Ponytail. And take off that stupid trench coat. You look like a bloody flasher." To the rest, she called out, "Lower your pants down 'round your ankles, and your underwear too, if ya got any. That's good, keep it comin…"

The four men glanced at each other and grumbled, but two pairs of trousers dropped and hit the floor. The two naked men looked at Krista and shrugged.

"…except for you two. Now put your hands behind your head and lace the fingers together and stand there till I tell ya different. I got plenty of lead to squirt, ya follow?"

Ada slipped into her boots and walked to the middle of the room, where Sundown was trying to rise from the floor. His arms shook, and his bloody, shredded legs quivered; his long beard grazed the floor as he grunted and strained to rise.

She bent over and said into his ear, "Brother, there's something you must see." When he turned to look, she drew back her foot and kicked him in the mouth so hard that he spun in the air. Bloody teeth sprayed from his mouth and clattered to the floor, and he landed on his back, staring up at the ceiling. "Gaze upon heaven, Brother Sundown," she said. "Hey, did you know that the letters in 'sister' also spell 'resist'? Now *that's* fascinating." She watched him for a moment and then walked to Krista's side rubbing her wrists.

"You okay?" Krista asked in a low voice.

"I think so," Ada said. "I'm really grateful Kick-Ass Krista showed up tonight."

"How's she doing?"

"She's doing fantastic," Ada said, barely above a whisper. "A real *femme fatale.*"

A Fall of Embers

"She read a lot of noir detective novels when she was a kid."

"It came in handy. She's so brave."

"She isn't. Weenie Krista is scared shitless, but the Life Force is empowering Kick-Ass Krista and keeping Weenie quiet."

"Not to yuck your yum, but you know that gun is empty?" Ada asked, shielding her mouth with her hand.

"That's why Weenie is scared shitless, kiddo."

"I love you," Ada said softly.

"You better."

Ada looked around the room and then at the back door. "What now?"

"We go to the front door and wait for the signal," Krista said. "Does it open?"

"I'll check. Why don't we just take the back door?"

"We'll need a quick getaway, and the front door is better. There's too much junk out back." Krista walked sideways across the room, keeping the four men in the gun sight as she did. Ada slid back the door latch and opened it after a few yanks.

Krista glanced out at the dark and silent countryside. "Okay, boys," she said. "When I tell ya, start countin backward in even numbers from a thousand." She pointed the shotgun at Chunk. "You, Wide Thing. That's your job, got it? 1000, 998, and so on till you get to zero."

"I got it, lady. I ain't stupud."

"When we leave, I'll be coming back in to check, and anyone that moves gets plugged. Got it?"

They nodded, and Girly Boy sneered. "We're gonna do exactly that."

Ada whispered in her ear. "They'll chase us as soon as we leave. Listen, I'll go boost the truck. Gimme five minutes, I'll honk when it starts, then you can jump in and we'll burn rubber."

Krista shook her head. "That won't work. Once we get the signal, we'll only have a few seconds."

"What signal?"

She leaned through the doorway but heard nothing but tree frogs. "The one we haven't gotten yet."

The room fell silent except for the whistling from Low Man's crushed windpipe. The men against the wall fidgeted and coughed, and Ada tapped her foot.

"Lady, my hands are going numb," Chunk complained.

"Tough shit. Shut up," Krista said.

"I'd really like to get outta here," Ada whispered, and Krista hissed for her to be quiet. One man started to whistle, which drew a sharp reprimand from Krista, and the others shuffled their feet and looked at each other sideways.

"Listen, bitch, you won," Girly Boy said. "You can go now."

"Shut up!" she yelled.

"You got a strange way of winnin," Chunk said.

"Ah think she just likes lookin at our johnsons," one man said.

"I said everybody shut up!" she screamed, and the room fell so silent that each tick of the wall clock sounded like a whip crack.

"Never knew that clock was so loud," Chunk muttered.

"SHUT THE FUCK UP!" Krista bellowed.

Low Man's whistling slowed and finally stopped, and Sundown lay still on the floor and gurgled. The heavy rifle numbed Krista's fingers, and her shoulders started to ache.

She tilted her head and listened again for a sound outside, and this time she heard a distant roar. She grabbed Ada, who was now wearing a strangely blank expression, and shoved her through the doorway. "All right, Wide Thing, start counting. And remember, I'll come back in and check!" Chunk began to mumble, and she backed through the doorway.

Ada stood on the porch and gazed into the southern sky, a small smile on her lips and her eyes soft and dreamy. "Happy, happy stars." She pointed to the south, where the fug glowed.

The rippling roar grew, and in the time it took for Krista to draw a breath, the sound doubled and four lights took shape. "Let's go!" she yelled.

"I wanna have sex," Ada murmured.

Krista yanked the girl off her feet and dragged her off the porch. The light and sound swelled and washed over them, and the ripping became a roar that shook Krista's chest. She ran around the pickup truck and threw Ada to the ground as a sizzling growl passed overhead, and then the crack of an explosion shook the dirt. A wave of pressure and heat blew over her, and glass from the shattered truck windows showered her head and shoulders. The truck rocked sideways so far that Krista felt the running board press into her back. She started to rise and run, but then another blast pushed her to the ground.

A Fall of Embers

When the explosions stopped, she shook the glass from her hair and looked around the dusty yard. Embers fluttered from the sky like glowing snowflakes, floating lazily to the ground and casting a soft, warm light over the orchard. Their beauty entranced her, but then she smelled gasoline and spotted a river of the dark liquid coursing toward Ada. As she pulled her off the dirt, she heard an odd whiffling somewhere in the fug above coming at them.

A burning wood beam fell from the mist and speared the dirt next to them, igniting the gasoline fumes with a soft crump. The river of gas flared into blue flame and raced their way. Ada jumped to one side and ran, while Krista reached into the pickup and threw their bags and the briefcase out into the yard.

She ran into the fug seconds before the truck exploded and knocked her off her feet. Shaking glass from her hair, she saw that her shoelaces were burning and batted the flames out with the bottom of her backpack.

The rain of embers had turned into a glittering blizzard that covered her hair and stung her eyes. She shielded them with her hand and peered into the fug, spotting the small shape of Ada in the orchard. Stumbling forward, she picked up their scattered gear and then ran for the cover of the trees. Ada took the bags and the blankets from her hands, and Krista leaned against a tree trunk.

She glanced back at the grange's cremains: The heat of the explosion had blown away the fug, and a roaring inferno blew embers into the air where the building had stood. A roof beam collapsed, and a tornado of embers whirled up into the sky.

Krista sniffed the air, and strangely, it smelled like burning hair. With all the wood burning across the yard, she expected it to smell like a campfire.

She shrugged off the contradiction and sat beside Ada. "So Vincennes wasn't scary enough, right? You just *had* to do something bigger and badder than me –" Ada swore and whacked her in the back, knocking her face-first into the dry leaves. "Jaysus, girl! Okay, it was a tasteless joke! You don't have to beat me for it!"

"Your hair's on fire!" Ada said, and then Krista felt the heat on her back and shrieked. She rolled into the leaves, and Ada covered her head with a silver blanket. After a minute of rolling and batting, she sat in the leaves beside her. "You're okay now," she said.

"Thanks for putting me out, kiddo. I was totally clueless about that." Krista sat up and brushed scorched leaves from her hair. "How bad is it?"

"That grange is toast, thank god."

"I mean, how bad is my hair?"

"Oh, that. You need to cut the burned stuff off," Ada said.

Krista pulled the singed hair back from her face and let out a slow breath. "Well, I'm sure I can find a decent salon in this town."

Ada sputtered and broke into a laugh, and Krista joined in until they were both howling. Once they were out of breath and their throats were raw, Ada found a bottle of water in her bag, drained half, and handed it to Krista. "Why are we laughing? That wasn't even funny," she said.

Krista shook her head and rested against a tree trunk. "I've finally gone free-range mental. I'm way off the pasture now. How about you?"

Ada nodded.

"You and me, we'll find a shrink with some fabulous drugs when this is over," Krista said. "The happy kinda shrink that keeps a bowl of sedatives next to the couch. We'll eat them like candy."

Ada didn't answer; she just slipped her shaking hand into Krista's, leaned against her, and started to sob. After a minute, she wiped her eyes, and they sat in the dry leaves and watched the grange burn, mesmerized by the ever-changing columns of embers and flames.

"Thanks for saving me," Ada said. Another roof beam fell inside the grange, casting twinkling sparks into the dark fug that diffused into soft orbs of light. "I wish we'd grabbed some of their food before we left, but that's okay. At least it's over."

"It's over," Krista said. "And this is a night I want to forget, believe you me."

"Yeah. Let's pretend this never happened." Ada puffed out her cheeks. "That was way too close."

Krista ran her fingers through her hair and pulled out more leaves, still feeling like she was on fire. "That sure didn't go the way I expected. I thought I'd hear the missiles coming sooner."

"Missiles?" Ada looked from her, to the burning grange, and back. "Damn! You called in an air strike using Tala's tablet for coordinates!"

"I had to concoct a Kobayashi Maru, but I couldn't build a bomb. So I got Bob Downs to deliver some."

"That was really clever!"

"It was, wasn't it?" Krista grinned and leaned back against the tree trunk.

"You definitely rock, sister. How'd you figure that out?"

Krista shrugged and drained the water bottle. Across the clearing, the apple trees burned like a row of Christmas lights. The embers rained down slowly, and some danced in the updrafts like a snowfall of dancing red fireflies.

"All this needs is a soundtrack, like some scary pipe-organ music or something," Ada said. "So what's next?"

"This is where my plan ends," Krista said. "But we've got to get outta here before someone shows up, and we can't take the road, so I guess we're going back into the Halloweeny orchard."

"Just give me a few minutes to calm down first," Ada said, and then the tree above them burst into flames. She looked up and sighed. "Yeah, all right, a burning bush. I get the hint." She stood and leaned against the trunk, brushing the leaves from her pants. "Like I need more Old Testament in my freakin life."

"We have four direct hits. The Talon is returning to base. Backup moving into place."

"Excellent, Tom. Ryan, what's our visual on this?" Raphael asked.

"Nothing yet, except the Blackeye picked up the flashes. Once the Blackwings move in, we should get a better view of the impact site." Ryan Beckmann slid his fingers over the monitor. "The thermals will obscure our visual acquisition, though. From what I can tell, the detonations set off a small forest fire. The area is blanketed with smoke."

Downs stood next to Raphael and tried to make sense of the input. "We need a Rapid Response Team in the air to confirm the kill, Raf. We also need to bring the other team in at daylight to scour the area for Warner's tablet."

"Actually, I had Tom order it the minute you signaled from the gym. Their ETA is four minutes, my friend. Relax."

"I know, but this kill is critical."

"Worrying about it won't make it work better, Bob. I have this under control, all right? We'll have eyes in the sky and boots on the ground in four minutes, and we hit the target with four times the killpower we needed. I think we're good here, assuming this isn't another Activist trick."

"That's why I worry. Warner isn't just any target. Every move she makes serves a strategic purpose, but I can't see what The Activity would gain from this gambit."

"Unless she was telling the truth," Raphael said. "There's always a chance of that. Don't overthink the problem, Bob. Wait for more intel, and we can build a better model."

"Wait, wait, always wait." Downs frowned and walked the edge of the podium a few times. He looked up at the Wall, and then the tablet in his pocket vibrated. A mail message on the screen read:

ENCRYPTED-----EYES ONLY-----ONE READ AND ERASE

FROM: ASTEIN / A4NTC

TO: RDOWNS / A1NTC; RVINOLA / A1NTC

WARNER USED TALA RIPLEY'S TABLET TO MAKE THE CALL. TALA RIPLEY IS DAUGHTER OF JACK RIPLEY, WHO IS SUSPECTED OF ASSISTING WARNER IN MARYVILLE. SHE'S ALSO AN OFFICER AT BANGOR NAVAL SUBMARINE BASE IN KITSAP, WASHINGTON. ADM. ADAM HARRIS COMMANDS THE PACIFIC SUBMARINE GROUPS THERE. BECKMANN IS CONNECTED TO HARRIS AND SO IS LANG AND NOW RIPLEY IS TOO. NO CAUSE FOR CONCLUSION BUT SUSPICIONS ARE HIGH THAT HARRIS IS ACTIVIST NEXUS AND BECKMANN IS COMPROMISED///STEIN.

Downs glanced at Raphael, who was reading the same message and shaking his head. "Still believe in coincidences, bud?"

"More these days, yeah," Raf muttered.

"That'll make your mind soft. It's a bad habit to get into."

Raphael turned to Downs with angry eyes and started to reply, but then Ari Stein swiveled in his chair to face the podium. "Out of an abundance of caution, I pinged the Ripley tablet," he said.

"Why? We hit it with four Hades missiles," Raphael said. "It should be nothing but computer atoms now."

Ari nodded, but his face was pale. "The tablet replied to the ping, Raf. It survived the strike. Not only that, it's moving."

GIRLY BOY ROLLED ONTO HIS BACK, and a sharp pain jabbed his shoulder. He looked up into the fug, which was glowing for a reason he didn't understand – but then, he didn't understand anything that had just happened. After the two women ran outside, he pulled on his trenchcoat, grabbed his pistol, and ran after them. He stopped at the door and wondered why the sky sounded like it was being ripped in half, and then something shoved him into the air and sent him flying. Now he was lying in a field and listening to the sound of grinding gears inside his skull.

His left shoulder hurt when he tried to move his arm, and he felt a sharp pain from his ribs when he tried to breathe. Turning his head to the right, he saw a pillar of flame in the field; blinking a few more times and squinting, he made out the concrete porch of the old grange.

With an agonized effort, he sat up and looked around him. His buddies had to be dead, all of them, because they'd been inside when the bomb went off.

He didn't know how the bitches planted a bomb. He'd watched everything the tall one did, and he knew the little one had nothing on her because he'd searched every inch of her body when she was unconscious.

The sound switched from third to fourth gear in his brain, and he shook his head as if he could fling it out of his ears. More sounds drifted from the trees on the other side of the grange, and he turned that way to listen; he wasn't sure, but it sounded like voices.

Then he heard laughter: the high-pitched, full-throated howls of two women celebrating. "Bitches laughing?" he growled. "Bitches laughing about this? This funny to you?" He reached into his right pocket, but his revolver was gone. He patted the dirt and found it lying next to the smoking head of Hackle.

"Bitches think it's over," he said, "but it ain't, not till this gun's empty." Grimacing, he climbed to his feet and limped toward the trees.

KRISTA AND ADA STUMBLED THROUGH THE ROT and dead leaves of the orchard, aiming for the river and keeping a watch for any more hanging men. However, the fug had thickened again, and they moved cautiously, fearing what they might bump into.

They ducked under the blankets when they heard a drone, but this time it didn't fly overhead. Instead, it sounded like it was flying in a circle over the grange. They heard helicopter blades buffeting the air far away and ran through the trees, forgetting about dangling stiffs.

Ada limped as fast as her legs would take her but begged Krista to stop after a minute. "Gotta catch my breath," she gasped. "Legs hurt. Where are we going? This takes us to the river."

Krista sagged against a tree trunk. "First, we've got to get away. Then we'll figure out where to go."

"The river's a dead end. We oughta turn right and go north."

"That won't get us any further away."

"No, but the river can't be far ahead, and we have to turn eventually." Ada took a deep breath and looked out into the fuggy orchard. "I think I hear water."

The tree next to her exploded and showered them with shredded bark as a sharp crack came from behind. Ada scrambled to her feet and crouched behind a tree, but then she heard Krista crashing through the leaves and ran after her.

"The tablet's moving west at three miles an hour, approximately one-half mile from the impact site," Ari said. "Whoever's carrying it is on foot."

"Tom, have the Executives follow that tablet. Send them the coordinates and get them into that orchard. Where's the second helo?"

"On the way," Tom said, "but they can't land close to the site. The fug's too thick, and they don't know what they're landing in. The first unit's turbines ingested debris when it landed. It's nonoperational now, so I'm keeping the second helo in the air."

Raphael nodded. "Fine. We can pursue on foot and push her to the river. When the second helo pulls in, send it there."

FOR SOMEONE WHO SWORE SHE WAS UNFIT, Krista moved fast when she was motivated, and Ada stumbled to catch up. The orchard ended after a few minutes of running, and she made out a shape in the fug as she staggered onto a dirt path. "Hey!" she rasped.

Krista turned and replied with a short yelp, and then she vanished. Ada crept to where she'd been, turned in a circle, and peered into the murk, but Krista was gone.

Leaves crunched and dry branches snapped from the orchard, and then a bullet whistled past her ear. She flinched and stepped back, and her foot found nothing but air.

She tumbled backward, feeling a queasy moment of weightlessness, and then hit wet dirt and somersaulted down a slope until she struck something hard with her shoulder. She rubbed her arm and felt cold metal behind her, and then she squawked as the shotgun landed on her sore leg and splashed into the water.

After feeling around in the dark, she wrapped her fingers around the gun and pulled it out. From the fug ahead, she heard Krista call her name. "Over here!" she yelled, but it sounded like a frog croaking.

From somewhere nearby, Krista said, "We're on the riverbank. There's no way to climb up the cliff we fell off, so we've got to go along the shore. C'mon, let's move."

Ada stood and ran her hand along the hard object behind her back. "Why don't we just take this boat?"

"Boat? Where?"

"I'm standing next to a rowboat, I think."

Krista walked over and then fell into it with a clatter, a thump, and a string of colorful curses. "Right, we'll do this instead," she muttered.

Ada threw her backpack and the gun into the boat and pushed it into the river. From the back of the boat, she heard the splashing of water and it began to move. "Did you find an oar?"

"I'm using your mom's briefcase. I hope it's waterproof."

"Of course it is. It's the Commander's, after all." Ada picked up the shotgun and paddled with the stock. The boat moved slowly at first but gathered speed when the current caught it. As they passed an outcropping of rock, they heard a sharp cry of surprise from the top of the cliff.

"What was that?" Ada asked.

"Maybe whoever was chasing us just found the same cliff we did."

SIXTEEN ALPHA LOOKED THROUGH HIS SCOPE again and tried to find the target far ahead in the fug. His scope used magnified night vision, but he was running and the image was shaky. Sixteen Beta was scanning with infrared goggles, though, and he confirmed that the target was less than fifty yards ahead.

"Good," Alpha said. "I'm taking my shot now." He knelt into the leaves and brought his sniper rifle to his shoulder. In the scope, the shadowy green-and-white image of a tall person took shape, and he corrected his aim for wind and drop. However, the target disappeared as he started to squeeze the trigger. "Where'd she go?" he asked.

"Dunno." Beta stood and squinted into the darkness. "Let's find out."

They ran to the end of the trees and onto a dirt path, and then Beta held his hand out. "Sharp drop, Jay. That's where she went, right over the edge."

Alpha scanned the shoreline below through his scope. "Damn, I can't see anything in this muck."

Beta pointed down to the riverbank. "Minus sixteen degrees elevation, ten degrees south of west, range forty-one yards."

Alpha knelt into the dirt and raised his rifle. In the scope, he spotted a tall figure with a ponytail standing on the riverbank and looking across the water. "That looks like Warner." He aimed at the Off Button – the sweet spot at the base of the skull that guaranteed a kill – and squeezed the trigger. The rifle cracked, and a cloud of green mist blew from the target's head. The body fell face-first into the river.

"One shot, one kill," Alpha said with a broad smile.

"Splatmaster Jay strikes again," Beta said, and the two bumped fists.

"We have a successful redaction, two miles west of the impact site on the Wabash River. Target is in the water and drifting south," Tom said.

"Good news, Tom. Congratulate Sixteen for me," Raphael said.

"We need to confirm it's her," Downs said.

"The second helicopter is coming downriver. We'll have them fish the body out." Raphael turned to his Tactical Chief. "Tom, how long until the helo's over the target?"

A Fall of Embers

"Three to five minutes. They'll have to approach slowly because visibility is poor tonight, and they need to avoid a railroad bridge that spans the river about a mile south of there."

"That sure sounded like a gunshot," Krista said.

"It was a high-powered rifle, but it was far away. I wonder who's shooting and what they're shooting at?" Ada asked.

"Not at us for once." Krista stopped paddling with the briefcase, tilted her head, and listened. "Do you hear a helicopter?"

Ada pulled the gun out of the water and let the boat drift for a second. "Yeah. It's coming from upriver. We're sitting ducks out here, y'know."

"I know. We need to get across the river right now. Let's put our backs into it."

They pulled with as much strength as they had, but the small boat was trapped in the current. "That did nothing," Ada said as she watched the helicopter's lights approach. "I say we head for the near shore instead."

They paddled again for another minute but got no closer to the shore. Shortly after they stopped paddling, though, a tall concrete wall appeared out of the fug. The boat rocketed past it, and then it turned back upriver toward the shore and into a pool of swirling water behind the wall. They pulled for the riverbank, and the bow of the boat ground against it after a few minutes of frenzied effort. They threw their gear out and jumped onto land.

Ada looked above them. "This is a railroad bridge," she said. "The abutment created a backwater here, and it drew us in."

"Good. We were stuck out there." Krista shoved the boat back into the river. It floated lazily for a minute but then caught the current and zoomed downriver again. She strapped on her backpack, picked up the briefcase, and looked up at the bridge. "These are the tracks we crossed on the way here. What do we do now?"

Ada pointed to the north. "The helicopter is just hovering out there, so let's take a minute to catch our breath and figure this out." She looked up at the bridge again; the concrete tower extended up past the tracks, which went through a hole in the side of it. "This is a bascule bridge."

"Splendid," Krista said. "Does that help us?"

"Nope."

The bridge ended about thirty yards inland, and the orchard they'd run through began beyond it. "I'm not going through there again," Krista said. "It's just a deathtrap. We should take our chances crossing the bridge and getting to the other side."

Ada nodded and exhaled a long, tired sigh. "Well, I guess we'd better get moving."

"The body is male. Driver's license is for a John Gilliboy of North Atherton, Indiana. He had Ripley's tablet in one coat pocket and a recently fired pistol in the other."

"Thank you, Tom." Raphael turned to Downs. "We're being played again, Kemosabe."

"I know, and it's a masterful play." A vein was throbbing on Downs' forehead and his face was red. "Too masterful. It makes me wonder if she's getting help." He glanced at Ryan Beckmann, who appeared to be working diligently. "She always gets away on your shift, Raf."

Raphael rubbed his face and sighed. "Will you get offa that? Look, this Gilliboy was obviously pursuing her, and she set him up for the kill. He was taken out on the riverbank, which means Warner's in the river somewhere." He looked at the aerial photograph on the Wall. "Tom, search the river for Warner's body, a boat, a raft, something she might be floating on, and check the riverbanks too. Move Sixteen down to this railroad bridge here and have them check it out. And move the drones down there too."

KRISTA AND ADA PASSED THE WALL where the tracks met land, and they were walking along the side when Krista stopped suddenly. She crouched and pointed up, where footsteps crunched on gravel. They backed quietly down the embankment and under the bridge, and then feet clomped across the railroad ties above.

Ada spotted a metal catwalk slung under the bridge that led to the concrete tower. "Let's take that and go under them," she whispered. "When we get to the tower, we'll find a way to get on the bridge."

They found a few divots in the concrete wall to use as handholds, and soon after, they were sitting on the catwalk's metal grate a few feet beneath the tracks. The footsteps stomped overhead again, and this time they heard low voices. Taking careful steps and praying the catwalk wouldn't creak, they crept to the concrete tower.

The drone's wail grew louder, and they felt a small tingle as it passed. The helicopter fluttered above the bridge and swept the riverbank with a spotlight. After searching the ground, it flooded the bridge, and sharp bands of light shone through the railroad ties.

Ada mouthed a curse and ran to the end of the catwalk. The concrete tower was solid above and to each side, and they had nowhere to go but down. She stamped her foot quietly, sank to the metal grate, and leaned back against the concrete tower. They needed to find a way out of the trap, but she was too tired to think. She closed her eyes and tried to clear her head.

When she opened them again, the steel beams of the bridge were moving. They pulled away from the bridge and thinned into long tendrils, their ends bending into fingers that probed the metal catwalk. One finger poked up and pointed at her, wavering in the air like it was sniffing for her blood; it hated her, and she felt its hate like heat. Then the other beams separated into tendrils and joined the leader, stalking toward her…

She banged her head against the concrete, but the hallucination refused to end. Taking a deep breath, she closed her eyes and banged it even harder. When she opened them again, the bridge was just a bridge.

"What are you doing?" Krista whispered, but Ada only shook her head. "Are you all right? Why'd you do that? I saw your eyes –"

A boat whistled downriver. Ada looked up at the concrete tower, and at the thick cables and massive steel hinges on both sides – and then she nearly yelped with joy. "This is a *bascule* bridge! I know what to do! Why didn't I see it before? Follow me and be quiet." Pulling the shotgun over her shoulder and strapping it tight, she crept to an opening in the metal grate. A ladder was set into the wall, and she climbed down the face of the tower.

KRISTA LOOKED AT THE LADDER, at the briefcase, and then at the rungs; she'd have to descend one-handed, which gave her flashbacks of the escape from her apartment. She hissed at Ada to stop, but she'd already reached the bottom of the ladder and was doing something to a small door set into the wall. With a silent whimper, she stepped on the ladder and started climbing down.

Helicopter blades thudded overhead again, and the spotlight played along the riverbank below – and then it crept up the concrete tower toward Ada. Krista pulled her feet above the catwalk and called softly to her, but Ada seemed unaware of the approaching light. It was almost to the bottom of the door when she swung it open and disappeared inside.

The helicopter flew away upriver, and Krista started down the ladder, trying not to bang the metal briefcase against it. She'd only descended a few rungs when she heard footsteps clanging on the catwalk, and she scurried down. After a few more rungs, she reached the door.

Ada grabbed the briefcase, and Krista slid through the opening into dusty-smelling darkness. She turned on her tablet light and saw a concrete room with two braided steel cables as thick as telephone poles connecting the ceiling to the floor. A recessed metal ladder in the far wall continued up beyond the ceiling. "That was too feckin close. So what now?" she asked.

"We wait and hope the boat gets here at the right time." Ada pointed at the ceiling and the floor. "A bascule bridge has two counterweights that drop when the bridge opens. You're standing on one, and the other is above you. By the way, you oughta turn off that light."

"I can't. I'm afraid of closed-in spaces."

"Okay, then close your eyes and imagine wide-open spaces," Ada said.

"I can't. I'm afraid of them too."

"Are you afraid of everything?"

"Not everything. Chalk doesn't bother me anymore, and I'm making steady progress with dust bunnies."

"Sounds like Weenie Krista is back. Listen, if you've gotta have multiple personalities, hold onto Kick-Ass Krista."

"Hey, kiddo, don't talk to me like I'm cracked!"

"You have multiple personalities, sister. That's normal?"

"The Life Force gets into me sometimes, that's all. It makes me do weird stuff."

"Listen, I'm not complaining, but you're more cracked than a bowl of dive-bar peanuts."

"Well, maybe it's my multiple personalities that are cracked and not me. Huh? Ever think of that?"

"That's gotta be the goofiest proposition ever –"

A Fall of Embers

Unseen machinery creaked somewhere far above, and then the floor shook. Krista grasped one of the cables and held on until the movement stopped with a shudder and a clang. "What just happened?" she asked.

"We descended when the bridge opened. These weights balance the load to reduce gear strain."

"How does that help us?"

"It makes us invisible, dummy. The idiots won't guess we're below their feet. Shhh." Footsteps walked across the ceiling, and voices filtered through the gaps where the weight met the wall. After a minute, the ladder clanged as boots climbed up it.

"They keep getting closer and closer," Krista said. "I'd like to stay in here for a while. This is about as safe as we'll get."

"Yeah, I know what you mean. A few hours of safety would be nice." The machinery creaked again and the floor rose. "Okay, so that's just our luck, isn't it?"

"I'm not surprised. I always have bloody awful luck after the full moon." The floor stopped with a jolt, and they listened for sounds outside the door and up the ladder.

"I think I still hear someone on the catwalk," Ada whispered from near the hatch.

"What's up the ladder, then?"

"That oughta be the bridge control room over the tracks. That might be our only way out now," Ada said. "Here, take my stuff and I'll go check." She climbed the ladder, and then faint light shone into the room as she cracked open a hatch at the top. "It's the control room," she whispered. "I don't see or hear anything up here."

"All right," Krista said. "Once we get up there, how do we get out? Where do we go?"

"I don't know. We'll figure it out later, I mean, it's not like we have any real plan or anything."

"True," Krista said. "It's worked so far, so why change now?"

"She's somewhere in the vicinity of the bridge, Raf."

"I agree. The footprints on the riverbank are conclusive."

"You need to do more," Downs said. "Don't just stand around and be passive –"

Raphael wheeled around. "And just what would you suggest? I have eight men, a helicopter, and two drones operating in the area."

Downs raised his hands and took a step back. "Easy, Raf."

"This is *my* Watch, and you're a visitor. If you can't do something productive, then leave." Raphael looked at the Wall and snapped at Ari, "Get me plans of that damn bridge."

"I've already tried. There aren't any."

"All right. Tom, send the teams through one more time, and I want real-time input from their headgear cameras. Detach a squad of Collaterals from the nearest border checkpoint and get them here. Ryan, receive visuals from the field and put all of this up on the Wall."

KRISTA CLIMBED THROUGH THE HATCH into a long, narrow room with dusty windows on one side. A long counter had once lined the windows, overlooking the tracks and the river below, but all that remained were stains on the linoleum where the legs had been. A large, white cabinet squatted in its place, with blinking lights and AUTOMATED BRIDGE OPERATOR BY WAGEX painted on the front. Light wandered through the windows, barely illuminating the empty room.

"I looked around while you were coming up," Ada said. "There's no way out except the hatch we came through and those stairs at the end, which I bet are being watched. There's a ton of men running back and forth down there. All that's left is this access hatch in the floor, which probably goes nowhere."

"So we're trapped." Krista ran her fingers through her hair and walked to the hatch. She raised the lid and saw a steel beam just beneath the opening, with silver tracks further below. The steel only extended a few feet in each direction and ended at concrete walls.

She heard men's' voices from somewhere below. Ada heard them too, and she tiptoed to the far stairwell and listened; she frowned and gave Krista a thumbs-down, and then she pointed to the open access hatch.

Krista reached down into the darkness with her feet until they touched the narrow beam. The space was only a few feet high, and she had to crouch to clear the ceiling. When she felt balanced enough to move, she shuffled sideways to make room for Ada.

Ada pulled the hatch down silently and crouched beside her. Inches above, heavy footsteps stomped across the control room, and then another pair arrived and they heard voices. "She's not here. We just checked here."

"Look down there."

The access hatch opened, a light shined down inches from Ada's side, and then it slammed shut again. "Nothing. Told ya so. Why are we doing this all over again?"

"Cuz we have orders, so that's what we'll do. Look, you stay here, and I'll go back into that weird room downstairs and see if she comes back that way."

"Yeah, yeah, fine," the voice said.

Krista's knees were throbbing and her toes were going numb, but she couldn't move because two Federals sauntered along the tracks fifteen feet below. When they vanished into the fug further down the tracks, she sat and dangled her feet into open space.

Ada sat as well and shook the blood back into her toes. "I guess we can stay here till they go, as long as nobody looks up."

"I hope they don't. There's nowhere else to go," Krista whispered, looking at the blank concrete walls to each side. "I hate being trapped. I'd rather fight my way out than sit here and wait to get caught."

"Definitely," Ada said. "I wish I had more shells for this gun so I could blast through this wall of dumbass flesh and get going."

Krista nodded and had just started to whisper an answer when the access hatch opened again. Ada edged over as a pair of feet wearing black ballistic nylon boots dropped through the opening. They kicked back and forth idly as the man they were attached to whistled *Duck and Cover*. His hands reached down and untied a boot; he turned it over and a few pebbles rolled out, and then he massaged the bottom of his foot.

"I could tie his shoes together," Ada whispered in Krista's ear.

"Do you think you could pull him through the hole and take his gun?" she asked.

Ada shook her head. They watched the man's feet swing back and forth. He began whistling a popular headbanger tune and used his thighs as drums.

"I hate that song. It's like a chainsaw chewing through a guitar," Ada whispered.

The beam began to vibrate, imperceptibly at first, and then the entire bridge shook and rattled. The Federals ran as a rumble rose from the tracks, and the feet pulled from the hatch and the lid slammed shut. "Train," Ada mouthed over the growing roar.

Krista nodded and pointed across the river – since the rumble came from behind, the train would be going west. Ada pointed at her chest and down, and Krista shook her head. Ada then pointed at Krista's chest, and Krista shook her head even harder; Ada stuck her tongue out and Krista replied with her social finger.

A train whistled, but the Federal stomped around above them and didn't sound like he was leaving. Krista looked up at the floor and then at the tracks; jumping on a moving train was stupid and dangerous, but it was the only way out. She gulped and nodded slowly.

Ada motioned that she'd jump first, and that Krista should follow. She tightened her gear, grasped the beam, and doubled forward to see the approaching train. Krista clutched the briefcase to her chest and made the sign of the cross on it.

"A coal train is approaching the bridge," Ari said. "Westbound, thirty-five miles an hour, with a scheduled speed of ten miles an hour at the bridge."

"Good," Raphael said. "She'll run for the train or use it as a distraction. Tell everybody to keep their eyes open. Warner will be moving soon."

A ROAR EXPLODED BELOW, and dense, gritty smoke enveloped them. After the cab of the steam engine flashed by, Ada jumped off the beam. A second later, Krista closed her eyes and leaped; a second after that, she slammed into sharp rock.

The air was dense with choking dust that stung her nostrils. She wiped the dust from her eyes and found that she was half-buried in coal in an open car behind the engine. "Ada?" she called over the roar of the engine, and from somewhere behind she heard a movement. "Where are you?"

The coal clacked and clattered as Ada scrambled over. "I'm all right! How about you?"

"I'm fine! I can't believe that worked!" She peeked over the end of the car at the bridge receding into the distance. The helicopter floated from behind it, and it switched on its spotlight as it reached the back of the train.

They swore in unison and burrowed into the coal. It seemed to get heavier with every handful they moved, but they didn't stop until every bit and bump of their bodies were covered in black rock.

IN THE NSF HELICOPTER ABOVE THE TRAIN, the door gunner squinted through his scope. He saw nothing except a lot of train out there in white light mode, and switching to night vision turned the image blindingly bright. Blinking his eyes, he changed to forward-looking infrared and scanned the coal tender and the steam engine in front of it, which glowed orange from the boiler's heat. "I can't see a damn thing!" he yelled to the pilot.

"That's okay!" the pilot yelled back. "This train's stopping at the Illinois border in eight miles! The Ironshirts will check it from top to bottom!"

THE HELICOPTER WHIRLED AWAY, and Krista sat up and spat coal dust from her mouth. Ada tried to wipe the grit off her face. "This gets into everything!" she yelled over the engine's roar. "I'm gonna have black boogers for the rest of my life!"

"Speaking of *having* a rest of our lives, we've got to get out of here!" Krista looked over the top of the coal tender. The steam engine was ahead of her, connected to the tender by a conveyor belt carrying coal to the boiler, but the platform wasn't even wide enough for two people to stand.

Ada clambered through the coal to the rear, where a white metal box about the size of a Hugo sat on a half-length railcar. Antennas and dishes sprouted from its roof. "I think this is the control cabin for the train!" she yelled.

"Can you break into it?"

"Of course!" Ada rummaged in her bookbag and pulled out the lock picks. She crawled to the edge, flipped her legs over, and vanished beneath the edge of the car. Krista waded through the coal, and then she half-climbed and half-fell down a dented ladder extending to the tender's platform.

Ada stood at the gap between cars. "You go first! Your legs are longer!" she yelled.

Krista stepped over the two-foot gap and then pulled Ada onto the platform. They edged along the side, holding onto a rail on the cabin, but the ledge was so narrow that their heels hung over the tracks. Trees flitted by and branches whipped Krista's back.

Ada reached the end first and hopped onto a metal platform behind the cabin. She rattled the handle of a small door secured by a barrel lock. "I hate these things!" she yelled. "This could take all night!" She pulled out her picks and bent over the lock.

"Well, the sooner you start, the better we'll be!" Krista crawled to the front again to find another way in but only found two tiny, dirty windows set into each side of the box. As she was edging back along the side, the engine's roar changed pitch and the train slowed. "Uh-oh! We're slowing down!" she yelled around to Ada. "We don't have much time!"

"I'm working as fast as I can here, y'know!"

Krista shimmied around the corner and onto the rear platform, where Ada was hunched over the lock, working a strange device with quick fingers and swearing under her breath.

"I don't want to be a bother, but couldja be hurrying a bit more?" Krista asked.

"Couldja shut the hell up? This isn't easy! These are the hardest locks in the world to pick!"

"It's just that I don't know why we're slowing down and –"

"You're breaking my concentration! Go talk to the voices in your head or something!"

Krista leaned around the corner and squinted into the fug ahead, and it appeared as if the train was rolling into a cold-white sunset. "I see lights up there! That's where we'll be stopping, I'll bet!" She watched the gravel slide by. "I'm thinking we should get off and run!"

"I'm already on the eighth pass! Just a minute!"

"There's just a string of coal cars behind us! We can't hide in those! If you can't get us into this thingie, we've got to get off and run, kiddo!"

"Zip it!"

The train slid into the floodlights and jerked to a stop. Krista shielded her eyes and tried to see beyond the lights, but then she heard voices at the front of the train and feet crunching across gravel. "Ada, dear," she whispered, "this would be a grand time to open that thing. Honey? Baby? Darling? Come on."

The footsteps closed in – and then the lock clicked, and the door bumped against Krista's shoulder. She grabbed the edge, ran into a small room full of blinking lights, and closed the door behind her. Ada turned the lock as bootsteps rang on the platform outside.

The door handle jiggled and the boots stomped across the platform, and then the small window darkened as someone peered inside. They pressed their bodies against the wall.

The bootsteps returned to the door and the handle jiggled again, and the silhouette of a man and a rifle barrel filled the opposite window. One soldier rubbed the glass and tried to shine his flashlight in; the other soldier rattled the window frame and tried to open it.

After a few more tries, though, the apparitions left the window, and the platform shook as they jumped off. They breathed for the first time in minutes and slid to the floor.

Men stomped past the cabin and called to each other, and Krista and Ada remained frozen in place waiting for the door to crash open. After the longest half hour of their lives, though, the steam engine huffed, and the train rumbled west again.

PATRIOTS

Day 37
Thursday evening, September 24, 2043
Bangor Naval Submarine Base, Kitsap, Washington

Across the continent, a tall man in a woolen coat walked along Delta Pier and looked beyond the dark hull of the submarine *Patrick Henry*. A few hundred yards away in the Hood Canal's black waters, the navigation lights of a tugboat blinked as it waited to push the *Nathan Hale* into the berth after the *Henry's* departure. The *Hale* was bumping hulls with the *Ethan Allen* up at the north berth because Bangor was packed: Five Patriot submarines and four old Tridents clogged the piers, and the harbormaster was shuffling boats into every available space.

Commander Ennis Quinn removed his cap and wiped the damp from his face and reddish-brown hair. A chilling, omnipresent fog and drifting rain filled the air, and the cold seeped through every seam in his coat. It always did when he was topside in Washington State.

A sharp breeze wafted off the water and blew a cold draft up to the shiver spot between his shoulder blades. He'd once loved wintry weather, but that changed in 2034 when the Navy perversely rewarded his heroism by giving him command of an Arctic Fleet destroyer.

He shivered again at the memory of five years playing chicken with Soviet Bloc frigates in the Northwest Passage, five years with a perma-frozen beard, five years with testicles that refused to drop from his warm abdomen. Much of the polar ice had already melted away, but thirty degrees below zero was still piss-freezingly cold.

A stronger gust blew up the canal, pushing a chilly mist over the hull of the *Patrick Henry*, and he ducked into the sail's lee and looked up at it. The first Patriot submarine was a deadly beauty, but the nanocoated hull absorbed light as well as sonar rays, and it was hard to see its outline even in the pier's floodlights. Only the gray '807' painted on the sail confirmed it was there.

The *Henry* was a fine boat – in his mind, the finest that ever floated – and if he were a lucky man, she'd be his when Captain Bricker retired next year. He glanced at the end of the gangway, where a slim woman with graying brown hair talked to a tall, athletic, blonde-haired man. They were Captain Juliette Bricker and Rear Admiral Adam Harris, the two officers who would decide his future.

Worrying about that wrecked his composure, which he'd sorely need for the next ninety days, so he gazed across the Hood Canal to clear his mind. He heard a familiar *tap-shh-tap, tap-shh-tap* from the dock. Clasping his hands behind his back, he waited for Lieutenant Commander Tala Ripley, who always dragged her left heel when she walked and didn't know it. The footsteps stopped, and he said, "Good evening, Tala."

"How do you always know it's me?"

"I have eyes in the back of my head. You'd better get yourself a pair if you want to be an executive officer."

Two fingers parted his hair. "Sorry, Ennis, I don't see them back here."

"I had them custom-made in Japan. They're miniaturized."

"Ahh," Ripley said. "Like the rest of your external organs, according to the rumors circulating around the crew."

He turned around and smiled. "They're already slamming me like I was the Old Man? That's good news."

She returned his smile and pulled her collar up to her ears. "Everyone's rooting for you, especially me, Ennis. And we all think you'll get her next June."

"The competition is stiff. There are so many qualified candidates from the Trident fleet and so few boats."

"Don't assume a Trident command is a qualification, Ennis. New boats need new blood – look at the trouble Bricker's had transitioning from Tridents. Besides, you commanded the *John Jacob Astor* for five years, and that's gotta count for something."

"That was a seventy-year-old rustbucket in the Arctic Fleet, and no one considers the Frozen Chosen to be real sailors anyway."

"You're wearing the Navy Cross, pal. That's not a real sailor?"

"That was years ago. What have I done lately?"

"Okay, look at it this way – every executive officer that Bricker's ever trained got command of a Patriot boat. Jimmy Columbo got the *Revere*, Bryan Pettit got the *Allen*, and Paige Pangelis got the *Hale*. I think the Navy's kept her at sea this long to train a new generation of commanders, and you're next. And on top of all that, your best friend is the Commander of Submarine Force Pacific."

He stifled a chuckle and bounced on the balls of his feet, his green eyes twinkling. "Admiral Harris is a dispassionate technocrat who'd never let feelings influence his decision."

She laughed and nodded over her shoulder to the end of the gangway, where Harris and Bricker stood. "Right. Dispassionate's the perfect word to describe him and Bricker. Like dry's a good way to describe the ocean."

"It's not wise to speculate about that. Besides, I wasn't his best friend. That was Ryan Beckmann's honor. He was the one Adam chose for his best man, not me."

"I've never heard of Beckmann. What ship's he on?"

"Oh, he's out of the Navy. He resigned his commission and went to some black-budget spook agency." The smile faded from his face. "Persia was tough on him. We were the only three that survived the *Vanderbilt* attack, which was bad enough, but our little vacation at the Hotel Hamadan afterwards broke him."

"I heard that the Persian interrogations were pretty aggressive."

He nodded and looked over the black waters again. "Interrogation. That's a euphemism for what they did." He watched the tugboat strain to keep its position, his eyes and lips hard. "The sick thing is that the bastards didn't even understand English. I don't think they wanted information. They just wanted to vent." He forced a smile to his face. "And that's in the past, so why don't we talk about something cheerier?"

"This usually cheers me up." She pulled a pack of nicotine bubblegum from her coat pocket. She'd never smoked, but there was something about the gum she liked, and she had a wad of it in her cheek every waking hour. She blew a bubble nearly the size of her head but sucked it back in before he could pop it. He lectured her about the unseemliness of a senior officer candidate chewing gum, and she answered by blowing more bubbles.

More wind gusted up the canal, and he stomped his feet. "I wish they'd hurry this up so I can get down below. The first thing I'm going to do when I get to my cabin is turn on the fireplace."

"It's just a video of a fireplace. How does that warm you up?"

"I don't know, but my hands always feel warmer when I hold them up to it," he said. "It's a psychological quirk."

"I just want ninety days of dry weather," she said. "I'm tired of living in this rainforest. I swear I have mushrooms growing out of my scalp." She pulled off her cap, and he made a show of looking through her shoulder-length blonde hair, but he found no fungus.

The crew bus pulled up, and a gaggle of junior officers jumped out and scurried aboard. They watched the boarding ritual for a few minutes and then turned back to watching the canal.

"Oh, hey," she said, laying her hand on his arm. "Guess who showed up at my door at four this morning?"

He looked at her blankly and shrugged.

"My parents!"

"Jack and Elise? Didn't you say they were staying in Ohio and doing the stiff-upper-lip thing?"

"I know, and that's where it gets interesting," she said, leaning toward him. "*Really* interesting. You won't believe this – it sounds like a plot from a cheap thriller."

"I don't like thrillers."

"You'll like this one," she said, wiggling her eyebrows. "Trust me, you'll get a kick out of this."

"Very well," he said, squaring his jaw and shoulders. "You may fire when ready, Ripley."

She snorted. "You're really getting into this Commanding Officer gig, aren't you?"

"I'm just practicing in case I get the nod."

"Okay," she said, popping another square of gum into her mouth. "Get this – Krista Warner herself was at their house!"

"The glamorous rebel with the great gozangas?"

"Is that all you think about, Ennis?"

"No, I also think about making hot, messy, monkey love with glamorous rebels and their great gozangas."

"Right. With your custom-made miniaturized weenie?"

"It's only miniaturized in standby mode, Mister Ripley," he said with a twinkle in his eye. "So Warner just dropped into the middle of Ohio for a spot of tea? Seriously?"

"No, she roared in with a squad of Federals on her tail, looking for a place to hide. She stayed overnight, and the next day the Federals swarmed into town – helicopters, drones, door-to-door searches, the whole nine yards. She barely got out alive, and then my parents had to escape too. They parked under the trees during the day and drove on back roads at night to get here, watching out for the Federals the entire time. They say they're never going back. The entire East is just falling apart because of this virus, and Dad says there's nothing for them to go back to. They're staying at my house while I'm on patrol. I'll help them find a place to live around here when I get back."

"That's unbelievable," he said. "That can't be true."

"They swear it is, and I think it is too. They're as giddy as teenagers about the whole episode. My dad even showed me a lock of long red hair that Warner gave him, and they both swear it's hers." She leaned toward him. "And Dad says he kissed her."

"Lucky guy, your dad."

"You might get a chance if you play your cards right," she said, and his eyebrows rose. "She's coming here, Ennis. She has a house somewhere around the base, and she's tight with my folks. I can arrange an introduction once she gets here."

"Hmm. I might consider that offer," he said.

"Oh, gimme a break. You're using her picture for your tablet wallpaper. It's obvious you have a crush on this bimbo."

He pulled the brim of his cap down to his nose and hunched deeper into his coat.

Her eyes laughed and she blew a big bubble, and then she leaned over until her mouth was next to his ear. "If you recommend me for XO, I'll even talk you up like you were the greatest man to ever strut this Earth."

"Despite the blatant illegality of that offer, it's unnecessary. I was going to recommend you for executive officer anyway if I made CO."

"Do I smell a deal?" She sniffed the air. "Yep, that's the sweet smell of a deal. Take a whiff, Commander."

"You smell salt air and creosote, Mister Ripley. Honestly, I don't know why you're in such a hurry to become XO. You need to let your ulcer simmer a few more years before you can appreciate the pain of this job."

"I just want something to do. I'm the Strategic Warfare Officer on a boat where the weapons system is automatic. If we ever release a missile, all I can do is sit back and say, 'Yup, thar she goes.' I get bored outta my skull."

"Your job is to maintain and oversee the systems to assure optimal performance and to assume control should something go wrong, Tala. That's an important mission."

She blew a bubble and popped it. "Yeah, and that's the problem. Nothing *ever* goes wrong."

"Julie, I'm worried about your cold rod."

"Adam, we've run the models a dozen times, and the answer always comes out the same. Ennis is a nuclear engineer, and he says as long as we keep the reactor under ninety-two percent output, the pressure imbalances are tolerable. He's already locked out the maximum power at ninety percent."

Harris crossed his arms and leaned back against the gangway. "Still, a cold rod in a reactor is unpredictable, Julie. Fission reactions aren't as stable as everyone thinks. A cold rod can go –"

"You can take the boy out of the reactor room, but you can't take the reactor room out of the boy. Is that it?"

Harris frowned at her. "I'm just concerned for my boat and my fiancée, all right?"

"Not so loud, Adam." Bricker looked around to see if anyone had heard this breach of Navy regulations, but the only people within earshot were Quinn and Ripley, who were laughing at some private joke. "Look, I'm not happy about this, either, but we'll never hit ninety percent." She gave him an impish look and said in a low voice, "Besides, I'll be on a ninety-day patrol, and it's *your* cold rod you should be worrying about."

He barked a short laugh. "Hey, if I get lonely, there's always the shipyard."

"Go ahead and swim with those whales. When I get back, you'll be swimming with the fishes."

"I love it when you get tough with me. Don't worry, I'll be good. I'm used to being a part-time virgin."

"You better be. I've got thirty-six nukes at my command, bub."

He wiped the mist off his face and pulled up his collar. "I can't wait till next June – warm weather and a warm woman, both at the same time."

"You know what I'm gonna do when I walk off this gangway for the last time? I'm gonna jump into your arms, give you a big smooch, and yell 'I'm engaged!' and to hell with everyone else. Then I can start planning our wedding without treating it like a military secret."

He cleared his throat and looked down at the gangway. "About that. I've had a change of heart."

She stiffened and eyed him warily.

"When you come down this gangway, I want to get right on my launch and head to Friday Harbor, find a Justice of the Peace, and get married right then. No more waiting. All I want out of a wedding is you, and the arrangements are getting in my way."

Her eyes watered, and she blinked back the tears. "You're a cruel man, telling me something like that in a place where I can't kiss you all over."

They leaned against the rails of the gangway with their arms crossed, but their eyes imagined passionate love and deep kisses, and they lost themselves in each other so completely that neither heard the junior officers approach the gangway. One of them cleared his throat politely, and they snapped out of their happy musings.

The first officer in line saluted. "Permission to come aboard, Captain?" he asked.

Bricker stood up straight, her lips a thin horizontal line. "Do I look like the Officer of the Deck, Mister Santos?"

"No, sir." His face grew rigid and blank, as junior officers do when they're about to get thrashed.

"Where does the Officer of the Deck stand when my boat is boarding, sailor?"

"On the boat, sir."

"And where am I?"

"On the dock, sir."

"Then why are you wasting my time?"

"I'm sorry, Captain."

"Don't apologize for failure, Ensign. Just get it right." He and the rest of the officers scurried up the gangway. "Give them three months ashore and they go soft," she grumbled. "It takes me days to whip them into shape once we're underway. Do me a favor – keep the world from going to Hell in a speedboat for the next few days so I can get them back into fighting condition."

"If I could keep the world from going to hell, I would." He gazed over her shoulder at the canal's far shoreline. "It wants to, Julie."

"There's that face again, Adam. You've had it ever since you went on that so-called fishing trip with Governor Wang. When will you tell me what really happened?"

"I don't *know* what happened. I'm still trying to figure it out." He shrugged and sagged against the railing again. "Politicians are bad enough, but inscrutable Chinese-American politicians – Lord, preserve me. Talking to her is like nailing fog to a wall."

"Maybe I can help you figure it out. It's better than keeping it to yourself."

"All right, but this is just between us," he said. "As you can guess, we didn't go fishing."

"Of course not. She's allergic to seafood."

"Right. We talked about California the entire time."

"And talking about California throws you into a weeklong funk?"

"No," he said, taking a deep breath. "But talking about the secession of California will."

"They're always babbling about that down there, and they never push the button. Why get worked up over it?"

"Because this time they mean it," he said. "Lieutenant Governor DaCosta flew up here from Sacramento and talked to Wang last week. He said a secession proposal is circulating in the Legislature, and a veto-proof majority signed a letter supporting it two weeks ago."

"And you think they'll do it?"

He nodded. "He says they have to. The taxpayers are screaming that they can't pay the skyrocketing state taxes, but California needs to tax them that hard because DC gives them less funding every year. Right now, California's getting back twenty cents of every federal tax dollar, and that's got everybody's ass hairs up. And as if that's not enough pressure, they've also got some dark-money group, the Californians for Fair Taxation, pushing everybody's buttons and pissing off voters about Washington. Governor Rodriguez hoped the tenpez recall would cool everybody down, but it didn't work. Now the only answer DaCosta sees is to send DC a breakup letter and stop paying federal taxes."

"They'd secede over money? That's all?"

"That's what triggered the first revolution, Julie. It's always about money."

She looked down at the gangway floor. "They're taking the short view. Sure, I hate flushing my tax dollars down the head too, and it'd feel good to flip Washington the bird. But what happens after that?"

"That's what DaCosta's concerned about." He shivered and tried to climb deeper into his coat. "Julie, he asked Admiral Dolan in San Diego where Naval Base Coronado's loyalties would lie if the state seceded."

"I'm not shocked. A secession could trigger a war. But did Wang ask you the same question?"

"No. She just let it hang, but she was definitely scrutinizing my reaction to the Dolan news. I think she was sizing me up in case she needed to ask."

"I agree." She gazed down the pier with unfocused eyes, her lips pursed. After a few moments, she said, "So Wang thinks California's gonna secede, and if they did..."

"Washington State would have to go with California. We'd have no economy without them."

"Right. You need to game this fast, Adam. Suppose she asks if you'd side with Washington in a secession. How would you answer?"

"The easy answer is that I'm just a sailor until the Chief of Naval Operations says otherwise. But the true answer isn't as simple. There are repercussions from any course I take." He sighed and tried to rub away a growing headache. "Politics isn't my thing. The best course might be to just retire and walk away from this whole problem."

"You and me and a cabin in the San Juan Islands sounds like heaven, Adam," she said. "Wang's leading you into uncharted political waters. That's why you feel confused. You don't have to follow her, though. You can walk."

"Maybe I should. The worst years of my life were in Washington. I couldn't wait to get away from that never-ending politicking," he said. "I don't understand why California is doing this. As if they're not making enough trouble with that tenpez recall, they add secession on top of it." He pulled off his cap and shook the water off it. "They can't ever leave well enough alone."

Three chimes sounded from the boat, and the officers turned to look up the gangway; the aft hatch was closed, and the Officer of the Deck stood

Patriots

by the forward hatch. Quinn and Ripley walked to the boat, and Bricker stood to attention and saluted Harris.

"Fair winds and following seas, Captain," he said, returning her salute.

A small smile flitted across her face. "As you wish, Admiral."

THE GESTAPO IN DRAG

Day 38
Friday morning, September 25, 2043
Near Springfield, Illinois

"Spiders!" Ada's body stiffened, and her feet scratched at the floor of the control cabin as she tried to scramble away from the apparition.

Krista held her shoulders and whispered in her ear. "They're not real, Ada. I don't see them."

"They have trunks like elephants," Ada moaned. "And they scream."

"Nothing can hurt you. I'm here and I'll protect you," she murmured. "It's okay. You've just got a few more hours and the hallucinations will be gone." Ada stared at the far wall, her eyes filled with terror, and shook her head as if to throw off the vision.

After Ada's first hallucination on the train, Krista checked a Base-M support group site on the SatNet. The addiction was brutal – the first warm, sensuous dreams degraded fast into phantasmagoric horrors that addicts banished by taking another Rock or committing suicide. The only way to break the addiction was to withstand at least twelve straight hours of intense fear.

Ada screamed and pushed away from the far wall. "There! See…get away!" She shrieked again, and Krista held her tight. The hallucination faded after a few minutes, and she sagged against her chest.

"Twelve hours total is what I read," Krista said in a soothing voice. "Only six more to go, and I'll be with you the whole time. We're halfway there, you and me, so you be strong, all right? I need your help with this, Ada. You hear me?"

She nodded, and Krista sighed in relief. In the last bout, she hadn't responded for ten minutes, and she'd had to hold her so she wouldn't bang her head or bite her already-bloody tongue. The kid was small, but she was strong and tough, and they were both exhausted from the struggle.

She stroked her hair and cooed soft words until Ada's muscles relaxed; her head grew heavy against Krista's chest, and she fell asleep soon after. Krista lay back and gazed at the blinking lights of the train's control panel.

The small space was barely wide enough for one, and spreading her legs to let Ada snuggle forced her knees to bang against the walls. She yawned and rested her head against the rattling metal of the cabin wall; once she relaxed, though, images from Revenge and Vincennes stabbed into her mind again. They'd nipped at the edges of her consciousness for the entire night, and she'd been seized by uncontrollable bouts of trembling until she discovered that staring at the blinking control panel lights blanked out her thoughts. Looking at the lights again, she felt her mind ease.

While she needed to stay strong, she'd also earned the luxury of a complete and final nervous breakdown once they got to California. She'd buy a seaside cottage, and there, she'd wave bye-bye to reality and its awful ways. It would be a full-scale version of the dollhouse she'd had as a girl – a white clapboard Victorian wedding cake adorned with towers and porches and gingerbread. With a happy shiver, she sighed and watched the twinkling lights.

You're doing well, Miss Kellen.

"Thank you, Figment," she whispered. "Where were you in Revenge when I needed a swift kick in the arse, though?"

You knew what to do. You didn't need me.

"I didn't, did I?" A warm glow spread up her back, one so welcome that she shivered again. "You can stick around if you want. There's plenty of room in my head."

Figment didn't answer.

The lights threatened to put her asleep, but she had to stay awake for Ada. She needed to do something productive, and a post fit the bill perfectly. She dipped her finger into the coffee jar and then unfolded her tablet.

The Rake
September 25, 2043

SORRY, I COULDN'T MAKE IT TO MY FUNERAL

At least the real Nazis were competent. This NSF crowd is as sharp as Gestapo cosplayers in an East Village drag show

Here I am again. Nine days after I started out on this jaunty jaunt, I'm still alive, despite everyone's expectations. Thousands of Federals and millions in blood money haven't done a thing, and even the NSF is impressed: I had a chat with Serial Wrongman Bob Downs, the Spook Supreme, and he said I've set some sort of record.

Huzzah!

The record almost ended last night. I became separated from my bodyguards in the thick fug in Revenge, Indiana, and I fell into a trap. Not an NSF trap – the Federals aren't good enough to catch me – but a garden-variety wrong time / wrong place trap.

It was dicey, but I got out of it by snookering the Federals. One thing that Downs has taught me is that it's easy to con a liar – all you need to do is play the opposites game with them, and they fall for it every time – so I called him and said I was ready to turn myself in. And as I expected, missiles landed on my location fifteen minutes later. Pow! Blammo! It was glorious! My problem was vaporized just like *that*.

Those boys really put the 'Service' in Civil Service. Try getting a pizza delivered that fast!

I hooked up with my beefsteak Activist bodyguards (not in *that* way, ladies!), and we crossed the river for a little picnic while we watched the Federals stumble all over a railroad bridge looking for me. We spread out the blanket, and my favorite hunk, Seth, handed out delightful chicken cordon bleu sandwiches, provolone salad, and a coquettish Chardonnay. Sure, the meal was cold, but Revenge is best served that way.

-KLW

The Gestapo in Drag

She leaned through the window to get an uplink and deliver her post. After it finished, she surfed *Midnight Sun* for a few minutes. The news was terrible – Philadelphia had seen riots, New York City was silent and dark, and the virus was becoming even deadlier. Some vigilante was also on a killing spree: Three Chalys Pharmaceuticals executives had been brutally murdered in the past few days.

After that, she checked her mail, which contained a message from the editor at *Midnight Sun*: He'd taken the Ottawa government to court, hoping to get an injunction so he could release the videos. But she knew that wouldn't happen now because Ottawa wasn't spiking her videos. Washington was. She felt Gabriel Cheyn pulling the strings.

She leaned against the window frame as the train glided through endless fields of corn, their stalks rippling in a light breeze like waves on a gentle sea, and imagined what might have been: Trope's videos might have aroused a flogged and fearful America to rise against its criminal government, and the world might have changed for the better. But that wouldn't happen now. Complacency and apathy would retain their grip on America.

Not long ago, she wouldn't have cared what happened outside her four walls, but those walls had been demolished. She was in the world now, and it was an ugly one, stripped of decency and humanity.

Sue McConnell, Jack Ripley, and the sheriff were counting on her for leadership, for change, for the smallest hope that America might become fair and right again once its long night was over. And she was pretending to be the leader they needed and deserved. That was wrong. She had to deliver on her promises, not play a Washington lying game.

But she was nobody, a self-absorbed, resentful agoraphobe in the fast lane to oblivion, and no matter how much Figment urged her, no matter how much she yearned to be the Anarchista of her fantasies, no matter how hard she hoped for a better world, she couldn't imagine the status quo changing. She gazed at the cornfields, crippled by the same sense of futility she'd felt in the Revenge junkyard, and unable to find a clever gambit to rescue her.

Ada interrupted her rumination when she bumped her leg. She seemed to be awake, but her mind was somewhere else. Krista waved her hands in front of Ada's eyes and she blinked. "Oh, hi," she said. "I just had the most amazing revelation."

"Really? What?"

"Take this down. I just saw a brown algorithm, brown and bubbly like English stout. Those are important."

Krista pulled out her tablet, and Ada recited a long and incomprehensible mathematical expression. Krista sat and tapped on her tablet, now and then asking for clarifications, and read it back to her when she was done.

"No," Ada said. "That part's a shiny yellow expression, like melting butter. Light speed is variable in shiny yellows, so it's a over the integral of s, not f. C is inconstant."

"Like melting butter. Right." She made the change. "What's all this mean?"

"It defines the relationship of energy to space in locally distorted timewells, enabling modulation of the truon feed and containment of the toron array."

"Okay. What's all this mean?"

"Duh. It makes time travel possible." Ada yawned and curled up in her lap. "Been wanting to figure that out for a while."

She began to snore, and Krista looked at the gibberish on her screen. *Right. This is just another Base-M hallucination.* She deleted the file and closed her eyes to rest them, but she fell asleep within seconds.

"Did you get any sleep?" Raphael asked.

"Some, but not much." Downs rubbed his eyes and yawned. "I'm ready for the Watch, though."

"There's a protest up in Anacostia later this morning, but we have light fug today and solid acquisition from Blackeye 2. Other than that, it's been slow. No news, of course, from Indiana."

"I know." Downs looked up at the Wall – the teams were still scouring the area, but they'd find nothing. Warner and the package had slipped away again.

"You read what Warner just posted, I take it?" Raphael asked.

Downs scowled and looked away. "I have."

"So *we* weren't played last night, Bob. *You* were. She pushed your buttons and made fools of us all."

"Watch that talk."

"You need to hear it. You want her dead so bad that you're letting her manipulate you. Your situational awareness is being subsumed by your passions, my friend."

"*If* what she wrote was true, Raf. Don't assume it is. I think this was an Activist operation to draw out our resources for another search and distract us from another operation. It was clearly planned. How else did she disappear at the river?"

"She was in the boat. We found her hair and we have a DNA match."

"Fine," Downs said. "But where'd she go from there? How'd she disappear at the bridge with all the assets we had deployed? It was a sophisticated operation, and Warner was using herself as bait, and that's all there's to it." He walked around the edge of the podium and watched as Ryan Beckmann briefed Buta on the status of Acquisition. "And I still think she had help."

"Look, take some advice. You're too engaged in this, and you're losing your perspective. This is dangerous, very dangerous. You have to stay detached to do this job, and brother, you are nowhere near detached."

"Detached? I'll get detached when Warner is dead and the cancer inside this Watch Room is cut out. That should be soon."

"Careful, Bob. We still don't know anything."

"Oh, yes we do," Downs said. "I know that Hogue and Beckmann are dirty. I feel it inside, and I'll find the evidence soon enough. Then we'll act and clean our house."

"Beckmann isn't dirty," Raphael said, his face reddening. "Listen to me – you're looking for a scapegoat because you're blowing it with Warner. You need to accept your failure and move on, not destroy things..."

"Watch where you're going, Raphael."

"...not destroy things in a temper tantrum because you've got some sorta hate-on for this chick, goddammit!"

"Enough, Mr. Vinola! Step off my podium, or I'll have you removed!"

Raphael took one step back onto the carpet of the Watch Room floor. "The Watch is yours, Mr. Downs," he said stiffly.

"Damn right it is, Mr. Vinola."

DISPATCHES

Molle's Hill
NewsHub Political Affairs Channel
Broadcast Transcript of September 25, 2043

Molle: Dr. Stanton, thanks for coming on my show. I must admit that I wasn't expecting you.

Stanton: It was a spur-of-the-moment thing. I came here to talk about the innovative stuff we're doing at the Respiratory Care Center up at Georgetown Hospital.

Molle: Tell us all about that.

Stanton: I can't. I've forgotten what I was supposed to say. Ever since they hooked me up to that machine at the National Tranquility Center, that's been happening a lot.

Molle: Why were you there? I thought only children were allowed to tour it.

Stanton: Oh, they wanted to talk to me about The Activity, but I told them I didn't know anything – after all, how could there be a resistance when there's nothing to resist? We don't have the Ironshirts of the bad old days marching the streets. And they wanted to talk about something else.

Molle: Yes? What was that?

Stanton: I can't remember. I think it was about that girl I was dating a few weeks ago, what's her name –

Molle: Krista Warner?

Stanton: That's it! They wanted to ask questions about her. They have this wonderful machine down there called a Mapper, which makes mind models or something, and it was terrific! It was like years of therapy in a matter of minutes! It drained all my worries and inhibitions.

Molle: Well, I'd like a few minutes of *that*. How do I get in?

Stanton: Oh, it's by invitation only.

Molle: I'll be sure to get myself invited! I have friends in high places.

Stanton: Speaking of high places, have you heard of the new restaurant, Brutus?

Molle: The one under the tracks at Union Station?

Stanton: That's the one. It's quite an experience – they slaughter, butcher, and prepare your beef right at your table.

Molle: Now that's as fresh as you can get.

Stanton: Absolutely. I've reserved a table for tomorrow night, and I'm planning to invite the most beautiful woman in the world to go with me. Are you free then?

Molle: Oh, yes, Dr. Stanton, I certainly am! What time is the reservation?

Stanton: I forget.

⊙═⊙═⊙═⊙

Midnight Sun
News Post of September 25, 2043

MASSACRE IN THE NATION'S CAPITAL

What follows is a transcript of a satellite phone message we received moments ago from our Witness in Anacostia:

"I'm walking a few feet behind the front line of the protesters as we march across the South Capitol Street Bridge. Mae Esteban stands in the middle, and they have their arms linked to make a single line from side to side.

"Lined up on the other side are Metro Police in riot gear, crouching behind their shields like they're expecting violence. They're wasting their time because Esteban told everyone to leave their weapons behind, and we're only going to the middle of the bridge anyway. I don't think the Metro Police understand that. Maybe they think we're stupid enough to storm their lines and try to take over the District or something.

"We're just taking our bridge back and saying that from now on, you're in our town and you play by our rules. And one of the rules is that if the government won't give us the vaccine, then they can't drive through our town.

"Hundreds of protesters are chanting what Esteban said at the rally last night – 'our town, our people, our rules'. Everyone's wearing masks, so it's a little muffled, but I think the police are getting the message.

"It's peaceful, but our side is a little hot. The Metro Police are just watching, and they're calm – they don't even have their nightsticks drawn, and it seems like they want to avoid a confrontation –

"A shot! I just heard a shot. Nobody's supposed to have guns…one of the men next to Esteban is on the ground…oh, fuck…some of the Metro Police are looking off the bridge and behind to the right, they're pointing like they heard where the shot came from…their line's breaking up…I see the man now, a young guy, bleeding…yeah, he's bleeding from the stomach and Esteban is kneeling next to him and doing something, yeah, that's right, she's a doctor.

"An officer just broke through the Metro line, and he's running over carrying something…a first-aid kit…Oh, Christ, someone shot him! There was a gunshot from our side, and he's down on the ground…Oh lord, oh lord, don't do this, people…Shit!

"They're firing back, all of them now, back and forth, this is madness, how could this go so wrong, so fast…gimme a minute.

"Okay, I'm back. I took cover next to one of the light poles, and Esteban is still in the middle of the bridge…she's alive, but the damn fools are all shooting at each other, oh dear Lord, stop this if you can…I see a few Metro officers down, but there are lots of our people out there, and they're not moving. I think they're hurt or maybe dead.

"Esteban's standing up now. She's standing up into the line of fire, for God's sake! Just look at that, she's holding up her hands to both sides and yelling something and bullets are whizzing back and forth…I've never seen such bravery anywhere…the gunfire's slowing down, and I just saw one of our men tackle another one with a gun and throw it off the bridge…Wait, a man just stood up and he's walking to Esteban…okay, no one's shooting now, and as Jesus is my savior, I hope that doesn't happen again. This is bad, the worst thing I've ever seen.

"There's more commotion on our side…I think the people behind us just figured out what happened and they're agitated. Two men are walking, now there's three, and they're holding their arms out to the side to show they have no guns…the middle of the bridge is, well, I thought those folks were just taking cover, but dear god, most of them aren't moving now…there's so many and they're so young…the Metro Police are pulling back now, and a helicopter is hovering over the river with guns aimed at us, but Esteban doesn't seem to care. She's telling people what to do and waving for more to come help, but no one wants to go out there.

"Okay, now I can see, it's two Metro officers and ten, no, eleven citizens…this is a massacre, there's no other word for it, and I can't believe this really happened…I saw history happen before my eyes. I wish I didn't.

"Sirens now from the District side, and I think I hear some from Anacostia, but it could be the echo…no, the crowd's separating, and a St. E's ambulance is driving up.

"Wait a few…*here, no, I'm okay, help the others, no, it's just a scratch*…the paramedics just picked up two people and they're putting them in the ambulance, I guess there's no reason to rush the others to the hospital…there go the two Metro officers now, and there goes the St. E's ambulance. Esteban is yelling at the men, and they're gathering around the bodies…they're picking up the dead, two men to a body, and now they're running off the bridge…Esteban looks sad and angry at the same time and…*yeah, I hear you man, I'm moving*…I gotta disconnect now."

THE AMERICAN MAIN

Day 38
Friday evening, September 25, 2043
Near Moberly, Missouri

Krista was enjoying a soft, happy dream of does and fawns, but it shattered when the coal hit the floor.

"Sorry," Ada said. "I didn't think it'd be that loud." She plucked a piece of coal from a bag, examined it, and threw it outside. It bounced onto the tracks, and then she picked up another and did the same thing.

Krista rubbed her eyes. "Are you all right?" she asked carefully, unsure whether this was another weird Base-M episode. Although the symptoms supposedly lasted only twelve hours, the SatNet advice could be wrong. It often was.

Ada scratched a chunk with her fingernail. "Don't look at me like I'm nuts. The spiders came back when you were sleeping, and I decided to do something to stay awake."

"So you got a bag of coal?"

"I cracked open that control panel and checked the train's route. Those cars behind us filled up with coal in Scranton, which was delivered to KLEPTCO Bellefontaine. The coal tender was also filled in Scranton, so I climbed over to check it out. By the way, there aren't any engineers or anything. We're the only people on the train."

"I figured it was automatic, like everything else."

"Yeah. Anyway, since this is Scranton coal, I grabbed a bag to see if there were any Hot Rocks in it. I'd feel better if I had high explosives on hand."

Krista smiled, relieved that Ada was returning to normal. "Were the spiders bad?"

"Yes."

"Did you find any Hot Rocks?"

"No."

"Are you mad at me?"

"No," Ada said. "I'm tired and hungry and I can't stop shaking and I keep getting the heebie-jeebies every time I remember that Blue Ball planted that chip in me. My scalp keeps crawling when I think they put one in my brain too, and then I freak, which together with the spider shakes is like proof that I'm effed up even beyond the reach of Sigmund-Freakin-Freud. *And* I didn't sleep for more than few minutes while you were asleep. I'm totally frazzled. I wish I had earbuds so I could let Blac Sac blow this away. God, I'd even listen to that Keriana crap right now."

"I wish you'd stop bashing my Keriana music. And even if you had earbuds, I couldn't let you listen to my Blac Sac. My battery is almost dead. It usually lasts for weeks, but I can't keep a charge on it anymore. I hope nothing's wrong." Krista slid her backpack over and pulled out the baby food can. "Well, at least we can eat. There's still most of a can left." She mixed a shake in her water bottle, and they passed it back and forth until it was empty.

"We need to ration that," Ada said. "This train's destination is a strip mine in Antelope Valley, up in Bumfuck Wyoming near the Montana border. We might be on it for three days."

"Three whole days? That's splendid news."

"But I could hack the controls and take over the train if you want. We could throw the hammer down and barrel into Sacramento." Ada sorted through the rocks again. "It wouldn't be all that hard."

"Someone would notice. We'd give our position away."

"I don't care. I don't want to see Bumfuck Wyoming again. I say we oughta go straight to California."

"And I don't, so we'll go to Wyoming."

"Hold on! Since when do you decide everything?"

"Well, if I've got multiple personalities, I get multiple votes. You only get one. That's the price of being sane."

Ada checked another lump of coal and frowned. "All right, that's fair. Kick-Ass Krista deserves a vote. Oh, by the way, did I ask you to write down an algorithm this morning?"

Krista found something to examine in her lap. "You said a lot of things."

"Maybe it was another hallucination." Ada threw all the coal chunks through the door and slammed it closed. "This isn't helping at all. It's just making me more jittery."

"Let's try something else, then. Come here," Krista said. "Get your briefcase and sit here, and I'll give you a neck rub and tell you what Bob Downs said about it."

Ada's eyes brightened. "He knows about it?" She slid her briefcase over and set it in her lap, and Krista massaged her neck muscles, which were as tight and knotted as if she'd been knitted by an angry sailor.

"He wants 'the package,' as he called it, so I don't think he knows it's in a briefcase. But he wants what's in it. I heard it in his voice, and I think he wants that more than my tablet."

"Mmm," Ada said. "Knowing my mom, I'll bet there's something really nasty in here." Faint clicks came from her lap as she tickled the combination dial. "Oh yeah, keep that up, I love neck rubs," she said. Five minutes later, she was asleep.

"See, kid?" Krista murmured. "I'm magic."

THE FAIRIES HAD TAKEN KRISTA AWAY AGAIN, and she gazed sightlessly at the blinking control panel lights, letting her mind drift. Despite being hunted for the past few weeks, she'd been feeling flashes of hope; if she survived, she might find her freedom and build a new life, which she would have never found in the fetid dungeon of Washington. The shackles of conformity had crippled her for too long, and she vowed never to return to that swamp.

She opened her tablet and sent a message to her attorney instructing him to sell her building and put the proceeds in her trust's cash account. It might not sell for much, but anything was better than nothing for a building she'd never see again.

The car's shaking had jiggled Ada to the floor, where she'd curled up in a ball between Krista's legs, her head on the folded hoodie. Krista extricated her legs and then stood by the control panel to stretch. It was made by WAGEX Corporation, like the box she'd seen on the bridge in Revenge. This machine had probably replaced ten men – brawny, hardworking men who were long gone.

She lit a cigarette and opened the window. Outside, a green carpet of corn stretched to the horizon and reached for the clouds, interrupted only by cracked roads and an occasional harvested strip. Dusk crept in from the east, and the few farmhouses and barns she saw were dark and empty. Dense vines climbed the walls, and sometimes even the roofs, so they'd been neglected for years.

Birds soared, and insects swarmed in dark clouds above the waving stalks. The Life Force was so rich here that she felt it fill the empty pores of her soul, but she felt repelled at the same time – this sea of corn and wheat was alien to human life, and she and Ada were the only two creatures with souls here. A sharp twinge of loneliness pricked at her heart.

A small town rolled past the window, and every house was empty. Grain silos flashed by, but like the ones in Maravelle, they were caved in or leaning drunkenly, slowly being demolished by nature. At the far edge of town, a beetle-shaped Producer churned away at the edge of a cornfield; a row of once-green farm tractors sat on a lawn next to it, each rusting and buried in a ring of weeds, their operators having moved on long ago.

An awful realization struck her then, and as she watched the land of maize but not men flit past, she wished that she could remember how to cry.

⊙═⊙═⊙═⊙═⊙

The Rake
September 25, 2043

THE AMERICAN MAIN
They toss our bones across the marble and read their fortunes, and they think themselves gods

I remember a long-ago October day when my mother and I took a drive to upstate New York around Halloween. She wanted a fresh pumpkin for the pie and another to make a jack-o'-lantern with me.

It was a crisp day, back when the falls were still cool, the kind of day that promised cold winters and warm holidays. I watched the farms pass my window, and I remember seeing tractors and trucks rumbling to and fro as they brought in the harvest. The sweet smell of burning autumn leaves hung in the air, and I drew in as much as I could hold. For a singular and sacred moment, I felt peace; for once, the world was right and good.

As day ended – and I remember so clearly the splendid orange sunset that night – lights in the farmhouses burned bright, and smoke lazed from their chimneys. In those homes, couples bickered, meals were eaten, small victories were celebrated, and life as we knew it carried on as if it always would.

I'm glad I remember this time because it's gone. As I sail the inland sea of corn and wheat that was once our vibrant American Main, I see no human life, no tractors, no farmhouses flying the flag. I only see automatic machines and empty houses, the residue of life that moved on, or passed on, so many years ago.

Having seen the bones of America's breadbasket, I now understand why Gabriel Cheyn unleashed the virus on us: He's cleaning up the mess left behind after the Great Correction killed that October Country I remember.

And you and me are that mess.

Long ago, so long that I read about it in history books, America had a 'middle' class. They had to go – all the historians agree they were an aberration – and the members of that class descended into the rank and file after the coronavirus slammed them and triggered the Great Correction. For a time, it seemed like a natural thing, the economic crisis being a necessary wildfire that would bring forth a new and healthier economic forest.

That's where we made our mistake. We discovered too late that this middle class was essential to the economy's stability. They married the aspirations of the wealthy to the brawn of the rank and file, making a fair economy possible for all. When they disappeared, so did half the American economy.

Faced with this crisis, our corporate masters did something we never expected of fellow Americans: They turned their backs on our balky economy and built new businesses in Asia. The jobs that the rank and file depended upon – farming, manufacturing, construction – disappeared overnight, and unemployment and discontent rose. The value of the dollar plunged, and the government, starved of money, cut assistance to the unemployed and elderly. In response, rioting spread across the land, a violence so severe that it took the heavy hand of fascism to stop it.

Those riots frightened our benevolent masters, who then embarked on a plan to crush the troublesome malcontents. Instead of giving them the jobs they needed, Corporate America gave even more work to the machines and overseas workers. The government contributed by shredding the social safety net and reducing government assistance to far below the poverty line. They probably believed that under such pressure, the rank and file would become extinct in a generation.

That plan failed. Unlike a tractor that will rust and decay by the forces of nature and time, the obsoleted worker will ask why he should be silent. Since he and his fellows resisted the fate imposed on them, they became an obstacle to the ambitions of *Homo Nobilis*.

So they had to die.

Money talks, I know, but sometimes Money whispers into its minions' ears and tells them to slaughter our fellow humans. That I didn't know.

I'm sure Gabriel has a splendid euphemism to mask this atrocity: Rightsizing the Republic? Downsizing our Democracy? Whatever he calls it, it can be better described in two words: Final Solution. Like Hitler, this ball-less braincase will do what humans never would.

Okay, I should curb the crude language, but it's hard when all I want is to wrap my fingers around Cheyn's skinny, wrinkled neck and squeeze till his head pops like the pimple it is. But I'll try to be good.

It's easy to feel enraged that our government and business leaders have resorted to genocide merely to gain more worthless dollars, but it's precisely at such a crossroads that we should step back and try to understand how we got here.

It's not completely unexpected. After all, it's a peculiarity of humanity, this morbid fascination with our extinction, especially by some extravagantly gruesome and violent death spectacle. It's been this way since the early days of Greek drama, and even today, scores of books wipe us out with an astonishing yet unlikely disaster.

But we consume it all with delight because *it isn't real*. We know that the authors write these stories to shock or seduce us into a greater, gentler humanity, not because they're pimping some diabolical plan. Perhaps this is how Gabriel missed the point: One must be human to grasp the concept of humanity, and that feckin chthonic gobshite is so far from human that Martian microbes would have more compassion…

Right, I mustn't let my anger get the better of me. Anyway, my point is that these writers titillate us with disasters and apocalypses we know will never happen. They don't write these books as damned how-to manuals, you know. They're bloody works of FICTION! Listen, when Jonathan Swift said we should eat the Irish, he didn't mean we should grab our forks and toddle over to the feckin Emerald Isle! For fuck's sake, Gabriel, isn't it bloody obvious that this shit is WRONG? Are you so…Can you be…?

Screw it. I did my breathing exercises and found my serenity, and I released the homicidal anger poisoning my soul. But now I can't think of anything to say.

I give up. Trying to understand this madman's motivations won't lessen this horror. It won't blunt the pain. It won't stop a virus. It won't bring back those we've lost.

Only the assassins can fix this now.

-KLW

DISPATCHES

Midnight Sun
News Post of September 26, 2043

NEOVIRUS CONFIRMED IN CHICAGO

Eight cases of Neovirus were confirmed inside Chicago this morning. Since the infected individuals were inside the city before the absolute cordon, experts believe that measure has proved ineffective, and Neovirus may already be spreading throughout the state.

The disease has spread to the American Midwest and South as infected individuals flee the Northeast. Neovirus is now suspected as far west as Kansas City and as far south as Jacksonville.

Midnight Sun has stopped receiving reports from our Witnesses in Indiana, Kentucky, Tennessee, and Georgia. This may be a more accurate indication of the disease's spread than MRC reports.

SOUTH CAPITOL STREET BRIDGE DESTROYED IN WASHINGTON

Our Witness in Anacostia reports on the dramatic events unfolding in Southeast Washington:

"About an hour ago, I got blown outta bed by two explosions. The windows rattled, and the bed shook so hard that I fell on the floor. I turned off the lights because I thought that anonymous 'they' was finally coming after us. I think I'm getting as paranoid as everyone else around here.

"I dressed and headed down to the river. I went down to the Anacostia River levee, and a crowd there was pointing up and down the river. I was stunned by what I saw.

"The South Capitol Street Bridge is gone. Not totally, but there's no center span over the river anymore. Someone blew it up, and it had to be someone from our side. I'd bet a week's salary on that. Everyone in Anacostia was hot and angry over the massacre on the bridge this morning.

"I hear that the other bridges were barricaded, but I'm not sure about that, and I'll be taking a walk up to the Eleventh Street Bridge to see for myself. They say all the other roads into town are barricaded too.

"I also got a phone call from a friend in Annapolis last night, just before I went to bed. He said Governor Molloy has mobilized the Maryland National Guard, and they'll be stationed along the border to keep the violence inside the District.

"And now it's down to violence. This is getting out of control, and I'm not sure if anyone is in charge here. I saw Esteban last night, and she had a group of people with her, so maybe she's running things. I'm just not sure.

"I wish I'd moved my family out of town when I had the chance. It looks like my window of opportunity might have just slammed shut."

LEGISLATURE TO VOTE ON TENPEZ, WHITE HOUSE THREATENS RETALIATION

The State Legislature of California will vote on the tenpez recall this afternoon. The chances of passage are rumored to be very high.

During this morning's press conference, the White House Press Secretary stated, "It is the Gibbon Administration's position that any State, acting against the Union's interests, should be prepared to accept reciprocal sanctions or unilateral actions, up to and including the use of force by the United States Government. This includes the withdrawal of Federal emergency assistance for natural or public-health disasters."

A reporter asked if that meant that California would be denied the vaccine if they passed the tenpez recall measure. The Press Secretary's answer was blunt: "Yes."

An hour later, the White House computer system was hacked. It is still offline as of this writing.

TAKING THE CURE

Day 39
Saturday morning, September 26, 2043
Near Bonner Springs, Kansas

After the South Capitol Street Bridge Massacre, many political observers expected The Activity to emerge from the shadows and retaliate, but the Activist voice was silent afterward. Dissidents and pundits speculated that the Federals had already eradicated the rebel movement.

The truth would have disappointed them: The Activity was asleep on a coal train, savoring a soft-porn dream of sweaty men beating glowing iron with mallets.

Clack-clack went the wheels and *clack-clack* went the mallets. Dream Krista, wearing a green ball gown, lounged on a rococo loveseat in a foundry. In the center of the floor, a brawny man raised his sweat-sheened arm, bicep rippling, and then he turned to her with a raised eyebrow. The upraised hammer remained poised for the strike as if he was unwilling to make noise in a lady's presence.

An unseen band started blowing soft jazz, and a dwarf wearing a floppy red tam o'shanter soft-shoed to her side, a silver tray with a coffeepot balanced on his stubby fingers. She poured some brew into a crystal cup, and she sipped with a pinky raised while eyeing the young man. He wanted her, she knew, but he wasn't picking up on the breadcrumb trail of come-hither cues she'd dropped. She realized that the boy wasn't too bright, which turned her on even more.

"Don't mind me," Dream Krista told the blacksmith. "Please, carry on, *my good man.*" She grinned inside – even he would understand a hint that bold.

He shined her a toothpaste-ad smile, complete with a sparkling *ting*, and then he pounded the hammer on the hot iron and...*clack-thunk*. The little cabin shook as the train bumped over a loose rail, and her head thumped against the windowsill. She swore and looked blearily through the window at the lightening eastern sky.

Stretching the stiffness from her muscles, she stood and yawned even though she wasn't tired. In the past twenty-four hours, she'd slept for more than sixteen and hadn't moved more than a few feet around the cabin. Ada was curled up on the floor at her feet, sleeping deeply now that the Base-M had left her bloodstream.

She rummaged in her backpack for water, but the bottle was only half full. They'd have to jump off the train to find food and water soon – if they could find a town with real people and not machines. While it was a relief not being hunted, the prospect of starving and dehydrating was just as bad.

She slid the small window open, lit a cigarette, and watched the monotonous Kansas countryside sail by. They were still rolling through farmland, but it was more depressing than what she'd seen yesterday. Even the abandoned towns and vestigial roadways were gone, replaced by unbroken expanses of cornfields.

She heard a rustle, and then Ada stood beside her. "Good morning," Krista said, and Ada grumbled as she flicked her lighter. "Feeling a bit jammered? Well, with what you've gone through, it's understandable."

Ada grumbled again, pulled a few stray hairs back from her face, and wiped grime from it with the back of her hand. "I've forgotten about Revenge already."

"You have?"

"Yeah, mostly. I have something like an asylum in my outerbrain full of prison cells, and that's where I stuff the scary things. I call them Sanity Cells. Once I lock something in one, it can't get out. That's where Revenge is now. I locked and bolted that door a while ago."

"I wish I could have a few of those. They'd come in handy right about now."

"I couldn't live without them," Ada said. "Literally. I'd be dead by now if I couldn't forget some things."

"Seriously?" Krista tried to look into her eyes, but Ada turned away from her and would say nothing more.

∞∞∞∞∞

Taking the Cure

KRISTA LEANED AGAINST THE RATTLING METAL WALL again, and Ada sat between her legs and fiddled with the briefcase on her lap.

"How many more combinations do you have left?" Krista asked.

"Just under a million."

"That'll take forever," she said, squirming to find a comfortable spot.

"Maybe, maybe not. I could hit the right combination anytime. It's an equal win/lose probability each time."

"You tried birthdays and all the usual combinations?"

"Of course," Ada said. She went back to turning the lock dial – tick-tick-*tick*, tick-tick-*tick* like a metronome, and together with the thumping of the cabin's wheels over the tracks, Krista's mind sank into simple blankness. She was staring sightlessly at the far wall when the briefcase clicked.

"You opened it?" Krista asked.

"Yeah! The combination was 01-14-75 – Albert Schweitzer's birthday! Why didn't I see that?"

"That's so obvious! Are you sure you're a genius?"

"Sometimes I wonder." Ada's fingers ran across the gray suede interior. "Two thick packets of papers. A pen and a pencil and that's about it, wait, there's something back here in the lid pocket. There's a picture of me, and there's another one…"

"What?" Krista asked, but she didn't answer. She looked over her shoulder again, and Ada held a silver-framed photograph in her hand. A tall man in a uniform and a shorter woman in a wedding gown smiled for the camera.

"Who are they?" Krista asked, and when Ada didn't answer, she looked closer. "Whoa, that's got to be your mom! You two are practically twins!"

"Yeah, Freak One and Freak Two," Ada muttered.

"At least you know what you'll look like when you grow up. Is the man your father?"

"I guess."

"You don't know?"

"If I ever saw his face, I don't remember it." Her grimy finger drew circles around the man's face. "They divorced when I was two, and Mom never kept any pictures of him."

"Except for one."

"Yeah," Ada whispered. "Huh. So I wasn't a baster baby, and Mom didn't get inseminated by aliens or anything like that. I had a real father." She pulled a square of toilet paper from her bookbag and wiped her eyes. "This feels weird."

"I can imagine. It must be surreal."

"I'm a little dizzy."

"You've just had a shock. Take a few deep breaths and you'll be okay. Here, lay back against me and relax."

Ada slid the briefcase off her lap and laid her head against her stomach, never taking her eyes from the picture. "He looks like a Jim to me."

"You don't even know his name?"

Ada shook her head. "As far as my mom's concerned, he didn't exist. She never told me anything no matter how much I nagged her."

"Okay, so that just plain sucks. There's no other word for it."

"Yeah. She's a bad mom sometimes, but still…" Her shoulders shook, and Krista pulled out a wad of toilet paper and dabbed at her cheeks.

"I'm screwed up. I'm a wreck," Ada said.

"Welcome to the human race, kiddo."

"Was it like that with you? Did you get the same feelings with your mom, y'know, love her and hate her at the same time?"

"She died when I was eleven. I never got a chance to hate her," Krista said. "I loved her and despised the Warners. I despised their feckin grand townhouse on Society Hill and their feckin fat faces. You know, I didn't eat a single meal their chef made because I figured they'd spike my food with roofies or something? For a year, I just ate chocolate bars, and did the Warners even ask why?" She laid her head back against the rattling wall, her mouth hard and tight. "They couldn't care less what I felt. They just wanted to keep me alive so they could suck bucks outta my inheritance. The bastards just shipped me off to some bloody hospital in Jersey and shoved a feeding tube down my throat."

"Why didn't you sue them?"

"I tried. I couldn't find a lawyer ballsy enough to sue Judge Warren Warner."

"Warren Warner?" Ada asked. "That's the douchenozzle who heard my case!"

"Get out! He was a national security judge? I always figured he did something with taxes."

"It was definitely Warren Warner. I remember him. He had a face like an overstuffed pillow with two teeny black buttons. And he was huge, like eight feet wide."

"Don't exaggerate," Krista said. "Four feet, tops. But that's what you get by eating a seven-course dinner every night. He literally ate my inheritance." Krista looked up at the ceiling. "The chocolate cake was tasty, though. Sometimes I'd sneak a piece in the middle of the night."

"I'm so sorry for you. I only had to suffer Judge Nozzle for an hour. You had to live with him for years. *That's* a galactic screw job."

"I know, right? Anyway, Judge Nozzle kept me in that hospital for a week till we made a deal – I still wouldn't eat their food, but I promised to eat something more nutritious than chocolate bars. I only ate at restaurants after that, a different one every night so they couldn't figure out my routine and drug me."

"You were a little rebel even back then, huh?" Ada asked.

"I thought I was, but I never changed a thing. All I ever did was make everybody as miserable as me. And the crappy diet screwed up my knees. In the end, I hurt myself more than anyone else. So you're not the only one with a messed-up childhood."

"All right, we're both screwed up. I feel better now." Her eyes turned back to the photograph. "So you think he's a Jim?"

Krista took the photograph from her hand. "More like a Dirk or a Thor."

She laughed and took it back. "Right, like anyone's named Thor."

"If you want to find his name, you should check your birth certificate. The father's name is usually listed, and since they were married…"

"The birth certificate in my records is fake," Ada said. "I've never seen the real one, and I never will. I have Q-Level clearance, which is like nosebleed level, so Los Alamos blackwalls my records."

Krista scratched her head. "I'm not following you. Back up a bit, wouldja?"

"Remember, Blue Ball created a false identity for me. But they also buried the real one behind a digital blackwall so the Reds can't learn who I am. Even *I* can't find out the truth now. That was one of the things Mom had to agree to in Bumfuck Wyoming."

"Wow, I'm sorry. It's like they erased you."

"Yeah, that's one reason I'm so screwed up." Gazing at the blinking control panels, a crooked smile crossed her lips. She snorted a soft laugh. "I'm gonna get them back for it. I know every nuclear secret we have, and I'm gonna be naughty and tell you some."

"Ooh! I like secrets, especially somebody else's!"

"It'll feel good to tell the truth for once. I'm *so* ready for treason." Ada wrinkled her nose and grinned. "Okay, the Hiroshima bombing? That was probably a mistake, but we'll never know for sure cuz *Emma Dilemma* and her crew vanished after the bombing. They were supposed to drop Little Boy –"

"Wait, wait, I know this! *Enola Gay* dropped the Hiroshima bomb! I'm right for once!"

Ada smiled serenely. "Are you?"

"That I am. I read it in my history classes, kiddo, and…oh, crap." Krista rested her head against the wall with a thump and looked at the ceiling. "That was all made up?"

"Well, yeah. Nobody was gonna admit Hiroshima was the worst FUBAR ever, so the government erased everything about *Emma Dilemma* and wrote in *Enola Gay*. Anyway, *Emma Dilemma* was supposed to drop Little Boy on Okurokami Island, an unpopulated rock eleven miles south of Hiroshima, just to show the Japanese that nuclear war would suck ass and they oughta surrender. But they dropped it smack in the middle of Hiroshima for some reason. By the way, speaking of nuclear oopsies, you know why we did all that so-called nuclear bomb testing in the Nevada desert a hundred years ago? That was World War Three."

"You're kidding!" Krista said, sitting up. "Tell me everything."

"The funny thing is, you know most of that story already, but you're conditioned to deny the truth. *But the truth is out there! Bwah-hah-hah!*" She wiggled her fingers in Krista's face, who shrank back. "But lemme tell you something you don't know – the lab at Los Alamos is emptier than Arista Molle's head. We just say we're using it to screw with the Reds. The real lab is five miles west underneath Pajarito Mountain, and you get there by underground trolley. Oh, and here's another juicy one – Klaus Fuchs actually wasn't a traitor."

"Klaus who?"

"Seriously, Krista? The guy who gave the hydrogen bomb to the Soviets in World War Two?"

"Oh, *him!* Right, right. I was thinking of somebody else."

"It was actually Roosevelt's idea for Klaus to defect. He gave the Reds so much garbage science, it set their weapons program back twelve years. I read that in a special library down on Level Nine named after him. Only the Q's can get into it cuz it stores all America's nuclear secrets, and boy, some of the stuff in there will straighten your pubes right out, trust me."

"Now *that's* a juicy secret," Krista said. "But weren't you only supposed to go there after you graduated –"

"Holy crap, look at that!" Ada said, pointing through the window.

"What?"

"A huge bird flew by, guess you missed it. So anyway, I checked my fake birth certificate, and it lists the father's name as 'unknown.' It also says I was born in Minnesota, but I know I was born in Virginia."

Krista patted her shoulder. "Okay, you win. Your childhood was way more messed up than mine."

"Great, so when do I get my valuable prize?"

"Your prize is more strength of character. Some crap like that."

Ada shrugged and sighed. "I wish I knew more about him. I mean, it's nice to see a picture, but it's driving me nuts now. This is like giving a starving person a taste of food and then taking the plate away."

"Let me see that." Krista took the frame from her and squinted at the man's clothes. "I can help. For one thing, he was a commander in the Navy."

"Duh. Really, the uniform's a dead giveaway."

"Do you want my help or not? I know a lot about military insignias and medals."

"Sorry." Ada turned to see the picture.

"I did a post once on veterans selling their medals for food money," Krista said, taking the pen from the briefcase. "I spent some time in a Georgetown shop talking to a guy who bought and sold them. I got to know the medals pretty well." She pointed to the ribbons on his chest. "This is a PRC campaign ribbon, so he was in the war. This is the Purple Heart, so he was wounded in combat. These two are unit commendations. These other ribbons, I don't know."

"So he was a war veteran."

"Ahh, but not *only* that. There's a ginormous clue in this picture."

"C'mon, don't torture me. What?"

Krista tapped the photo. "See this gold star hanging from the blue ribbon around his neck?"

"Yeah?" Ada fidgeted and squinted at the picture. "What is it?"

"That's the Medal of Honor."

Ada held the picture up to her nose and whistled. "Wow. My dad was a war hero?"

"That he was."

"Wow." Ada's gaze became soft and dreamy.

"And here's the best part – only four hundred people got the Medal of Honor in the PRC, and I'm sure there's a list of them somewhere," Krista said. "That'll make him easier to find."

ADA PROPPED THE PICTURE AGAINST THE WALL and started reading. Krista delved into a packet as well but found pages of numbers looking so much like freshman algebra that her brain froze up. She only understood a few of the words – a, and, the, but, and Recombin.

However, Ada knew what she was reading; she smoked nervously, and her neck muscles bunched in knots as she swore blistering Zulu insults. She leafed through the packet again to see what was agitating her, but it still made no sense, and she closed her eyes to doze for a few minutes.

After she awoke, she leaned against the windowsill and checked her mail, as well as *Midnight Sun*, which was becoming more depressing every day. Ada appeared by her side a few minutes later and stared out at the passing fields.

"What's your diagnosis, Doctor?" Krista asked.

"Fuckery," Ada said with a dark look. "Plain ole fuckery. But you don't need me to tell you that. You read it."

"Why don't you give me your take?"

"It's obvious that Chalys knew about this for years," Ada said. "They had to. You're right – this was a planned biowar, and Chalys was part of it. They made Recombin from March through June of this year and then stopped before they had enough to vaccinate the entire population." She lit a cigarette and puffed furiously. "They were never planning to save everybody."

"They didn't. They had a list, and a lot of people weren't on it. They offered salvation only to the ones they picked. And they're still at it. I read that the White House is threatening to deny the vaccine to California if they pass the tenpez recall this afternoon, so the Administration isn't even trying to hide the fact that they're using the vaccine as a bludgeon."

"Actually, Recombin's not a vaccine. It's a virophage, a virus that feeds on other viruses," Ada said. "That's a crucial difference in a lot of ways. For one thing, it's not manufactured, it's grown. That means we could grow our own Recombin if we had the feedstock."

"Really? We can make our own?"

"Not us, personally, but a technologically advanced state like California could." Ada took Krista's packet from her hand, thumbed through it, and stopped at a diagram. "This is the design for the Chalys continuous-tube bioreactor. Anybody could make one with enough time and money, and I'd bet California would sink a ton of time and money into this." She closed the packet and frowned. "The problem is that they don't have any feedstock to grow in it."

"Well, we have it in our blood, don't we? Why can't they just use that and grow it?"

"That's the problem with viruses. They mutate," Ada said. "The Recombin that's in our veins isn't the same we were injected with, and we don't know what it would do. Besides, there's nowhere near enough of it – maybe only a few milliliters between the two of us."

"I read that Neovirus mutated. *Midnight Sun* says it's become deadlier. It kills in a day now."

"That's no surprise," Ada said. "Take trillions of viruses and expose them to a living environment with billions of influences, and mutation is inevitable. You can't predict what a virus will do when it's released into the wild. Those idiots!" She threw the packet into the briefcase on the floor – and as it fell in, a flap loosened on a compartment in the lid.

They knelt to see what was in it. Ada pulled up a leather flap, and a dull silver box about six inches long lay in the foam-lined compartment beyond. She pulled it out and turned it over. "This is a Cryogenie. It's still working, but the battery is low."

"What's a Cryogenie?"

"A refrigerated transport container. I had about fifty of them at home. They didn't work anymore. Mom brought them home so I could keep my toys in them." Ada turned the thumbscrew on the front, and a faint hiss escaped the box. "Still cold." She opened the lid and then drew a sharp breath.

"What is it?" Krista asked.

She turned the Cryogenie around so Krista could see. Inside, six vials of Recombin lay nestled in their padded niches.

"Holy crap!" Krista said. "Is that the real stuff?"

Ada pried a vial out and held it up to the light, swirling the clear liquid inside. "Of course it is. You don't know The Commander. She has contingency plans for her contingency plans, and this was her Plan B. If the meeting at St. Elizabeth's went bad, she was going to take this to California and help them reproduce it."

"But how'd she know they'd need it? She must have planned this weeks before the epidemic hit." Krista took the vial and turned it over in her fingers. "Maybe she heard something at Chalys and figured out that an epidemic was coming."

"Yeah, and she decided to save the world all by herself. I totally love that woman." She sniffed and slipped the vial back into its niche, and then she looked at Krista with glistening eyes. "She left me feedstock. She wanted me to take it to California and save the freakin world, and that's what I'm gonna do. No matter what."

Krista took her hand. "And I'm going to do my best to help."

❮━━━━❯

The Rake
September 26, 2043

TAKING THE CURE
Cheyn and his minions better pray for poop lube because Big Bubba in Cell Block E goes in dry. I feel so bad for them

What a meal! I just ate a huge dinner at an Activist ranch out here: fresh breadsticks, vast bowls of steaming pasta drowned in the most delightful marinara, a fresh Cobb salad, and then a perky red to wash it all down.

But then I got to thinking, as I always do in postprandial contentment, and I realized that the Federal Fiends have proven to be so bloody incompetent that I can reveal a few details of my mission now.

Many of my readers know I'm taking my tablet with the original videos to another jurisdiction. I plan to pursue the prosecution of Gabriel Cheyn and other officials.

That jurisdiction is the State of California, and I'll place this evidence in the hands of the State Attorney General in Sacramento shortly.

But I'm not just bringing my tablet.

I'm also bringing three hundred milliliters of pure Recombin and the plans for the continuous-tube bioreactor required to produce it. This will give California the ability to grow a steady supply of the life-saving vaccine. In a matter of weeks, the people of California will be immune to Neovirus, and the State of California will be immune to Federal extortion.

Not only that, I've got all the receipts. I have abundant written evidence that proves the complicity of Chalys Pharmaceuticals in a genocidal conspiracy, one fomented by our own government. I can prove that Chalys knew about Neovirus six months before the epidemic began, and a thousand people will go to jail as a result.

Clang!

Did you hear that? It was the sound of a thousand sphincters slamming shut in Washington. Oh Gabriel, my Gabriel, it'll take so long for yours to relax again! It might even take tools! But take heart: If you aren't hanged, the booty bandits in Attica will open you up nice and wide.

Cling! Clong! Ding!

Ahh, I love the ring of rectums in the evening air. It sounds like Victory.

-KLW

DISPATCHES

Molle's Hill
NewsHub Political Affairs Channel
Broadcast Transcript of September 26, 2043

Molle: We're talking to Giulio Sclerota, CEO of AnalSys Global Strategies. How are you today, Mr. Sclerota?

Sclerota: I've had better days, Miss Molle, what with this rain and wind.

Molle: Hurricane Yolanda won't reach you in here. We're high and dry in the Capitol.

Sclerota: Yes, but my offices are in Newport, Rhode Island, and they might not be high and dry in a few hours. That's the root of my concern.

Molle: If you can tear yourself away from your worries for a few moments, we can finish our talk and have you on a plane back to the Big Apple.

Sclerota: I see, yes. The Big Apple.

Molle: As you know, a vote is underway in Sacramento on whether to make their gold tenpez the state's official currency. If it passes, this move would force Californians to exchange their dollars for tenpez, which could cause the dollar's value to drop. Many economists are concerned this will lead to financial instability in the other forty-nine states. As a noted economist, what's your prediction?

Sclerota: I don't need to predict, Miss Molle. It's already happening. The dollar began a plunge against world currencies yesterday, losing about thirty percent of its value. Asian debt holders are dumping their Treasury holdings – discreetly, of course, but enough that a significant increase in interest rates can be expected in the next Treasury debt auction. I believe the government's borrowing rate will triple, at least.

Molle: Is this bad news for America?

Sclerota: Well, yes, of course. The government will be insolvent in a few weeks or months at the most. I can't think of any worse outcome.

Molle: What are the implications of Federal insolvency?

Sclerota: The US government will default on its debt because it's using new bond issues to pay off the old ones. Initially, expect a shutdown of nonessential government offices and assistance payments.

Molle: And in the long run?

Sclerota: We'll witness a breakdown in civil order similar to what happened inside the Containment Ring in New York. The economic pain will impact the Ranks the most, and as we all know, your typical Rank will revert to his innate brutishness in times of crisis. I'll need to stay at my Grand Bahama property till they succumb to the virus or they've been brought under control. I'd rather my children didn't witness either event.

Molle: I didn't know Ranks were like that. I don't associate with them myself. They're not like real people.

Sclerota: They *are* real people. Let's not forget that. But they resist change and reject their economic responsibilities, which makes them markedly less civilized than you and me. Much like a tribe of lesser apes in the wild.

Molle: I wouldn't know. I don't have personal experience to draw on.

Sclerota: I do. My household staff is comprised of hard-core Ranks, and they can be quite coarse at times. The only thing elevating them above the level of savages is that they're gainfully employed, although they don't seem grateful for that or for the vaccine I got them. All the same, one must live with these types, no matter how much a trial it is, unless one wants to mow one's own lawn or discard one's own trash.

Molle: I wouldn't want to take out my own trash. Eww.

Sclerota: So we need some Ranks, and it makes sense that those with even minimal economic value get priority over the unemployed, the elderly, and the ex-workers. This is why I don't understand this controversy over the list Warner's blathering about. Let's face it: The ex-workers don't help the economy, so why should the economy help them? And the employed aren't much better.

Molle: I don't understand. They have jobs.

Sclerota: I've prepared a chart that illustrates my point. See where the Labor Cost line crosses the Output line? The Chinese workers, and even the Indians, cluster around this ideal target zone. But the American worker is way out here.

Molle: That's not a worker. That's a dot.

Sclerota: It's not a real American worker, Miss Molle. It just represents one.

Molle: Shouldn't you give it arms and legs, then? And the Chinese worker should have a funny cone hat. It'd be easier to understand that way.

Sclerota: Perhaps we should move on. As you can see, the American worker isn't competitive in the globalized labor market, and corporations can't keep giving them handouts forever. A cut in wages of perhaps eighty percent would be a good starting gesture, but –

Molle: When the American worker begins to starve, does his dot get smaller?

Sclerota: You really aren't getting this, are you?

Molle: I'll admit, I was never good at algebra, so I...hold on, I'm getting a news flash...yes, the California Legislature has unanimously passed the tenpez recall measure. Governor Rodriguez is expected to sign it into law tomorrow.

Sclerota: Well, the riots won't be far behind now. I hope your apartment is high enough that the rocks and the torches won't reach it.

Molle: Oh, don't worry, I'll be safe. I have my own army, thanks to General Esteban. I have the stars around here somewhere. Well, thanks for coming today, Mr. Sclerota, but that's all the time we have. Speaker Hayborn, hello and welcome to my show.

Hayborn: A pleasure as always, Arista.

Molle: We're here with House Speaker Noah Hayborn. You look exhausted, Mr. Speaker.

Hayborn: There's so much to do in this terrible time, and I haven't slept for several days.

Molle: Mr. Speaker, how do you feel about the actions the State of California has taken?

Hayborn: Today's events are the natural result of the indifference this do-nothing administration has shown. I'm not sure we can survive another year of this, and I wish the Founding Fathers had written a clause to allow impeaching a president for sheer incompetence. Unfortunately, President Gibbon has to commit a high crime or misdemeanor to be impeached, and he has committed none, as far as I know.

Molle: What do you think he should do?

Hayborn: California has voted to reject the dollar as legal currency and use their own. This is a violation of Article I of the Constitution, and the Justice Department should seek an emergency injunction from the Supreme Court on those grounds. After that, the president must sequester all tenpez currently circulating in the forty-nine States. The public, and the Corporate-Americans that make America great, must be protected from this senseless economic attack.

If he won't take these necessary measures, then I call on him and Vice President Cheyn to resign and allow a temporary government to take the helm – before the State of California does the next logical thing and secedes. The Gibbon Administration allowed them to go too far, like it allowed the Anacostia insurrection to build until it exploded into violence. This is a national emergency, Arista, and it should be treated as one. All necessary measures must be taken, and all necessary force must be used. Now.

Molle: Strong words from a strong man, Mr. Speaker.

Hayborn: I'm sorry, but I have a conference in a few minutes. I'll have to cut this short.

Molle: Thanks for sharing your perspective with us, Mr. Speaker, and you're welcome back anytime.

Hayborn: Thanks, Arista.

○─○─○─○─○

Midnight Sun
News Post of September 26, 2043

HEALTH CORDON TO TAKE EFFECT AT MIDNIGHT ACROSS WESTERN STATES

The state of California, in concert with Washington and Oregon, has announced that a health cordon will be implemented at midnight tonight along the ridges of the Sierra and the Cascade Ranges. All air, road, and rail traffic from regions east of the mountains will be denied entry.

Citizens east of this cordon are urged to cross into the protected zone before then. California will provide bus service for those without transportation from high schools in the following locations: Adin, Susanville, Truckee, Lee Vining, and South Lake Tahoe in the north, and Inyokern, Barstow, Indio, Yucca Valley, and El Centro in the south.

The cordon will be enforced by each state's National Guard, and deadly force will be used to prevent individuals or vehicles from approaching within fifty yards of the barrier.

However, a spokesperson for Vice President Gabriel Cheyn states that the Administration will block the cordon in Federal court: "No state may prevent the passage of American citizens across its borders. This so-called cordon is in flagrant violation of two clauses in our cherished Constitution, and this Administration will seek an emergency injunction from the DC Circuit Court on Monday to prevent California's National Guard deployment. California isn't its own country, no matter what they might believe out there."

When asked about the forthcoming legal action, an anonymous source in the California Lieutenant Governor's office said, "Cheyn sends us an injunction, I'm gonna use it to wipe my ass cuz you can't find a piece of toilet paper in this friggin town. He's just pissed off cuz of the tenpez recall, and now he's acting like he's friggin Don Gabriel of Flatbush, or whatever hellburg inflicted this goombah on us, and he's makin all sorts of threats. Lemme tell you – where I grew up in Brooklyn, there was a don on every block, and we all knew the code. The don thought you were okay, he didn't whack you. He thought you weren't okay, he whacked you in front of your family. I haven't gotten whacked, so I figure Cheyn must like me, which is really ironic cuz I dropped ten large into the office pool for his assassin's defense fund – whassiname, Shirazi? What was I saying? Oh, yeah, if Cheyn wasn't a whiny *gavone*, he'd be going to the mattresses, not the magistrates, amirite? And this injunction? Talk about chutzpah! He says *we're* violating his cherished Constitution, y'know, the one he loves so much that he's pissing all over it every chance he gets? So we're gonna ignore all his agita, do what we gotta do. Our troops are driving up to the Sierras now and laying down the cordon tonight. The curtain's comin down and the fat lady's singin, Gabe. Get used to it."

In the coming days, California will commence construction of refugee camps along the eastern slope of the Sierras to accommodate those who are turned away. A spokesman for the city of Reno, Nevada, says the city welcomes all refugees and hopes they will take advantage of the numerous amusement, entertainment, and gaming opportunities the Biggest Little City in the World has to offer.

IDJITS

Day 39
Saturday evening, September 26, 2043
Near Wamego, Kansas

Krista was reading the news. Ada sat across from her and read the packet from the briefcase.

"Feckin splendid." Krista swore and dropped her tablet into her pocket. "I was just getting to some interesting news, and the battery blinks out."

"There's Murphy's Law for you."

"Isn't that superstition? You beat on me for being superstitious, but it doesn't apply to you?" Krista asked.

"The science underlying Murphy's Law isn't understood, but that doesn't make it superstition. Murphy was onto something, and someday I'll find out how his freakin law works. So what news is so interesting?"

"There's a new cordon up in the West, and they're not letting anybody in. The tablet croaked before I could finish reading, though. We've got to figure out how to get through that."

"We have valuable bargaining chips – you have the evidence to put Cheyn away forever, and I have Recombin feedstock," Ada said. "You know, it's so weird that we each had half the answer, and we found each other in the middle of nowhere. That's got to be a one-in-a-billion chance."

"Right. That's why it's not a coincidence, not with one-in-a-billion odds. The Life Force brought us together so we could do this, and that's all there is to it."

"Life Force," Ada said. "Don't start with this New Age stuff again, all right? I like you, and I want to keep liking you."

"Why does the Life Force have to be superstition? Why can't it be some new science like Murphy's Law?"

"Cuz I'm a scientist, and I said it can't."

"That's cheating!" Krista said. "Aren't you supposed to be all rational and objective and stuff?"

"Okay. I'll admit, your so-called Life Force does have some characteristics equal and opposite to Murphy's Law –"

"Aha! I was right!"

" – but Murphy's Law is real and the freakin Life Force is made up, so it doesn't matter! End of inquiry!"

Krista lay back against the wall and gazed at the ceiling. "Fine. Believe what you want, even if the facts say otherwise."

"Facts? What facts? Are you full of..." She opened the packet and buried her nose in it. "Forget it. I won't argue. I'm letting it go."

"Finally. Will you let me relax now?"

Ada slammed the packet into her lap. "And I just don't understand why you had to tell everybody we were going to Sacramento! It makes us easier to find, and I like being lost! What sort of dumbass idea was that?"

"You're not exactly letting this go," Krista said.

"It just makes no sense to give the bad guys our freakin itinerary."

"Trust me on this, all right? You know science and I know propaganda. I've seen this game played by the masters in Washington, and giving them our destination embarrasses the Federals and forces them to save face. They'll make mistakes because they'll be desperate to stop us."

"And you made it easy to find us cuz you gave our destination away," Ada said. "Sounds like a toaster-in-the-bathtub idea to me."

"They won't find us. They'll be scouring the eastern border of California expecting us to cross there, but we won't. Once we get off in Wyoming, we'll steal a car and go to Washington, and then we'll drive south through Oregon while the Federals have their thumbs up their butts somewhere in Nevada. All we've got to worry about is that cordon."

Ada dropped the packet into the briefcase and rubbed her eyes. "Okay, whatever. If it works out like that, I'll be surprised."

"We've got to figure it out as we go along, kiddo. It's worked so far."

"Yeah," Ada said. "But if we don't get any food or water, we won't have to worry about that. I'm getting lightheaded, and now that we're out of water, my throat is totally parched."

"How long till the train stops?"

"It keeps going till tomorrow night, I think. Hang on, I'll check." Ada stood and squinted at a small monitor inside the control panel. "We'll be in Antelope Valley around three in the morning the day after tomorrow, about another thirty-four hours or so from now." She tapped the monitor a few times. "This is interesting."

"What?"

"This shows that the train is stopping soon to refill the boiler water."

"Will there be people there?"

"How would I know? Do I look like Zoltar the Magnificent or something?" Ada tapped the monitor a few more times. "It doesn't say anything except Siding 773W. That doesn't sound like a maintenance yard or a station, so there might not be too many people around. Maybe we can sneak off and find food and water."

THE TRAIN JERKED TO A STOP, inched forward, and then stopped again. After jiggling Krista and Ada for a few minutes, it hissed a long sigh, and the engine throttled down to a rumble. Krista opened the door a crack and peered out, but nobody was in sight. She crept onto the platform and peeked around the side.

The train had stopped alongside a metal gantry. Inside it, a long metal tube unfolded toward the engine. It couldn't decide where to go and oscillated near the engine like a charmed snake, but then it found the target and thrust into the boiler's side with a clang.

She couldn't see much, as it was dusk and the fug was thick, but the railroad siding seemed abandoned. Hearing nothing except mechanical whirring and grinding, she stepped down and walked to the engine. The metal tube shook, and squinting through the fug, she saw water dripping off the end that connected to a metal tank on the gantry.

"There's a water tank up yonder," she said to Ada, who had dropped to the ground beside her. "I'll see if I can get to it."

"Make it quick. We're only here for thirteen minutes. While you're up there, I'll look for food."

Krista walked to a ladder on the side of the gantry. It climbed to a catwalk, and she spotted a spigot on the tank's side; the problem was that the first rung was three feet above her head.

Behind her, the tube splashed water over the gravel, and she walked over and cupped her hands under the trickle. It was warm and rusty, but she was too thirsty to care. She filled their bottles with brown water and then sipped more from the trickle.

When she was on her third handful, Ada walked up holding two withered ears of corn. "There's a cornfield back there, but it's already been harvested. But I found these." She handed the ears to Krista and cupped her hands under the trickle of water. "Gah. This water will give me lockjaw, I just know it."

"Don't worry. The Federals will probably kill us long before that." Krista ripped the husks off, and the kernels inside were shrunken and dry. "Not exactly appetizing."

"But it's edible." Ada dried her hands on her pants and bit into the cob. "This is feed corn. If cows can eat it, so can we."

"I'm too hungry to be picky." They leaned against the engine and ate. After they finished, they guzzled more rusty water.

"That was good, but I'll be making corn dogs for weeks," Ada said. "I'll probably get hemorrhoids."

"Aggh! That was *way* too much information!"

"Well, it's true. The hull of a corn kernel is indigestible."

"You don't need to be a scientist to figure that out," Krista said. "It's obvious to anybody."

"I suppose so," Ada said. "All you have to do is turn around and –"

"Can we change the subject, please?"

"Why? Poop is interesting."

"Not to me." Krista sipped more water and splashed some on her face to wash off the coal dust. "You find more corn, and I'll fill the rest of the bottles."

"All right –" She froze and peered toward the back of the train, where she'd heard faint men's voices. "Uh-oh. We're not alone. Time to bounce, sister."

They kicked their corncobs under the train and sidled back to the control cabin, and then they climbed to the platform quietly. Once they were inside, Krista closed the windows, and Ada locked the door and leaned against it.

The cabin rattled as someone jumped onto the platform. "Toldja. They always stop here for a drink."

"You sure this is going west, Billy? I don't wanna go back into that virus."

"It's pointing west, so it's going west, idjit." The door handle jiggled. "Nah, it's locked."

"Lemme try." The door shook so hard that the cabin wall vibrated and Ada's head bounced against it.

"Still locked, ain't it?"

"It was worth a try, Billy."

"Nah, this won't open. Let's ride up in the engine, dude."

"Wicked pissah! Can I blow the whistle?"

The cabin shook again, and footsteps trod toward the engine. A minute later, the robotic arm whirred back into the gantry, the steam engine throttled up, and the whistle wailed across empty fields as the train chugged west.

A FEW STIFF SHOTS

Day 39
Saturday night, September 26, 2043
Potomac Landings Estates, Fort Washington, Maryland

Victoria Lang sipped her whiskey and gazed through Simon Rance's bedroom window. Entire trees floated downriver, along with pieces of houses, as the river flushed away the waste from the last hurricane. She'd never understood why people worshiped the Potomac; it could be an angry beast during the floods, and it was a muddy brown mess even when it was tame.

"Muh," the guard on the floor grunted. She knelt and examined his injuries. *Depressed basilar skull fracture, seizures, probable hemorrhaging. He has less than an hour to live. Maybe I shouldn't have swung the baseball bat so hard.*

She stood and considered how to end the man's suffering. Whacking his skull again with the baseball bat made her stomach turn, so she placed her foot on his throat and shifted her weight onto it to collapse his windpipe. Her mission of mercy underway, she returned to sipping Simon's scotch.

Over on the bed, Rance gasped. She flashed him a boozy smile. "Simon, you're awake! Good." She raised a finger and looked at the guard – he wasn't even straining to breathe through his constricted airway, and he'd be gone soon. "Gimme a minute."

Rance thrashed but couldn't pull free of the ropes binding his hands and feet to the bedposts. "Tor-eee!"

"One minute. First things first."

The guard finally stopped breathing, and she walked to Rance's ornate bed, drained her whiskey, and set the glass on the nightstand. He didn't look like the hard-charging CEO of Chalys Pharmaceuticals anymore but more like a pudgy and pasty businessman with a bondage fetish.

She reached into her shirt pocket, felt for the pen shape of her digital voice recorder, and switched it on. "We're going to have a little chat, and you'll be honest with me. If not, I'll kill you." She sat on the edge of the bed.

"You're mad."

"No, I'm feeling serene." She leaned forward to inspect the cannula she'd inserted into his arm while he was sedated.

"You're insane!"

She taped the cannula down tighter because his thrashing had worked it loose. "It doesn't matter. You'll answer my questions whether I'm insane or not, right? Because you like this whole 'life' thing?"

"You killed Dave, Tom, and Lev. You'll do the same to me. Stop with the charades." He turned his face away.

"Not necessarily, Simon. If you answer my questions and try not to piss me off, I'll let you go."

"Except I can identify you as a murderer. I just saw you kill my bodyguard. Why would you let me live?"

"I've killed ten men so far, and the NSF has enough evidence to convict me. It won't bother me if you talk. On the other hand, it won't bother me to kill you, either." She looked up from his arm. "Or your son."

He opened his mouth to speak but only managed a raspy whisper. "You're a monster."

"My child's a playing piece in your game, and it may have even killed her. These last few nights, I've felt..." She looked at the headboard blankly and her lips tightened. After a few heartbeats, she blinked and turned her attention back to his loosened cannula. "But I'm not playing some damn game. I'll happily waste your little brat if you don't talk. All it takes is one little pinprick as he's going back to the dorm, and your boy's just another stiffer. *Hoc est bellum*, Rance – you kill mine, I kill yours, everybody mourns."

"I don't have anything to do with your daughter!"

"So maybe his death will be senseless. Who knows, who cares? That's how war rolls." She double-checked her pen recorder and saw the green 'record' light. It was time to ask the tough questions. "Simon Rance, multiple sources tell me you ordered the engineering and production of Recombin. Who contracted this work?"

Rance glared at the ceiling, his nostrils flaring.

"Do you love your son? Tell me the truth or he dies. Make a rational choice, Simon."

Rance let out a long breath. "It wasn't contracted. It was an understanding. A twenty-billion-dollar understanding, the kind you don't refuse."

"All right," she said. "That wasn't a complete answer, though, so tell me who made this understanding. I want names and specifics."

"It was with the Working Group, a task force of officials high up in the Gibbon Administration. They made the wheels turn, Tori."

"It's Dr. Lang to you, Rance. Now, who's in this Working Group?"

"It's a group of thirty-something people. I never met them all. I only know a few – Cheyn, his chief of staff Grimes, Plover from the FDA, Pill from the HHS, and Grovenor from Fort Detrick."

"Was Tommy Talbott involved? Deputy Inspector General of the FDA?"

"He was brought in by Plover after you played Nurse Nightingale at St. E's. You're lucky he signed on. We wanted you redacted, but he pleaded for a chance to bring you into the group. I guess he saw redeeming qualities in you that the rest of the world missed."

She pursed her lips and her eyes narrowed. "That wisecrack pissed me off, Simon. Don't let your ego get in the way of your answers." He stared the ceiling again and pulled at the ropes binding his arms, so she drew them tighter. "Back to business. So you're saying you were a part of a group of powerful Americans that planned and executed a genocidal assault on its own country?"

"Genocide is a loaded word for it. We prefer to call it Economic Selection, and look, it would've happened anyway. The next natural pandemic was bound to wipe us out, so what's wrong with inducing one and preparing to survive it instead of waiting to get blindsided by another random bug? Didn't we learn our lesson last time?"

"What's wrong with killing people? Let's see – ethics, morality, basic humanity…"

"It's moral and ethical to allow indiscriminate and rampant bloodshed over resource shortages? That would've happened within a year – there's just not enough money, energy, or food to go around. Every city would end up like Detroit. Cheyn came up with the idea of creating a managed pandemic so he could take the ex-workers and the obsoletes off the economy before a backlash brought down the government. The science supported that – there are plenty of studies proving that the land and the economy can only support 325 million people, and we have seventy-five million more than that. And most of them are obsoleted Ranks that don't even contribute to the economy anymore. The numbers are persuasive, you have to admit."

She sat back, shaking her head. "You say that like it made sense."

"It does. You just have to see it from a macrobioeconomic perspective."

"And studies alone persuaded a group of thirty powerful and rational people to perpetrate the most inhuman crime the world has ever seen? Just for that?"

"You don't see the responsibilities we leaders have to bear or the problems we have to solve." He struggled to sit up, and his face twisted and became flushed. "Look, you're nobody. You don't see the thirty-thousand-foot view. Well, damn it, we do! This land can only feed so many, and with the loss of cropland from climate change, we're pulling three crops a year from ground that was meant to deliver only one! We're poisoning ourselves with this toxic fug because we need too much energy for too many people, and we're forced to burn coal! It's just not sustainable! The Earth is crying from this abuse, and you don't hear it." He sagged against the headboard. "Well, I hear it. I heard the call and I answered and I don't expect someone like you to understand why."

She examined his face for a long moment and then shook her head. "Amazing. You actually believe that justified this crime."

"It wasn't a crime. It was a population reduction, that's all, and they happen all the time. When the deer population gets too large, we hunt them and bring the numbers back to a sustainable level. It's not even a moral gray area in my mind."

She stood and walked to the bar, picked up a crystal carafe, and poured a few fingers of whiskey. "Marvelous booze, Simon."

"Eight hundred bucks a fifth, it better be," he grumbled.

She took a sip and studied the glass. "It's interesting that you just employed an Aluminati argument to justify your acts. You're one of those tinfoil hat types, aren't you?"

"I'm an Elder of the Second Creation," he said. "I'm not ashamed of that."

"You're one of those Arkie loons who believe they can make a second Eden – something you can't do in a polluted world suffering from a scarcity of resources." She swirled her drink and watched the patterns in the amber. "A world burdened by too many people. Kill off a lot of them, and the resources will be abundant for the survivors."

"You don't know what you're talking about."

"Sure I do. I'm an Archangelist too, and I've heard that bullshit, but I didn't think you guys were so cracked that you'd engage in genocide. No, it's worse – it's indiscriminate democide. At least genocide has a point."

"I won't dignify that with my consideration," he said. "You're grasping at straws, Dr. Lang. You want an answer so bad, you'll believe anything."

"I'll believe any conclusion that fits the observable facts, and this does," she said. "It doesn't make sense that the Working Group would kill millions of people because of some stupid studies. No, they'd do it for the reasons you just expressed with such passion – to rebuild Eden, the population has to be reduced. The driving power behind this must be Aluminati."

"Bullshit."

"And you went along with Cheyn because you have a common goal. Cheyn needs to purge ex-workers for economic reasons, and the Arkies want to get rid of them for environmental reasons. As long as you don't have a shred of humanity, it makes demented sense."

Rance closed his eyes and turned away, his lips pressed so tight that they turned white.

"Where were you planning to stop, Simon? After you offed the ex-workers in America, were you going after Canada? Europe? I'll bet you wouldn't stop with America. If you reduced the population worldwide, you could reverse global warming, end starvation, all that. The whole world could be Eden. And since you control the cure for Neovirus, you'd have immense power too."

"And what's wrong with that?"

"Nothing. You'd just have to wipe out a few billion people. But that's worth it, right?"

"This planet doesn't need humans. They aren't important to any ecosystem, and we have plenty to spare. Don't get sentimental with me, *Doctor* Lang. We kill people every day for lesser reasons, and you know it. How many did you kill in your drug trials?"

"That was so many more could live!"

"What's so different about this?"

"Because I never made a life-and-death decision for my test subjects! I didn't pick who lived and died!"

"And we did, and we selected only the weakest animals –"

"Is that really how you see us, Rance? We're nothing more than animals?"

"Look at your typical Rank and tell me he's not more animal than human! They're not real people, for chrissakes! They're just weak animals that harm the larger herd! And there are too many animals in this herd for all of us to survive! Some had to be culled, so we picked the people that did nothing for the economy, and we're all better off for it!" He sat up and strained against his bonds. "Someday, humanity will thank us. When this is a green and vibrant planet with clean food and water for all, they'll be grateful!"

"Bullshit, Rance! That's complete –"

"They'll forget about the dead, and the living will thrive! They'll thank us for having the vision to know what had to be done, and for having the balls to do it!"

"You're out of your fucking mind!"

"They'll raise statues to us," he said, lying back on the pillow. "And they'll forget all about insignificant, bleeding-heart specks like you. You and your ilk are a dying species, Lang, like dinosaurs watching the comet crashing to Earth. Enjoy what little time you have left. But after you're gone, we'll remain."

She knocked back a slug of whiskey and let out a slow breath. "You're a disease, Rance, you and everybody like you. I hate you. And I thank you for delivering me."

"Well, I'm glad to be of service, whatever I did."

"You did something magical – you made my killings pure and right. You proved that I'm a decent person, and all I doubted about myself was untrue."

"Hooray." He turned away and pulled at the ropes holding him to the bed. "That's all I'm going to say, so just loosen these and I'll get myself out. I'll give you enough time to get away, but this is over."

"Hmm," she said with a mouth full of whiskey. She gulped it down and set it on the bar, and then she picked up the baseball bat and rested it against the bed's footboard. With her right hand, she felt for a syringe in her pocket and sat on the side of his bed again. "Simon, I've learned some hard lessons over the past few weeks. I've learned that all we love, and all we are, can be stripped away for making a simple mistake. Mistakes like trusting the wrong person, like I trusted Tommy Talbott." She pulled the syringe from her pocket and slipped off the cap. "And like you trusted me."

"Shit!" Rance squirmed at the ropes and tried to wriggle away. "We made a deal!"

She pushed the needle's tip through the cannula seal. "Correct. I won't kill your son, but I always planned to kill you. Doesn't betrayal feel awful?" She pressed the plunger and injected the respiratory paralytic into his veins. "You have ten seconds for your last words. Make your peace, Simon."

"You said...you said..." Rance strained against the ropes, shaking the bed, and screamed, "Let me go!"

"I *am* letting you go." Victoria patted his cheek. "There'll be one less mouth to feed. Aren't you happy?"

THE LUCKIEST TOWN IN THE WEST

Day 40
Sunday evening, September 27, 2043
Near Seven Up, Colorado

Krista leaned against the wall and watched the world pass by the window, fascinated with the horizon. Without moisture to weigh it down, the fug had risen to become a thin layer several thousand feet high, and she could see the sky meeting the land from east to west. The light of a crescent moon shone through and cast a cold blue light across the arid land.

With each passing mile, the grasslands were growing sparser and drier. Small cactuses now stood among a few rough patches of thatchy grass that had clawed into the cracked earth. For the last eight hours, that was all she'd seen as far as the horizon.

Nevertheless, it was a horizon, and she couldn't tear her gaze from it. She'd been frightened when she first realized how vast the prairie was, but that had faded, and a gentle contentment had dispelled the fright. She was lost in the outside world at last, and she wasn't afraid.

The moonlight revealed no signs of human life, and when they'd rocketed past a small town a few minutes before, one with streetlights and a paved road, she was elated to see any sort of civilization. Now, though, the desert landscape was flat and featureless once more.

The steam whistle shrieked again and shattered her reverie. She grabbed the window frame and tried to calm her racing heart; the boys in the engine wouldn't give the whistle a rest, and she hadn't slept all day. It didn't wake Ada, though, who was still curled up on the floor by the control panel.

As she reached for her cigarettes, a boom shook the train. Metal screeched outside, and the cabin shuddered. It slewed from side to side, breaking her grip on the window frame, and she flew into the opposite wall. Flames and smoke and sparks shot past the window. The cabin shook violently and rolled over, throwing her body against the wall and then the ceiling. She clutched for a handhold but was flung headfirst into the control panel. Her mind filled with flashing lights for a second, and then her world faded to black.

SMOKY DUST FILLED THE AIR, and she covered her mouth with her hoodie sleeve. She stood slowly and clutched a doorknob, unsure if the car would turn topsy-turvy again. Every part of her was sore, which was no surprise since she'd been bounced off the cabin walls like a racquetball, but nothing was broken or bleeding. She leaned against the wall until her head stopped ringing and then looked around.

The window she'd been standing at was now above her head, and the cabin door was horizontal, with the bottom edge at her shoulder. Through the window, she saw orange lights drifting overhead in a cloud of thick dust. She turned the doorknob she was holding, and the door swung down and clattered against the wall. After wiping her eyes again, she looked outside.

On one side, the platform of the car rose in a rusty wall; on the other, tiny, blinking orange stars covered the desert floor. In the darkness beyond them, long, black shapes tilted sideways and slammed into the dirt, groaning like mating dinosaurs. Pungent, eye-stinging smoke washed over her, and she ducked back into the cabin.

The floor felt soft and uneven, though, and she looked down to see that she was standing on Ada's leg. She felt around and found her curled up near the control panels.

"Are you okay?" She shook her, but the only response was a soft, raspy moan. Finding her armpits, Krista heaved her up against the control panel and saw the girl's head lolling to one side.

"Ada! C'mon, wake up, the train got into a wreck. We've got to get out of here!" She shook her a few more times, with the same result, and then she grabbed her armpits again.

She climbed into the doorway and pulled Ada through. Holding her ankles, she slid her gently down the side of the cabin headfirst. When her head was touching the ground, she let her go, and the girl crumpled into a heap. She jumped out and rolled in the hard dirt, and then she staggered over to Ada and grabbed her arms again.

Far ahead, the constellation of orange stars stopped, and she spotted the dark slash of a gully in the moonlight. She dragged Ada toward it, and then she accidentally stepped on an orange star she hadn't seen. Pain and heat lanced through her shoe and into her toes. She stomped her foot until a smoldering coal fell off her foot and into the dirt.

When she'd almost reached the gully, she looked back and saw the engine sitting on the tracks, a glowing hole in the middle of it, with the coal tender lying on its side behind it. The control cabin they'd been riding was also lying on its side. Beyond it, dozens of derailed coal cars were strewn haphazardly across the sands.

She slid into the gully and lay Ada against the side. "C'mon, kid, wake up. Wake up, please, something bad happened and I can't do this alone. We've got to get out of here, please, wake up. You're scaring the crap out of me, Ada, don't do this." She pulled Ada's hair away from her face and felt breath on her hand.

As she did, a spell of dizziness struck her, and she suddenly felt every bruise. She bowed her head and closed her eyes, praying that the pain would go away, that the Federals would leave her alone, and that Ada would wake up and make sense of everything.

"What the actual fuck?" Ada mumbled. "Is that the moon?"

"Oh, thank the stars," Krista said, stroking her cheek. "That's the moon, kid."

Ada blinked a few times. "Why am I looking at the moon?"

"Well, that's the weird part," Krista said. "We got in a train wreck while you were asleep."

"A train wreck?"

"I think the Federals blew up the engine with a missile. It's totally destroyed."

ADA WALKED ALONG THE MOONLIT SIDE of the engine and examined the glowing hole. "We weren't hit by a missile, so you can relax. See the way the metal bends out on both sides? That's from an internal explosion, not a missile. I think the boiler exploded. The coal's been blown all over the place."

"What did this?"

"I guess there *were* Hot Rocks in that coal. It's a shame. I needed a few." She rubbed her leg. "God, I feel like somebody stomped all over me."

They walked past the engineer's station, which had been flayed by shrapnel from the exploding boiler. "It was a quick end for the boys," Ada said. "At least they didn't feel anything."

"At least they won't be tooting that feckin whistle anymore," Krista said under her breath.

"Wow, *that* was cold."

"Couldja focus? We're dead if people show up and find us here. We've got to get away, and fast. I saw a town a little ways back, and I think we should head for that and steal a car."

"But we need to stay far from the tracks in case the emergency services are coming from there," Ada said. "We'll walk there through the desert."

ADA THREW THEIR GEAR into Krista's arms and then jumped through the doorway holding the wedding picture. She stuffed it into her bookbag and shouldered the shotgun.

Krista picked up the briefcase, and they started limping east. The walk took more than an hour because they kept tripping over prairie dog holes. However, they were still alone: Aside from the distant flickering glow from the train, no lights appeared in the sky or on the ground.

"There's something off-planet about this," Ada said. "A train's been derailed on a main line, and nobody's showing up."

"Maybe they don't know it blew up. We were in the control cabin, and maybe it stopped transmitting when the train crashed."

"Whatever. They're not here, and that's good for us," Ada said. "I think I see lights up ahead, over there on the right."

"That's probably the town I saw."

They walked for another half hour, and then Ada squinted into the darkness. "That's definitely a town, but it looks empty. There's a diesel station on a road that crosses these tracks, and there's other buildings along that road, so it's a main street. Let's cut across here instead of walking down that."

"Maybe we can find a car and get the hell out of here."

"Absolutely. Keep your eyes open."

THEY CROSSED THE TRACKS and looked in both directions; the wreckage of the train glowed in the distance to one side, and red crossing signals blinked on the other. The lights of the diesel station burned brightly ahead, but they saw no cars or people there. However, Ada noticed dozens of surveillance cameras around the store and pumps, so they stayed far away. ·

They skittered down the gravel slope into a weedy ditch and then through a field of patchy grass. In the glow from the filling station, they spotted a row of houses ahead and walked toward them. After a few minutes, they found a swing set in the backyard of a house.

Ada sat in a cracked plastic swing. "I need a break before I go in there."

"Good idea. We don't know what we're in for, although I can guess." She pointed to a wooden house whose back door was swinging in the breeze and slamming against the side.

"That freakin door's loud," Ada said, and then it slammed again. "You can hear it all over town. This place is either empty or everybody's deaf."

"It's deserted. We've seen this before."

"Yeah. It definitely has that infected atmo, doesn't it?" The wind caught the door and slammed it shut, and then it opened and smacked the house's side again. "Do you know if the virus has gotten here yet?"

"I don't," Krista said. "My tablet battery's dead, but I don't need the SatNet to tell me the virus hit this place. They split and didn't even bother to close the doors. I just hope they left a car behind."

Ada ran her finger along a swing seat beside her. "They've been gone awhile. There's dirt on everything."

The wind picked up and drove a wall of dust across the yard, and they hunched over and covered their eyes. Within seconds, it was whistling and howling, and then it ripped the door off its hinges and blew it end over end across the yard and into the gully. The gust stopped as quickly as it started, but the unearthly whistling remained as the wind tore through a distant part of town.

"Now there's a spooky sound," Krista said.

"Yeah. All we need is a freakin *Day the Earth Stood Still* theremin soundtrack. *Ooo-wheee-ooo!* There you go. Now it's a sci-fi B-movie."

The Luckiest Town in the West

"Weird. Who thought the B-movie guys were such visionaries? It turns out they showed exactly how the world would end."

"Not exactly. If they wanted to give their viewers the complete experience, they'd make them give up eating and drinking and showering and crapping for a week, and then the usher would whack them all over with a tire iron before they entered the theater. That might come close."

"I know, right? Well, I can't wait for the end credits, I'll say that. I detest this flick."

"Detestify, sister. But horror movies don't end like this. This kinda scene usually means the shuffling horde of undead is coming. The heroines run, the slow one gets eaten, the fast one kills her with some improbable weapon she finds at the last second, and then she goes all Serengeti on some zombie ass. *That's* where the movie usually ends."

Krista scanned the yard and peered into the doorless house, but she saw no zombies. "Let's change the script, then. We'll stay close together and watch each other's back. Keep your gun ready. Look like a desperado."

Ada nodded and reached into her bookbag to check the Cryogenie – it was scratched and dented, but the Recombin vials inside were still intact. They checked the rest of their gear, and then they stretched their aching muscles and examined each other for injuries. Neither was hurt, although they found sore spots that were certain to become bruises.

Krista stood and squared her shoulders. "I'm not ready for this."

"Yeah, but we need to find a car or a place to hide before somebody comes to work on that wreck." She stood and slung her bookbag over her shoulder. "Unless you have another clever Kobayashi trick in mind."

"I don't. I wish I did, I truly do," Krista said, picking up her backpack.

They walked through the weedy backyard to the house. Creeping through the doorless doorway, they found a kitchen with a thick layer of dust covering the floor; the cabinets were empty of anything edible, but the taps still worked. The water was refreshing and clean, and they drank until their tummies sloshed. After that, they filled their bottles and washed the remaining coal dust off their faces and arms.

After searching the rest of the house and finding nothing, they left through the front door and walked toward the lights of the main road. Krista poked her head around the corner and looked up and down it. "This place is empty. There aren't even any tire tracks in the dirt, yet the streetlights are still burning."

"Lots of lights are on. There might be somebody here, somebody we don't want to meet."

"Right," Krista said, looking at the wooden sidewalk running along both sides of the street. "We need to be careful, and really quiet." She placed her foot on the sidewalk and gently put her weight on it. The wood planks creaked and groaned. "That won't be easy."

Old-fashioned wooden buildings lined the street, but neon signs filled the windows and blinked cheerful messages about fat slots and happy jingles. They tried to open each door they passed, but they were locked.

"It's like a Wild West town," Ada said. "It's creepy now that it's empty – like somebody just finished a brand-new ghost town. Just built one from scratch without bothering to live in it first."

Krista nodded. "Like a Hollywood stage when everyone's out to lunch. This is some sorta casino town. Every store's advertising slot machines." She peeked around the corner into a short street of houses, but lights shone in only one.

After checking the darkened ones and finding no food or cars, they approached the lighted house. Krista opened the front door a crack, while Ada aimed the gun and tried to appear ferocious, but nobody inside reacted.

They crept into a litter-strewn foyer. Faint sounds drifted from a front room, and they tiptoed to it, only to find a young but dead man sitting on a couch and staring slack-jawed at an old TV. On the screen, a buff and mostly naked young man holding a glowing spear yelled war chants and vowed to return with his enemy's scalp.

"This is stupid." Krista rested her hands on her hips. "I should make some mordant comment, like he wanted to wait till the feckin *Fight for Your Life* marathon was over before he fled for his life."

Ada knelt in front of the corpse. He showed all the classic signs of Neovirus – bloody eyes and the remains of his stomach covering his shirt. He was also holding a beer can in his hand, and bees flitted in and out of it. "Why didn't this guy get up and go?"

"Maybe it hit him so fast that he couldn't get up?"

Ada spotted dried blood on his hair and his turned-out pants pockets. "Or somebody knocked him out and stole his car keys, and then the virus killed him while he was unconscious. That means the virus took him out real fast, faster than it used to. Just a few hours."

A gong resounded on the TV screen, and they turned to see the *Fight for Your Life* episode in full swing. A beautiful teen starlet clad in gold-lamé and armed with a high-tech bow raced into battle, presumably with the beefcake boy who planned to scalp her.

"I totally hate this show." Ada sneered at the screen. "Try going into battle when you're tired and hungry and filthy, bitch."

Krista squinted at the sprinting nymph. "Well, she *does* have a smudge of mud on her arm. That makes it authentic."

"Right. I'd like to see her in a fight where the bad guys really want to kill you. Real wounds hurt a lot. Real guns go empty just when you need them." She looked at the tablet in the man's hand. "He was just a decanus in the Desert Legion. Talk about lame! I made praefectus in the Forest Legion in less than a month."

"I thought you totally hated this show."

"I do, but the app is addictive. I couldn't stop."

"Nobody can. I knew a guy who walked into traffic and got hit by a car because he got anxiety attacks for even missing a minute of it. How'd you stop?"

"I think Blue Ball erased my character. I guess they figured I have better things to do. It was frustrating, though – our Screen Tribune was *this* close to capturing the Tessera Orb. But I finally let it go." A gong rang three times on the screen, and Ada's face twisted into a scowl. "Aww, hell! The Mountain Legion scum got it!"

"Sure. You really let it go." Krista picked up her pack and looked through a dark doorway. "There's nothing here. Let's see if there's something to eat."

They found a small galley kitchen with mostly bare cabinets beyond the doorway, but Ada spotted a can of beef stew and a box of crackers in the back of one. They ripped open the box and devoured the crackers, and then they stuffed the stew and a can opener into their bags and walked through the back door. To one side of the yard, a weather-beaten wooden garage leaned precariously at the end of a dirt driveway, and they walked over to check it out. An old pickup truck was parked inside with its engine sitting on a stand nearby.

"Just our luck," Ada said.

"Don't talk to me about luck, kiddo," Krista said. "It just depresses me. Y'know, now that we have this stew, my tummy's rumbling like crazy.

Let's take a break and have lunch." The can opener was in Ada's hands in an instant, and they sat on the floor and passed the can back and forth.

"This town's totally empty," Ada said.

"It sure feels empty. We've got to find a car, though. Before the train wreck, I saw nothing but cactuses. We're in the middle of the desert, and I've got no idea where the next town is. Hell, I don't even know where *this* town is."

"No way to make this thing run," Ada said, pointing over her shoulder at the truck. "Our only option is to keep checking. We oughta get moving so we can get done before sunrise. What time is it?"

"Just after four, I think."

"Not long till sunrise." Ada stood, stretched, and then winced. "Speaking of train wrecks, how are your aches and pains?"

"Achy and painful." She stood and rubbed her shoulder. "How about you?"

"I'll cry like a baby when this is all over," Ada said, picking up her bag and shotgun.

They'd just walked a few steps when they heard helicopter blades thuttering far away. A minute later, a spotlight flicked on and headed down the tracks toward the train.

"Time's up," Ada said. "This place will be swarming with people soon, and not the kind that'll help us."

THE TOWN WAS ONLY SIX BLOCKS LONG, and it took them less than an hour to check every house. Each was empty, and they found only one car, its front end mashed into the side of a brick building and green antifreeze dripping from underneath.

They trudged to the end of the wooden sidewalk and looked down the road into the empty desert. Something snapped and cracked above them, and Krista looked up at a banner fluttering from a light pole. "'Seven Up, Colorado – The Luckiest Town in the West.' That's ironic. I should write a post about this someday."

"Focus, okay? The sun's coming up, and we need a way outta here. Unless you don't mind spending the day in that stiffer's house."

"Nuh-uh. That place gave me the creeps. In fact, this whole town has been giving me the willies. It feels like the Black Dog is watching every step I make." Krista pointed down the road. "What's that?"

"What's what?"

"Way over there, a white light off to the right. It hasn't moved since I've been watching it."

Ada squinted into the distance. "It looks like a light pole. Maybe a mile or so away."

"Let's go check it out," Krista said. "That feels like what we should do."

THE LIGHT WAS FURTHER THAN ADA THOUGHT. After a half hour of walking, it was still as far away as it had appeared in Seven Up.

"Distances are deceiving in the desert," Ada said. "Hot, flat terrain is perfect for creating optical illusions."

"Well then, here's your proof. This is like that nightmare where you run and run, but the door keeps getting further away. Did you ever get that one?"

"I don't have nightmares," Ada said. "God, my feet are killing me. I'm getting blisters, and now my stitches are aching. I'm filthy and I stink and I'm tired."

"We'll be there soon." Krista scanned the horizon for aircraft, but the sky was still empty. However, it was changing from black to bluish gray, and she hurried her pace.

"Slow down, my legs aren't as long as yours," Ada said. "Show some mercy, Gigantor."

"I don't want to get stuck out here. If the helicopters come, we've got no place to hide. We need to get moving."

"I'm going as fast as I can."

"I know," she said. "I hope this isn't just a light pole we're heading for."

"Thanks for that, Commander Optimism. Could you keep that to yourself? My mojo meter is almost at zero." Ada tried to rub a cramp out of her shins but stumbled and nearly fell over. "I take it back. My mojo meter is officially zero."

"All right. Y'know, maybe something good is right ahead. Maybe we'll find our Xanadu, like some desert resort where the beds are soft and fluffy like a cloud stuffed in a mattress…"

"I'd love to sleep on something soft for a change."

"…and they have huge bathtubs with bubbles and lotions and endless hot water, and we can soak till we look like prunes…"

"I'd love to open my pores and give them a scrub. If I don't get this coal dust out, I'll get blackheads the size of raisins."

"…and they'll have a dinner buffet with roast beef and baked potatoes and apple pie. Dutch apple pie, all crumbly and sweet –" Ada's stomach rumbled so loudly that Krista stopped walking and laughed. "Holy crap, what a gutquake!"

"You just *had* to bring up food, didn't you?"

"You already ate. How can you be hungry again?"

"It was half a can of stew and that was hours ago and I already digested it," Ada said. "I'm digesting everything a hundred percent anymore. I haven't pooped since Ohio, and I even ate corn! I usually pass a knobbly dookie after –"

"I don't want to hear this!" Krista said, jamming her fingers into her ears.

"Well, when was the last time you pooped?"

"In Ohio, but I don't tell anyone."

"You just told *me*," Ada said.

"Is it child-beating if you beat someone else's child? I don't think so."

"Aww, c'mon, you love me."

"Right. Wait here while I get a blunt instrument."

Ada rubbed her stomach, and her lips twisted into a scowl. "I'm so constipated it hurts, like the Loch Ness Monster crawled up my butt and started growing. What I wouldn't do for a little diarrhea right now."

"Just shut up about your BM's, wouldja? Please?"

They walked in silence down the middle of the road as the eastern horizon lightened, the hot, dry wind blowing small tumbleweeds across the pavement. Suddenly, they both shivered violently.

Ada stopped walking and looked at Krista. "Did you feel that?" she asked.

"That was just the chillybones. I feel that sometimes when I'm about to get lucky. It's a waning moon, so maybe something good's coming my way."

"Superstition can't explain this away. That was a physical event. It felt like my bones turned to ice, and then it stopped. Something seriously off-planet just happened." Ada turned in a circle, looking at the surrounding desert. "See that big, lopsided tumbleweed? It wasn't there when we walked by."

"There's tons of tumbleweeds around here. We're in the desert, kiddo."

"But I woulda noticed that. We just came that way, and I'd remember a tumbleweed bigger than me next to the road."

Krista laughed and took her hand. "You're hallucinating, maybe from hunger or something. Let's keep going, okay? We won't find that all-you-can-eat buffet standing around here."

Ada frowned and trudged down the road. "I'm not hallucinating! People hallucinate about pink unicorns and spiders with elephant trunks, not tumbleweeds." She looked back at the hulking bush and intoned in a deep voice, *"Imagine, if you will, a world where humungous tumbleweirds appear out of thin air…ooo-wheee-ooo!"*

Krista pulled her arm, and shortly after, they spotted lights approaching on the road far ahead. They took cover in a ditch, but the lights disappeared shortly after, and they began walking again. After five more minutes, though, Krista groaned. "Aww, don't tell me that's just a light pole in the middle of the desert."

Ada squinted into the dark and frowned again.

"Well?" Krista asked.

"You said to *not* tell you that's a light pole in the middle of the desert."

"Splendid, just feckin splendid." Krista swore and kicked a small tumbleweed. "Now what?"

"There's a mailbox under it. It says 'Castle Something' on it, but I can't tell from here."

"Well, we can't go back, so maybe we can hide in the mailbox. *You* can fit in it, at least."

"Oh, shut it! I'm just small for my age, all right? I'm not some teeny dwarf or something."

"And I'm not some colossal Gigantor either," Krista said.

"Listen, if there's a mailbox, there's a house somewhere nearby."

"I know that. I'm just trying to keep my expectations low so I'm not disappointed if we've got to hide in a ditch today."

"Maybe you should say that, Krista. I'm not a mind reader."

"Maybe you should say nothing, Ada."

"Maybe *you* should say nothing."

"This is getting childish. I'm not talking to you anymore."

"Same goes for me," Ada said. "You're annoying."

"You're talking to me again. Didn't you say you'd stop?"

"Well, you're talking to me too!"

"Are you sure you're a genius? You don't sound like one right now."

"How would you know?" Ada said. "Besides, I thought we weren't talking."

They limped on, listening for sounds of life in the desert, but they heard nothing besides the occasional whistle of the wind.

"I remember now. I'm pretty sure I asked you to write down an algorithm the other day," Ada said.

Krista stared at the road ahead.

"You didn't write it down, did you?" Ada asked.

"We're not talking, right?"

Ada kicked a rock and sent it skittering down the road. "I thought so. You didn't write it down, and now you're dodging the question." She found a tumbleweed and gave it such a savage kick that it turned into a cloud of dust. "You really suck. Let me count the ways you suck. No, I can't – I'd need to use a supercomputer."

"Oh, are we talking again?" Krista snarled. "Can I bitch at you now?"

"Tsa mor kaka an eefa, zulinghu!" Ada slapped her hand over her mouth. "Did I say that in English?"

"Whatever that was, it sure as hell wasn't English."

"Whew, thank god. That woulda totally wrecked our relationship," she grumbled. After a few more steps, she slipped her hand into Krista's. "I hate this bitchy crap. Can we stop?"

"We're tired, sore, and hangry. I haven't got the energy for a squabble."

"Me neither." Ada opened the collar of her blouse and fluffed it. "Are you boiling too?"

"I am. Maybe we got a shot of virus from that stiffer," Krista said.

"Yeah, but he was dead for hours. How could he still be shedding virus after that long? Releasing this bug was so monumentally stupid, and stupid people shouldn't play with viruses."

"I can't be saying much about that," Krista said. "Stupid does as stupid is, I guess, and that's why we shouldn't trust humanity to people. Maybe the dolphins can hurry up and evolve and run this place for us. We've sure as hell effed it up."

After a few more minutes of trudging, they walked over a slight rise and saw the light pole on the road before them.

"Optical illusions," Ada said. "See?"

A LIGHT ON THE POLE SHONE on a dented mailbox, its wooden post ringed by dry weeds. Cracked vinyl letters on the side said CASTLE HERRERA. A hard wind whistled from the south, rocking the box from side to side.

"So I thought you were getting lucky or something," Ada said, peering at the empty surrounding desert. "This freakin blows."

"Maybe I just haven't gotten to the lucky part yet," Krista said. "How'd you see this from so far away?"

"I have 20/10 vision."

"Do you know how irritating it is to walk around with somebody who's beyond perfect in every way?" Krista opened the box and found it empty. "Either no mail, or someone's been here recently."

"Or the mailman's dead."

"There's always that." The wind gusted again, and something under the box tinkled.

"I wonder what this is for," Ada said as she pushed a chain back and forth with her finger. "Maybe it's like a wind gauge, or maybe the owner ties a dog out here."

"That's not it." Krista crouched and eyed the dangling chain. "It's brand new, and it's just screwed to the bottom of the box, so it wasn't meant to hold anything. This is a symbol, Ada – someone hanged Cheyn, get it? We might have a friend around here." She stood and peered down a path through the thatchy grass. "I think there's a fence down thataway, but I can't tell in the dark."

"The sun will be up soon, and we need to get off the road anyway."
Ada slipped the shotgun off her shoulder and headed down the trail. "Just
in case we don't find a friend, pretend this thing's loaded, all right?" She
turned her head left and right, listening for sounds under the whispering of
the wind. "I hear an engine up ahead."

They stumbled down an uneven, rutted dirt path. After a minute of
walking, the path dropped into a bowl in the earth with a metal picket
fence ringing the rim.

They walked along it to an open gate. Krista peered around the corner
and saw a small white truck idling in a dusty yard with a bunker-like
concrete box sunk into it. A wall at the end of a short ramped driveway was
exposed, and a garage door in it was open.

"This looks seriously coldwar," Ada whispered.

"I half-expect a rocket to come blowing out of this thing."

"Missile. A rocket is unguided, and a missile is guided. But this isn't a
silo. It looks more like a blast shelter with those sloped concrete walls all
around. See? They're designed to deflect a shockfront."

"I see that," Krista said. "I also see a truck, and it's running."

"And we need wheels."

"Right. Friend or not, we need wheels."

They crept to the back of the truck and peeked around the side. Its
headlights shone into the garage, illuminating walls lined with racks of
plastic containers, but they didn't see anybody. Krista looked through the
dark rear window, but the truck was empty. She motioned that they'd run

and jump into the front seat, and she held up three fingers and mouthed a countdown.

When she reached one, Ada ran for the passenger door and Krista ran for the driver's side. She was about to slide into the seat when she stopped and looked into the garage.

In the light of the headlamps, a man wearing a dust mask lay on the floor at the side of the garage. He raised his head to see them, and then his leg twitched and he sagged back against steps leading up to a door.

"There's a guy in there," Krista said. "He looks hurt." She jumped from the car and ran into the garage. When he heard their footsteps, he raised his head again.

He was a large, swarthy man in his early forties, but his face was pale and drained, the skin almost translucent; when Ada laid her hand on his forehead, it came away hot. "He has the virus," she said. The man nodded once.

"He looks sicker than a plane to Lourdes," Krista whispered. "If you give him a shot, will it help?"

"He's still in the early stages, but I don't know long they last anymore. It might be too late already."

"Too late. Gimme water...get away," he whispered. "You don't want this."

"We can't get it. We're vaccinated," Ada said, reaching into her bookbag. "Do you have any syringes?"

He nodded and blinked a few times. "Why?"

Krista unscrewed the cap from a water bottle, lifted his mask, and put it to his lips. "We've got a few vials of the vaccine. We can give it to you."

He took a few pained sips and scrutinized her face. "Warner?" She nodded, and a weak smile appeared at the corners of his mouth. "Damn. My hero." He turned back to Ada. "041697. Door code. Radio room on right. Medikit."

Ada clambered up the steps and punched the numbers into a keypad. The door lock clunked, and she pushed it open and vanished inside.

"What...are you doing here?" he croaked. "Middle of nowhere."

"You know us heroes. We show up where we're needed."

She raised the bottle to his lips again, and he sipped a few more times and then laid back on the steps. "Ken Herrera." He tried to smile but then grimaced in pain. "Hope it works."

"Of course it will. The stuff's like magic, Ken. Don't worry. You'll be back on your feet in no time."

"Almost made it inside, but…I collapsed. If I'd made it in, I'd be dead. Wouldn't have found me."

"Luck's a strange thing, Ken. Trust me on that."

The door clicked open again, and Ada ran down the steps carrying a large white plastic case. She laid it on the floor and then pulled out a plastic-wrapped syringe. "Okay, got it. You find a vein and swab it and I'll pump this right into his bloodstream. That's the fastest way to get the virophage to the scene of the battle." She took out the silver Cryogenie and removed a vial of Recombin. Holding it upside down, she pushed the needle through the seal and pulled the plunger until it filled. "Vaccines usually go into muscle, but this is a risk we have to take."

Krista found a vein easily; while Ken was tall and broad-chested, he had no body fat, and his blood vessels stood out like highways on a road map. She swabbed one, and then Ada pushed her hand out of the way and jabbed the needle into it. Ken gasped, and she pressed the plunger down until the syringe was empty. "Enjoy the meal, little buggies," she said, taking two small bottles from the medikit.

"You'll be okay now, Ken," Krista said, and she took his hand.

"I can't thank you –" He winced as Ada jabbed another needle into his arm.

"Antibiotic. Just to knock out any bacteria," she murmured, as she wiped another spot on his arm.

Ken turned back to Krista. "I can't thank you – Oww!"

"That's happy juice. In a minute, you won't have a care in the world," Ada said.

"Like I said, I can't thank you two enough," he whispered. His eyes crossed and he smiled shakily. "Oh, wow, lookie that."

"Not a care in the world," Ada said. "Krista, he has a bunker in there with everything, and I mean *everything*. But right now, we need to get him into a bed. He'll be dead weight soon. C'mon, help me get him inside." She looped her arm under his, and Krista grabbed his other arm.

"Okay, Ken, we're going to help you up and get you inside," Krista said. "On the count of three. One…two…three!"

They pulled him up, and Ken's legs skittered until he got them underneath his body. He wavered for a minute, but they kept him on his feet and walked him up the steps to the door.

"I love you," he said, and then his head lolled to the side.

"Which one of us?" Ada pushed his head upright.

"Both of you."

"Now that's so sweet of you, Ken." Krista grunted as she tried to keep him vertical and punch the code into the keypad at the same time.

"Marry me."

"Which one of us?" Ada asked.

"Both of you."

"Wouldn't that be polygamy?" Krista punched the right number and the door clicked open.

"Not in Utah. Not far away." His head fell forward and thumped against the door, pushing it all the way open, and they struggled to pull him upright again.

"Hurry," Ada said. "He'll be out soon."

They half-walked, half-dragged the man to a small room near the door. Radio equipment, TV monitors, and gun racks lined one wall, and a cot lay along the other. They lowered him onto the bed, and he smiled narcotically, lay back on the pillow, and started snoring.

"What'd you give him?" Krista asked.

"A shot of prescription-grade Synthopia. He'll get some deep sleep and have really colorful dreams," Ada said. "Hey, I know what that's like. C'mon, I'll show you what he has. I think he's one of those preppers. He has enough gear to survive World War Nine."

"So we found our Xanadu. I was right for once."

Ada pointed a finger at her face. "Don't get smug. Nobody likes smug."

They left the radio room and walked into a square concrete-walled space ringed with storage racks. Right behind the radio room, a metal stair descended to a lower floor. They clanged down it and found a large bathroom at the bottom with a soaking tub for two. On the other side of the stairs, kitchen cabinets stretched along the back wall and ended in a pair of refrigerators big enough for Krista to do jumping jacks in.

Ada opened one and saw stacks of frozen, blister-packed meat. The other refrigerator was also jammed with food containers, and she pulled one out and lifted the lid. "Roast beef with baked potatoes. And there's an apple pie in there. Dutch apple pie, of course, and I bet it's all crumbly and sweet."

"See? I told you I get lucky sometimes."

"This isn't luck. This is exactly what you said we'd find. How'd you do this?"

Krista smiled and shrugged, and then she opened a door at the end of the kitchen and walked into a wide room nearly filled with a round bed. A plasma screen display covered the wall from floor to ceiling. "Omigod," she breathed. "You've got to see this."

Ada peeked through the door at the bed. "As soft as a cloud stuffed in a mattress?"

Krista flopped onto it and sank in a foot. Ada laughed and opened the door to a floor-to-ceiling cabinet that filled the side wall of the bedroom; inside, sacks of flour, pasta, and rice were jammed into every available space. Behind the next door, she found cans of every vegetable she knew of, and some she didn't. "Awesome as fuck," she murmured. "You've got a weird magic going on, but I'll take it."

"Sometimes I'm just lucky that way. It's a Life Force thing."

"Or maybe it has something to do with those chillybones and the tumbleweirds. I'll have to spock that." Ada strode back to the kitchen and pulled out the roast beef container. "But that's for later. Right now, I'm gonna eat till I pop!"

THE MUSHROOM FARM

Day 40
Sunday night, September 27, 2043
Pacific Ocean, 460 miles south of Anchorage, Alaska

Tala Ripley slid her plate across the table and pulled up a chair across from Quinn, who was watching his table-mounted monitor as he ate. She munched on a slice of bacon, and then she twisted a monitor around and tapped it on to see what was so fascinating.

A submarine control room looking like a spaceship bridge flickered onto the screen, and a rock-jawed man with three-day stubble and a cigar in the corner of his mouth squinted at the camera.

"Oh, no," Ripley moaned. "Not *Mushrooms over Moscow* again. I hate this movie."

"C'mon, it's hilarious," Quinn said, dipping his biscuit in gravy. "This is the best part coming up. Shh."

Back on the screen, the chiseled commander swiveled in his chair and pulled the cigar from his mouth. "Sailors, tonight the *Patrick Henry* makes history."

A blonde and busty officer laid a hand on her cheek, her breasts heaving. Her other hand hovered over a red button the size of a dinner plate. "Commander, you don't mean…?"

"Yes, Lieutenant," he growled, flaring his nostrils. *"Fire all rockets!"*

Howls of laughter bounced off the wardroom walls, and Quinn raised his coffee cup to the junior officers across the room. "Gentlemen, if I ever say that, please shoot me."

Ripley shook her head and dove into her pile of bacon. "Rockets," she muttered. "That movie's so awful, it's not even funny. The credits are the only good part."

"It never gets old for me." Quinn sipped his coffee and grimaced. "Where do they get this pisswater?"

Ripley tried hers. "Tastes fine to me."

Quinn pulled a foil packet of instant coffee from a pocket and poured black grains into his cup. He stirred it and let go of the spoon, which clinked against the side. "See?"

"That's what it's supposed to do, Ennis. It's called gravity."

"No, no, no," he said. "In a proper cup of coffee, the spoon stands straight up and quivers in fear as it's slowly dissolved." He sniffed it and took a sip.

"Gimme some. It might keep me awake for the next six hours."

He handed her a packet. "If it's any comfort, we'll be running two release drills on this watch, and one of them is Strategic."

"That'll be interesting. And next year, it'll get *very* interesting."

Quinn rolled his eyes. "It's going to be a long year. I wish they'd make you XO just to shut you up. Why are you so aggressive about this?"

"You know where I grew up. I spent my whole life getting out of that trap."

"You're not going back to Maryville. You can relax."

"It gets built into you after a while – keep moving, keep reaching up, never back down." She looked into a corner of the wardroom and shrugged. "I wouldn't expect someone like you to understand."

"Someone like me," he said.

"Yes, someone like you. You never appreciate how many doors got opened for you on the way up. Well, lemme tell you, when you work your way up from a place like Maryville, you have to bust down every door and fight to keep from being shoved back through. You don't appreciate how hard that is. You take your advantages for granted."

Quinn drummed his fingers on the table. "You think being the son of the Manhattan Mattress King was an advantage? Did you see the commercials my dad made? The kids at school never left me alone after that one with the dancing cow."

Ripley snorted and pinched back a laugh.

"That was a real cow, Tala. Did you know that the Humane Society came to our apartment and asked me if I'd ever seen my dad sexualize an animal?" He gulped his coffee and set the cup down with a thud. "I still don't know what that means. Don't talk to me about advantages."

"He had the money and the connections to get you into Canoe U, though, and Annapolis opens doors. Ohio State doesn't. That's what I mean."

Quinn sat back in his chair and leveled a dark look at her. "That's insulting. A lot of Annapolis graduates got blown off the *Vanderbilt's* bridge at Bushehr Bay. I only survived because of dumb luck, not because of my so-called advantages. And after I was released from Hamadan, the Navy pinned a medal on me and then told me to go work my ass off. They cut me zero slack, Tala."

"Precisely, Ennis. But your hard work was recognized, and it moved you up. When you come from the rank and file, your hard work is taken for granted. You have to force people to pay attention to it."

"Lighten up. You'll never master the politics of this job if you don't." The junior officers stood and walked into the corridor, and Quinn sat back in his seat and crossed his arms. "Mister Ripley, recite the First Law of the Conservation of Happiness."

"Once the hatch closes, happiness can neither be created nor destroyed," Ripley muttered as she looked down at the table.

"Correct. Don't squander your happiness. If you don't keep a positive attitude, you'll be a wreck by the end of this patrol." He stood and straightened the wrinkles from his jumpsuit. "Ten minutes to the watch change. Why don't we continue this chat some other time?"

QUINN AND RIPLEY FOLLOWED THE OTHER OFFICERS to the Control Room. Ripley turned right through the hatch and sat at the Strategic Warfare console.

The Control Room was nothing like the starship fantasy of *Mushrooms over Moscow*. It wasn't sleek and polished; the small, square room was crammed with monitors, with cables and piping stuffed into every space between them. The command platform only held a chair and a charting pedestal, not the sweeping console of blinking lights the movie showed.

Ripley relieved the officer on duty and scanned her console. Her station was the same as the other eleven in the room – a touch screen console at her lap and a monitor at eye level, with a larger monitor above displaying the station's status to Command. She performed a quick diagnostic of her missiles and then started a war simulation to test the

Missile Release Control System's response. Turning to a small monitor at her side, she double-checked the readiness of the Mushroom Farm. Her thirty-six Joe Slicks were snug and sound in their tubes. She leaned back in her seat and watched numbers flit across the screen, but she'd find nothing amiss – the MRCS always operated flawlessly and didn't need her attention.

That grated on her nerves. She'd become an aeronautical engineer so she could tinker with the Navy's exotic harem of zoomies, not stare at a screen and watch them sleep in their tubes, all the while chewing nicotine gum just to keep from dozing off.

And the Slick missile was the most exotic of zoomies. It went by many names: The Defense Department called it the 'Missile, Joint Ops / Strategic Low Observable, Cruise Type K5' or M-JO / SLOCK-5, but it was known to the public as the Lancet. However, neither name rolled off the Navy tongue as well as Joe Slick, and the nickname had stuck.

The missile was a fantastic piece of engineering, a scramjet-powered demon invisible to radar that exceeded Mach 14 at cruising altitude. However, the Slick had two significant drawbacks: It had a strike range of only three thousand miles, but even worse, it could only carry an eighty pound payload. With modern American nukes tipping the scales at five hundred pounds, this limited the missile to carrying conventional explosives. Nobody in the Navy could see a practical use for an eighty million dollar missile that delivered such a tiny bang to its target.

Four years previously, though, a breakthrough in nuclear weapon engineering changed the Slick's role. That was when an ultra-light 950-kiloton strong-fission / fusion bomb was successfully tested – the W104 Mark 3 thermonuclear warhead. It was rushed into development, and the featherweight Mark 18 version, weighing in at a mere seventy-nine-point-eight pounds, was fitted on a Joe Slick a year later. The most unstoppable weapon ever made was installed on the new Patriot class boats shortly after.

Nobody knew where the revolutionary strong-fission technology had come from, but the rumors abounded: Some believed that Area 51's last surviving Little Green Man had coughed up the secret on its deathbed, while others were convinced that the technology had been discovered in an ancient Mayan codex where ancient astronauts had secreted the plans three millennia ago. Ripley laced her fingers behind her head and smiled – if she started believing that kind of baloney, she might as well put in a bid on the Brooklyn Bridge.

QUINN WALKED UP THE LEFT SIDE OF THE ROOM and saw that Communications and Countermeasures were operating smoothly. He continued forward into the Sonar Suite and found a young man sprawled in a seat, wearing headphones and staring at the ceiling – the customary posture of sonar specialists.

He backed out of Sonar, around the helm in front of Command, and turned in to Acoustics, where another man wearing headphones and virtual reality goggles gazed at numbers on a holographic sphere. The *Henry's* spherical acoustic array, which took up the entire nose dome of the boat, was sensitive enough to hear and identify vessels as far as a hundred kilometers away. Interpreting the data was an immersive experience, so he left the Acoustics nest without disturbing him.

Returning to the Control Room, he checked Engineering and saw that they were only drawing forty-one percent from the reactor. The Warfare stations were situated behind Command, and Tactical and Strategic were both running simulations and preparing for the drill later in the watch.

He stepped onto the Command podium and reviewed the crew report. Bricker briefed him on the condition of the boat, and then she and her watch headed aft for breakfast.

Quinn walked around the edge of the podium and rechecked the status monitors, and then he scanned the digital charting screen over the helm. They were still on schedule, and the *Henry* would transit the Aleutians near Akutan Island tomorrow and enter the Bering Sea.

Navigating the Bering Sea was difficult this time of year because fishing trawlers worked the area in fall. All commercial vessels were required to broadcast their location, but Russian trawlers often turned off their transponders to fish the rich migratory paths along America's Aleutians illegally. When the Red trawlers drifted on the currents, their nets became a silent danger that sometimes fouled the communications buoys of missile boats gliding a hundred meters beneath the surface. Four patrols before, the *Henry's* comm buoy had been snagged, and they'd had to surface to clear it.

If they made it through the Bering Sea untouched, he'd guide the boat through the shallow Bering Strait – the most exciting part of the trip because the Strait was littered with Soviet Bloc hydrophones. The Reds had long ago learned that the best undersea detection system was the human ear, and their acoustic specialists listened around the clock for the screw sounds of passing boats. However, the *Henry* used a laminar-jet propulsion system, and the only screws the boat possessed were packed in a box in the machinist's shop.

The Reds also filled the Strait with sonar, but that didn't worry Quinn. Most sonar rays slid off the boat's composite metamaterial hull like water off waxed glass, and the metamaterial was cloaked with a resilient nanocoating to absorb the few rays it didn't deflect. He only paid attention when the sonar transmitter was within a thousand meters, and they'd be ten times that far from the Red stationary sonars.

After the Bering Strait passage, though, the patrol would descend into a mind-numbing routine. The *Henry* was scheduled to sail across the Arctic Circle, take up station east of Novaya Zemlya in the Kara Sea, and then meander in a random pattern. After seventy-two days, they'd return to Bangor, spend three months ashore, and then get in and do it again.

"Ahh, but a little bit of Hollywood wouldn't hurt every now and then, either, would it?" He sat in the chair, still warm from Captain Bricker, and sighed.

CHOKEPOINTS

Day 40
Sunday evening, September 27, 2043
National Tranquility Center, Fort Belvoir, Virginia

Downs watched the Wall and waited for the chokepoint map to appear. Cochon and Mochyn had been working on it for hours already, and they were close to finishing.

Warner hadn't shaken their web once in the last forty-eight hours, and after that long with no workable leads, it was time to admit that pursuit had failed. However, she could only get to Sacramento by crossing a mountain pass, so they planned to monitor each one. More than seventy roads crossed the Rockies, but most were impassable by car, and Cochon was analyzing and mapping the road conditions of those Warner could drive. Speed cameras monitored the passes where the Interstates crossed, leaving only a few minor mountain crossings to cover with human eyes.

It would be much easier if they knew what vehicle she was driving because the fug was light in the Rockies. The Blackeyes could pick up her car easily there, but they didn't know what vehicle to search for, and their greatest capability had been rendered useless. Warner seemed to know precisely how to confound them – no matter what advantage the NSF had, she found a way to neutralize it.

The status monitor showed that the assault and surveillance drones would be landing soon at Fort Carbon, outside Durango, and they'd be ready for operations by sunset. The Executives and Special Activity Groups from Fort Wayne would be landing there later in the day – the Washington-based teams were being held in reserve to thwart The Activity's potential eastern offensive – and they'd be ready for deployment in the evening. A company of Collaterals and their equipment would arrive from North Carolina later. Although that much force shouldn't be necessary, Warner and the Activists were surprisingly resilient, and it might take a sledgehammer blow to squash them for good.

The chokepoint map still wasn't up. "Cochon? What's the holdup?" he asked.

"Almost done, sir." A map shimmered onto the Wall. "We need to cover thirty-eight passes, most of them in Colorado. Satan's Saddle, Widowmaker, and Purgatory Passes can't be crossed by anything except an experienced mountain driver with specialized equipment. The Syllogic Engine predicts that Warner will avoid them. There's no need to deploy assets there."

"Excellent," Downs said. "Hogue, deploy the Special Activity Groups to these other locations when their boots hit the ground."

AN HOUR LATER, Downs watched the repositioning of Blackeye 1, which monitored the New York City area and the Northeast. The Watch Room no longer needed to surveille the mostly empty streets; most corporations there had known about the virus beforehand and sheltered their key employees, and they wouldn't expose them to the few Rank survivors prowling the streets looking for food or fuel. The city would be stable until next week, when corporate security forces would throw the remaining Ranks off the island.

The NSF needed enhanced surveillance elsewhere, so he was sending the airship on a twelve-hour journey south to Baltimore to provide more detailed imagery of the tumultuous corridor between Richmond and Philadelphia. Even though the forty cameras on the Blackeyes could monitor activities almost four hundred miles away on flat terrain, the dense metropolitan areas were anything but flat and needed better coverage, especially now.

These Mid-Atlantic cities couldn't be allowed to fall into chaos or ruin; they had to survive the virus intact and form the administrative and economic core of the new nation. However, riots had torn through them, and Downs needed to minimize the amount of property damage. In another two months, the virus would kill or break most of the rioters, but they could do irreparable harm to the cities before then.

The riots might never end if Warner got the vaccine to California in the next three weeks, and they started to reproduce it. The Transition might even fall apart. Containing vaccinated rioters would be impossible without invading the cities and killing them on the streets– a nightmare scenario that would require using the Collateral Tactics Unit, who were more destructive than the rioters.

His mood darkened as he thought of the direction the Transition was taking. To make it worse, he was as responsible as anyone for this developing crisis.

The Activity is behind this, and we all missed it, he thought. *I even missed it, and I miss nothing. I've never made a mistake, and the first time I do, it's at a critical juncture in the Transition. I should feel shame for my mediocre performance.*

He took a deep breath and returned to watching the world. "Cochon. Have you finished your investigation into this Adam Harris?"

"I've almost completed it, sir. I'm awaiting verification on a few small items of information."

"Give me the executive summary, then."

"His records are clean, sir. Twenty-five years of spotless service. He has no motivation to resist the established order and is the model naval officer."

"Nobody's spotless. Elaborate."

"That's impossible without resorting to colorful metaphors, sir," Cochon said. "He's the prototype of the All-American Boy. Eagle Scouts want to grow up to be Adam Harris."

"That's the bulletproof cover every deep-insertion agent seeks, Cochon." Downs stroked his chin. "He was a prisoner of war with Beckmann, wasn't he? Is there a possibility of a Persian Candidate scenario?"

"How would you explain Victoria Lang, sir?"

"Perhaps Harris turned her," Downs said. "And that could explain why we can't find records for Warner before she was eleven. She could have been in Persia then. If the Persians have infiltrated the Activists, the strategic implications are disturbing, Cochon. Run an analysis –"

"Sir!" Hogue turned in her chair and ran to the podium.

"Why have you left your station?" he asked.

"I just received a directive, sir," she said quietly. "A presidential directive, and I confirmed it verbally with the White House Chief of Staff."

"That's unusual. Gibbon plays tennis in the afternoon, and other matters of state haven't stopped him before," Downs said. "What does he want?"

"He's ordering us to enter Anacostia and suppress the insurrection there. Using the *Collaterals*, sir."

Downs stiffened and scanned her face for any clues about the coming punchline. "This is the wrong time to joke, Hogue. It'd be a disaster to send the Collaterals marching into a city again."

"Check your tablet, sir."

He glanced at the screen of his small computer and grimaced. "Thank you, Miss Hogue." He turned away and dialed Raphael's number.

RAPHAEL LEANED BACK IN HIS CHAIR and rested his feet on Downs' desk. "It's what he says, Bob. I know it's hard to take, but Noah thinks this can work to our advantage."

Downs pulled off his glasses and rubbed his eyes. "Sending the Collaterals to wreck Anacostia is a public relations nightmare, Raf."

"Noah thinks we can contain the damage to the Anacostia side of the river, and it won't matter in the end," Raphael said. "We can raze the place once we take over and use it for upscale housing. The key thing is that we have a written directive from Gibbon, and Noah can tag him for it when this gets ugly. It's a gross miscalculation, and as Noah says, 'Never interfere with your adversary's suicide.' I couldn't agree more." He dropped his feet and leaned over the desk. "I know you're concerned with keeping a low public profile, but we have no choice except to do it and deal with the fallout later. And it *is* a presidential directive. We can't refuse."

Downs stared at the featureless gray wall of his office. "Something bad will come of this, Raf. Open suppression of a city results in a popular backlash we might not survive. The backlash from Detroit nearly wiped out the NSF, and it took skillful marketing and political spin to keep our heads above water. Some fallout can't be dealt with."

"Political spin is no prob, Bob. That's my strong suit," Raphael said. "Trust me on this. It'll all work out to our advantage."

OPPOSITES MONTH

Day 41
Monday morning, September 28, 2043
Castle Herrera, Seven Up, Colorado

Krista threw the covers off her sweltering body and looked up blearily at yet another unfamiliar ceiling. Groaning, she rolled off the bed and stretched. From how tight her muscles were, she'd been asleep for a while.

She stumbled to the kitchen for a drink, running her fingers through her hair and yawning. The water from the tap tasted terrific, and she was on her second glass when she glimpsed heaven out of the corner of her eye – a baristomat. She started it up and then found that the hopper was filled with stale, dry Italian Roast beans.

"Beggars, choosers, whatever," she mumbled, rummaging through the wall cabinets. She found a mug, slammed it into the machine, and held the extra buzz button down until a LaBrea-like brew plopped from the spout. When it was ready, she sniffed the steaming mug and took a sip. She shivered with delight as the coffee swirled in her mouth, but it also awakened her bladder, and she grabbed her backpack and potty-danced to the bathroom.

When she saw the grimy apparition in the mirror, she nearly screamed – red welts covered her back and shoulders from the grange's embers, her neck was scratched from flying glass, and her hair was tangled in knots.

Pawing through her pack, she found her shampoo and conditioner and then searched the drawers under the sink for shaving gear so she could shave her furry legs. Sure enough, Ken had stocked ten of everything she needed for a complete grooming.

She bent over to fill the tub, and her hair fell forward; the ends were burned to a crisp and fused into clumps. Saving it would be impossible.

With a sigh, she turned back to the sink and searched the drawers for scissors.

KRISTA OPENED THE DOOR to the smell of frying bacon. She followed her nose to the range and found Ada pushing bacon strips around in a pan.

"Morning," Krista called.

"Morning. We're having a real breakfast if I can manage the eggs. They're powdered. I don't know how to make those."

"Don't worry, I'll do the eggs." She dug into her pack and pulled out the charger for her tablet. "Is there an outlet around?"

"Here by the counter. I plugged the Cryogenie into it."

Krista plugged in the charger and connected the tablet. "I've got to charge this up. I need to find out what day it is and what's happening in the world. Besides that, I'd like to do a post on Seven Up."

"Do you think that's wise? We're still near it. You've given away enough clues, Krista. Why don't you wait till we're gone?"

She grunted and watched the charging indicator.

"I heard you singing in the shower. You do a fantastic imitation of Keriana, y'know."

"Really, now?" Krista's eyes brightened. "Well, that's –"

"Yeah, you moan just like her."

"Aren't you the crabby one? Do you have a bad case of PMS or something?"

"No, I'm in a good mood."

"Well, come up with another excuse, then," Krista said, stepping into her sweatpants. "Oh, hey, guess what? I cut my hair short! I took at least two inches off!"

"That's not short," Ada said. "That's just less long." She peeled the foil off the spout of the powdered-egg carton. "My hair's totally ruined. Later on I'll chop it, maybe above the shoulders. You need a chop too. That ponytail's gotta go."

"I don't want *short* short hair. I had that once, and I looked like a boy. The schoolkids started calling me Christopher because they thought I was transitioning to male."

Ada looked her over from top to bottom. "You went to a school for the blind?"

"I was ten. I was kinda tomboyish back then."

"Get over it," Ada said. "By the way, I checked on Ken, and he's still asleep. He has a high fever, but it's lower than yesterday. Honestly, the fact that he's even alive is a miracle."

"That Recombin really works. I hope he'll be okay –" Her charger popped and flashed, and blue smoke curled from inside it. She grabbed a potholder and pulled it from the outlet, and the back of it was charred black. "Damn. This charger's a corpse."

"Look in that drawer next to the refrigerator. Ken has a few chargers in there. That's where I found one for the Cryogenie."

Krista rummaged through the tangle of wires, but none fit her tablet. "So much for that. Damn. It just gave me a ten percent charge. I won't have the juice to post."

"The news is never good anyway. No big deal," Ada said. "Since you have nothing to do now, come over and help me with these eggs."

ADA WALKED INTO THE GARAGE and found Krista sitting against the concrete wall near the garage door. She sat across from her, humming a few bars of Blac Sacrament's *Sticky Stuff*.

"You're in a good mood," Krista said.

"I just took the most epic poop," she sighed. "Talk about a backlog. And it really *did* look like the Loch Ness Monster. You shoulda seen it."

"I miss all the good things in life. Say, did you do something to your hair?"

Ada stood and pirouetted like a fashion model. "Whatcha think?"

"Wow! That looks nice. It shows off your face."

Ada flung her hair from side to side. "I look good with a bob. I like how I can toss it around now, and my head feels so light! *And* I don't look like a boy."

"I like it. Tell you what – you can cut mine like that tomorrow."

Ada giggled and sat against the wheel of Ken's small truck. "Pissin. We'll be all twinsy."

Krista laughed, lit a cigarette, and blew a plume out of the garage into the bright afternoon sky. "I love looking at the desert. You can even see the tops of the mountains from here. This place is so pretty, in a hardass kinda way."

"But it's too bright," Ada said. "I'm not used to this much sun. I spent most of my life in the fug, and this light's giving me a freakin headache now. And I keep feeling like I have to sneeze." Her nose itched, and she pinched it and held her breath. Her face grew redder and redder, and then she sneezed so hard that she doubled over and her hair flew forward. "I'm allergic to sunlight," she said.

"You can't be allergic to sunlight, kiddo. It's not like pollen."

"I definitely am." Her nostrils twitched, and she pinched her nose again.

"You'll get used to it," Krista said. "It's getting to me too, but I like it. The shadows are so sharp, and everything's so clear. And you can see forever."

Ada scanned the horizon beyond the cactus ringing the bunker. "I keep expecting missiles to come roaring out of the sky again."

"Now that would suck." Krista edged back from the opening a few inches.

"This place could take a direct hit, though. It was designed to withstand overpressure, in fact. It's a lot more solid than it needs to be."

"I'd like to not find out," Krista said. She rubbed her hand along the wall to her side. "The walls are solid cement. That's seriously strong."

"Concrete. If you made a wall just out of cement, it would fall apart."

Krista sighed and leaned back against the cool concrete. "Y'know, I really love you."

"Even despite me being me?"

"Bingo!"

"Okay, I'll accept that," Ada said. "Fair deal."

"It sure is. I've been looking for that deal all my life, and I haven't found it yet."

"Me neither," Ada said, resting her head against the knobby tire on Ken's truck. "Why does love have to be so tricky?"

"I don't know why," Krista said. "I'm not sure anyone does."

"It just makes a lot of people lonely." Ada looked down at her hands and spoke in a small voice. "You're the only one I've ever met that…" She finished the sentence with a shrug.

"Maybe I'm the only one you've met so far," Krista said. "Who knows what might happen? I hear the guys in California love blondes."

"And I'm a natural platinum blonde!"

"Even better. They treat platinum blondes like goddesses there." Krista gazed through the garage door again; a cloud moved across the sun, and the land suddenly lost its vibrant color. "You know, it's strange. Not long ago, I was so unhappy trying to make a good life in my tiny, tiny box. I was terrified of the unknowns in the outside world. In the past two weeks, I've learned why I should be terrified of it, but now I feel better than ever. Maybe I cured myself by going batshit crazy, but I'll take it."

"I don't think you're crazy. A little loopy, but not *seriously* crazy."

"Oh, I've definitely gone away in the head. I felt it happen in Ohio. It was like a spark jumped from ear to ear across my brain, and I've been different ever since. Now I sometimes feel a power running through me, some odd strength I never knew was there, and I wonder if that's just lunatic strength, or if the Life Force got into me. But whatever it is, I want more."

"Don't jump into superstition and mysticism for answers, Krista. I think there's a rational explanation for all this. When there are known threats, you stop worrying about pointless unknowns. I think you feel better cuz you're free from all the trivial stuff now. That's why I feel better too, and this is where I want to stay – on the edge, where everything is clear, everything is free, everything makes sense, where failure and death look you in the face and you can spit right back, where you're so close to the edge that you're afraid you'll burn up or break apart – this is life, Krista, and for the first time, I love it." She leaned back against the tire and closed her eyes. "But it worries me sometimes that I do. Do you think there's something wrong with me?"

Krista barked a short laugh and shook her head. "You think you're crazy too?"

"No, I just wonder if I'm…" She wrapped her arms around her knees and looked at the floor. "When I was in Bumfuck Wyoming, after I got caught with Baby Bang Bang, Project Blue Ball sent shrinks in to talk to me every day. They said I have a destructive personality, and I could only live in a so-called constrained environment."

"Weren't they part of the same crowd that was trying to make you an atom bomb slave?"

"Those douchenozzles. I heard them talking outside my room after one of the sessions, and you know what they called Baby Bang Bang? A 'Weapon of Miss Destruction.' Hah. *So* very funny. Let me pencil in when to laugh." She pulled back her hair with one hand and looked at the ceiling with a dark expression. "Miss Destruction. Everybody still calls me that. But anyway, I think there's something to what they said. I worry if I'll ever fit in anywhere, or if I'm just too dangerous and I'll always be a freak."

"That's bullshit. They were trying to get you to sign that contract. They'd say anything."

"Still…"

"It's bullshit, Ada. I don't think you're dangerous except when you need to be. I don't feel in danger around you. In fact, I feel safer with you around."

"Yeah?"

"Definitely. There's nothing wrong with you. You're exceptional, that's true, but that's a long way from being a freak that's got to be caged."

Ada slid over to the concrete wall and sat next to her. "Thanks."

"Don't thank me for stating a fact. Don't you always say that?"

Ada nodded and stared at something light-years away. "I think I was just built backwards, and now that the world is backwards, everything works the way it should. It's been like Opposites Month – everything about me that was a problem before is a good thing now."

"Ada, you're great the way you are, and I don't want you to change," Krista said. "You can be Little Miss Opposite as long as you want."

A black bird flew over, riding the thermals, and Ada watched it wheel in the sky far away. "I'd hate to find out that the only way I can be myself is to be a lonely freak."

"Well, we're free to be what we want now, aren't we? Maybe if we live through this, we'll stay free." Krista watched the bird dive with a screech and then rise with a small creature in its beak, and she closed her eyes – she and Ada were as likely to live free as they were to die gruesomely in some predator's claws, which was a thought she'd been suppressing. "Maybe everything will be better. When we were on the train, I felt like I was sailing over an ocean of corn to a faraway island. Maybe we're sailing to some exotic land where all the rules are different, and we won't have to live in tiny boxes. Maybe even the rules of Fate are different there too."

"I hope so."

"I hope so too. But no matter what we find, we'll handle it together, you and me."

Ada snuggled into her shoulder. "Yeah, you and me."

They looked out at the desert until the sun slid behind the mountains; a glorious orange sunset flared, and they watched the spectacle grow and then fade to night.

KEN WAS STILL ASLEEP, and his fever ran dangerously high. He'd also wet his pants sometime in the afternoon, which Ada said was a sign of recovery. "He's kinda cute for an old guy. I can see that rugged Aztec warrior face under a feather headdress. But right now, he's helpless as a freakin baby. We have to remove his pants now, or he'll get a rash." She reached down and unbuckled his belt.

"Nuh-uh. You're not looking at his junk."

"Don't treat me like a child," Ada said. "It's not like I've never seen a penis."

Krista pulled a blanket from a shelf and fluffed it open. "Well, you won't be gandering his tool on my watch." She laid the blanket over him, reached under it, and slipped his pants off.

"You suck," Ada scowled. "You suck like black holes wish they sucked."

"I won't be corrupting your morals, kiddo."

"After Vincennes and Revenge, you're still worried about my freakin morals? Seriously?"

"Sure." Krista tucked the edges of the sheet under his legs. "Corrupting the morals of an Arkie minor is a serious offense."

"I never believed in their crap," she grumbled. "First church I see, I'm resigning or whatever it is you do."

Krista smiled and took his wet clothes to an alcove behind the front door, where they'd found a laundry room and a decontamination shower booth earlier that day. As soon as she left the radio room, Ada lifted the blanket and glanced underneath.

"Stop peeking!" Krista called.

"What kinda creep do you think I am?" she asked, tucking the sheet back in.

"Well, stop peeking anyway and help me get this feckin washer going! It's like the one in my apartment! It's gone all Swede!"

Ada stomped to the laundry room, looked at the Swedish scrolling across the screen, and then double-tapped one corner. Her fingers flew across brightly colored icons, and then English words appeared while the machine whistled a jaunty rendition of *Battle Hymn of the Republic*.

"Now tell me how you did that, wouldja?" Krista asked. "I could never figure it out."

Ada smiled and shrugged. "Like I said, show me a machine. I'll make it work."

After the washer was running, Ada opened the medikit, wiped anesthetic on Krista's leg wound and removed the stitches, and then changed the dressing on hers. They walked downstairs and made pounds of pasta, slathered it with a gallon of meat sauce, and ate all of it. Krista even drank a *cerveza* after Ada nagged her to try it.

Pleasantly full and slightly drunk, they lounged on the bed and clicked through Ken's digital movie collection, but most of it was porn except for a few old Marx Brothers flicks. They finally settled on *Duck Soup* and laughed until the end.

When it was over, they returned upstairs and explored Ken's treasure trove. Ada found shotgun shells in the radio room, and she reloaded her gun and slipped a spare box into her bag.

In the main room, cartons of food with freeze-dried gourmet meals were stacked to the ceiling. They debated what to take, and then just picked two of everything and set them aside. On a far wall, they found two well-padded hiking backpacks hanging from hooks, which they filled with bottled water and food packs.

Ada started emptying her bookbag into the backpack, and Krista watched as Ada pulled pack after pack of cigarettes from the seemingly bottomless bag. "Where'd you get all those?" she asked.

Ada jammed a roll of toilet paper into the hiking pack. "Toilet paper and cigarettes. Never flee cross-country without them."

"Ahh, the things you learn in life."

"I'll leave the briefcase here." Ada stuffed the picture and the papers into a front pocket of the hiking pack. "It's too heavy."

"It's your mom's. You wouldn't mind leaving it?"

"No, I have what I want. Besides, it makes me a target. What if the NSF is looking for this thing now?"

"True." Krista reached into the overstuffed racks, pulled down a cardboard box, and found cartons of cigarettes inside. "Breathless Menthols. That's a femme brand. I think Ken had a playmate in mind when he stocked this place."

"He came alone, though, so I bet she's dead. Lots of that going around," Ada said, ripping open a case of water bottles.

"Also true." Krista shrugged and threw them into her pack. Opening another box, she found an assortment of lingerie: a red leather bustier that didn't fit her, fishnet stockings she wouldn't be caught dead in, and a black lace teddy. "This is my size," she said, holding it up. "How is this survival gear?"

"Maybe he needs sex to survive. He certainly didn't want to suffer through the Apocalypse. He set himself up really well – food, clothing, a sex den, everything."

"Well, that's for sure. I didn't find any bras in that box, though. I'm getting a different picture of our friend now." Krista slid out of her sweatsuit and shimmied into the teddy. "Do I look sexy?"

"Don't ask me. I don't get why that's supposed to be sexy," Ada said. "Y'know, the lace-and-sweats look doesn't make sense."

"Sure it does. It tells a man that if he can get over my outer slob, he'll be rewarded by my inner tramp." She swiveled her hips and crouched. "This is really comfortable. It keeps my jigglies in place, and it's even more comfortable than a bra. And look!" She pulled a tab at the crotch, and a lace panel between her legs fell away. "When I've got to tinkle, I won't have to take the whole thing off!"

Ada giggled and sat back on a box. "That's not what it's for, y'know."

Krista's mouth twisted into a frown and her cheeks flushed. "Jaysus," she grumbled as she pulled on her sweatpants. "It's better than wearing nothing."

"Sure it is. Ask any guy."

LATER, THEY OPENED THE GARAGE DOOR and walked around the compound in the crisp night air. The fug had vanished overnight, and stars splashed across the sky. They spread a blanket on the ground and gazed at galaxies and talked about mothers and men and love.

After a time, the eastern sky began to lighten, and they walked back into the garage to keep from being seen by the airship cameras. The bowl of night sky and stars slid back, slowly revealing a light pink dawn, and they watched it grow into a beautiful desert sunrise.

SPARRING PARTNERS

Day 41
Monday morning, September 28, 2043
US Route 50, one mile east of Gunbelt, Colorado

Mark Mason squirmed in his seat and gazed blearily at the truck's monitor. The dashcam displayed the face of every westbound driver, and when the traffic was heavy, the faces flicked by so fast that he hardly had time to see them. "I gotta go water the horse," he told his partner, and she gave him a puzzled look. "Y'know, pay the water bill? Hose down the porcelain? Siphon the python?" he asked.

"You mean you gotta take a piss?"

"Well, if you're gonna be crude about it, yeah." He opened the door and walked to the rusting water tank they'd parked behind. It gave deep shade this time of day, and cars coming from the east couldn't spot them, but the sun was peeking around the tank already. They'd have to move to another spot soon – even a white X-Urban broiled in the unrelenting high-country sun.

Colorado was already getting under his skin, and he'd only been in the state for half a day. Gunbelt sat at the head of a long, empty valley with no crops, no people, no houses, and no livestock. It felt creepy to see land just sitting there doing nothing, and he couldn't wait to get back to civilization.

He rubbed his eyes and looked past the scrubby grass at the highway. It was pointless to wait here for one woman to drive by, but it was their only chance.

After a yawn and a stretch, he zipped his pants and sauntered back to the driver's seat. "This is stupid," he said, and his partner grunted. "We hurry up, then wait in the baking sun for nothing to happen. We'll never find her this way."

"What else can we do?" Dani Frye asked. "The woman wants to be a needle in a haystack, so it's gonna be difficult. That doesn't mean we shouldn't try."

"Yeah, there a chance this might work. Maybe Warner will just fall into our laps," he said, rubbing his forehead with his palms. "Never mind me. I'm just grouchy this morning."

"Bad sleep?"

"Bad sleep, bad breakfast. The hotel's packed to the rafters and everybody was noisy, and the guys next door were smoking pot all night, so I didn't sleep. And the eggs were terrible this morning. I hate fake eggs."

"They were real eggs, Mark."

"They were pretty rubbery for real eggs." He squinted at the monitor again.

"They were real, rubbery eggs, then."

"If they were real eggs, they came from a rubber chicken. That's all I'm saying."

"Fine, but you need to eat or you'll get a blood-sugar crash," she said. "Why don't we get some donuts when we reposition? I saw a place down in Gunbelt that probably had good frying saucers."

"They've gotta be better than the ones at the hotel. They tasted like little spare tires. They looked like them too. I saw one that actually had tire treads around the outside."

"Lemme guess – you didn't like the donuts, either?"

"There's that woman's intuition." He yawned again and rubbed his eyes. "So what's the latest intel?'

Dani tapped a few times on her monitor and frowned. "Intel? That's a big word for it. I've got nothing." She turned off her tablet and yawned. "Shit, I'm catching these from you. Would you cut it out?"

"I can't," he said. "I'm exhausted."

She rolled her neck and got a few cracks. "Oh, that felt good."

"You got a stiff neck? Let me see if I can loosen it," he said, and she leaned toward him. He rubbed his fingers into the back of her neck. Gently, he ran his fingers across the clipped auburn hair at her nape. She'd had it buzzed before they'd left, and it was driving him wild.

"This isn't a neck rub anymore, Mark," she said. "Now you're just waxing your carrot."

"C'mon, you like how it feels."

"Mmm," she said, "Yeah, I do."

"It feels like soft fur," he said. "Anyway, you know that chicks with short hair turn me on."

"What a coincidence! That's what Jennifer says too! That's why I got it cut!"

He pulled his hand away and sat up in his seat. "Why do you always have to be a buzzkill?"

"Cuz you have a bad buzz, Mark," she said. "This'll never work out."

"I just don't get it, you and Jennifer," he said. "It's just two sockets and no plug."

"You don't get it cuz you're male and straight and you're not supposed to understand," she said. "And I'm not explaining it again. The last time I did, I lost my sex drive for a month."

"Well, I wouldn't want *that*," he grinned. "Look, you should give me a chance to make an honest woman of you, Dani."

"An honest woman!"

"Okay, how about bisexual, then? I'm flexible. We'll meet halfway."

"We tried that. Total fail."

"It wasn't enough," he said. "That's the problem. It's like therapy. You have to do it all the time, or your muscles atrophy."

She looked at him with a raised eyebrow and a half smile.

"Three, four times a day at least," he said. "For years and years."

"You're an animal," she said with a laugh.

"Yes," he said. "Yes, I am. That's why you love me."

"I never said that!"

He turned his attention back to the monitor and watched a pack of cars heading west on Route 50. "Hey, there's a redhead." He leaned forward and played back the captured images. "No, look at that proboscis. That's not Warner."

"Right," Dani said, and she laid her head against the headrest. "Proboscis?"

"Why are you looking askance at me?"

"Don't tell me you're using that Word Builder again," she groaned.

"Indubitably. I plan to have an indomitable vocabulary in three short months."

Dani snorted and covered her mouth.

"What are you laughing at? What's wrong with a guy trying to get smart, get a little sophistication?"

"Nothing, nothing. It's fine, really. So next you'll be shopping for a tux and a walking stick?"

"Now there's an idea. You think I'd look good in one?"

"You'd look like a six-foot-four penguin," she said. "Now, I'm not into guys, but penguins..."

"Penguins are cool. So they turn you on?" he asked.

"Penguins are polar, dude."

Mark scratched his head and grinned. "I wonder if there's a tuxedo shop in this burg. When we go for donuts, I'm gonna check."

"You'd reduce yourself to bestiality for this?" she asked. "You're pathetic, Mason."

"Hey, you said I was an animal." He sat up when an image flicked by on the truck's monitor. "Nah. That's not her."

"Not unless she grew a mustache." Dani sat back, lit a cigarette, and stared through the windshield glassy-eyed. "You're right, this is totally futile."

"Yeah, it is," he said with an easy smile, "but it sure as hell beats chasing cars."

NIGHTMARE ON EAST CAPITOL STREET

Day 41
Monday evening, September 28, 2043
St. Elizabeth's Hospital for the Indigent, Washington, DC

Victoria sat at the Orderly's Lounge computer and checked the SatNet for information on Ada. Her aggravation had been building ever since she'd felt the pull of Ada's mortal crisis, and panic was nipping at the edges of her consciousness. She'd started sneaking in here to check the news, hoping to find some way out of her anguished limbo.

Killing Simon Rance hadn't resolved anything – perhaps it balanced an unseen scale of justice, but it didn't relieve the ache of losing Ada. In fact, the killing made her feel worse. She no longer had a mission, and now she was sucking down two bottles of whiskey a day just to blunt her frustration.

That was growing by the minute. Even though she'd recorded a damning confession from Rance, she couldn't do a thing with it. She'd thought again about contacting Mae, but she was working around the clock organizing the people of Anacostia and was probably under surveillance. It would be suicide to attempt contact. And even if she did get his confession published, it wasn't the only one on the recorder – she'd admitted to multiple murders as well. She needed an exit plan in place before contacting anybody.

She leaned back in the creaky chair and gazed at the stained ceiling of the lounge. Consequences didn't matter anymore. She had to sneak up to the surface tonight and try to contact Mae, or the waiting would drive her into full, gibbering insanity.

It was still daylight, though, and the spy cameras could see her, so she turned her attention back to the computer. On *Midnight Sun*'s sidebar, the icon for Krista Warner's column showed that a new article had been posted on Saturday. She'd been busy interrogating Rance that day and had missed it.

She clicked the icon, but the server was busy again, which was happening much more since Warner had come out as an Activist leader. The woman was a master of deception; Victoria had known about Warner's non-conformist streak, but her rebellion had seemed to flow from the end of a pen. She would never have suspected that the writer was running a rebel cell. Shrugging, she clicked the icon a few more times, and then a post called *Taking the Cure* flickered onto the screen.

When she finished reading, she walked from the lounge in a daze. Ten minutes later, she stumbled into her cell, fell onto the mattress, and forced her mind to work rationally.

Warner had described the exact contents of her briefcase. By itself, that meant nothing because she might have just found it somewhere. However, she'd also said that the diagrams were plans for a continuous-tube bioreactor, which only a handful of scientists on the planet could know – and one of them was Ada.

She gave the ceiling a shaky grin and wiped the tears from her cheeks. Her daughter was alive, and she was going to Sacramento.

A minute later, she sat bolt upright. "Why the hell am I still here?" She grabbed her bag and began stuffing clothes into it.

THIRTY MINUTES LATER, she was pulling branches off Dave's pickup truck, which she'd hidden in the woods behind the power plant. She tossed them to the side, hopped behind the wheel, and backed out of the underbrush.

The roads were clear, and she arrived at the East Capitol Street roadblock in ten minutes. After driving around the overturned trailers barricading the street, she drove to the Maryland National Guard checkpoint. The soldier on duty waved her by without looking, and she continued on, thinking about what she needed to do.

By the time she'd finished packing her clothes at St. Elizabeth's, her plan was complete. Trying to drive cross-country in a dead man's pickup truck would guarantee a short trip and another date with the infernal Mapper, but there was another route to Sacramento that the NSF couldn't watch.

She unscrewed the cap from her whiskey and swallowed a gulp. To escape to the West, she'd start by going east, and then she'd travel most of the way to California in luxury. But first she had to murder a man.

As she passed the Metro station, she jerked her head to the right – a line of large, six-wheeled trucks with turrets, painted with blue-black camouflage, sat idling behind the building. Standing beside them were dozens of armed men in gray body armor and black visored helmets.

She rubbed her eyes and looked in the rear-view mirror, but her view of the lot was blocked by trees. After another mile of driving, she decided that she couldn't have seen a military assault force. It didn't make sense.

"This shit's gonna kill me. I'm seeing nightmares when I'm awake now," she said, tossing the whiskey bottle through the window.

DISPATCHES

Midnight Sun
News Post of September 28, 2043

NSF IRONSHIRTS INVADE SOUTHEAST WASHINGTON

We have just received a series of communications from our Witness in Anacostia. The first call was timestamped 8:52 PM Eastern Time:

"I'm down on the Suitland Parkway, near the Southern Avenue Overpass. Like all the main roads into Southeast, it's blocked by overturned trailers.

"There's no traffic on the Maryland side of the barrier, just a few jeeps from the Maryland Guard there. On our side, there's a few folks patrolling, mostly guys from the DC Guard pitching in to defend the District border.

"There's not much defending going on cuz most of the National Guard, ours and theirs, are hanging out over by the jeeps yappin at each other like this was just a normal day. I'll talk to a few and see what they think of the War That Never Was. I wonder if they feel the same way the rest of us do in Anacostia about this sitzkrieg –"

The post ends at that point with no explanation. At 8:57 PM, we received a second message:

"I had to pull back cuz something's going down on the Parkway. I hear big engines, and down around the bend, I see a lot of trucks. At least I think so. I can't see them clearly in this light cuz they're painted black, maybe blue...big trucks, I can see one now. They look kinda like beetles. Big wheels and tiny windows along the front and it looks like...yeah, there's a turret on the top! This might be the new Powell Fighting Vehicle they talk about on the SatNet.

"Who are they and what are they doing here? Is this the Army? Are we getting our war?

"The Maryland Guard doesn't seem to know who they are, either. One of their jeeps is driving down the Parkway toward them, and the other three are inching back to our trailer barrier...a jeep with a big machine gun is backing up too, but the soldier manning the gun has swiveled it around to face down the Parkway. They know something's wrong. I feel it too.

"The first jeep is almost up to the beetle-trucks, maybe fifty yards away, and it's slowed down. The others are pulling back around to our side of the trailers now and I can...the first jeep just turned in the middle of the road, and it's coming back like a bat outta hell! I don't know what they saw. They can't be Guard trucks if that jeep is turning tail and running.

"I'm getting off the road and up to the trees. Something's gonna happen here and –

"A rattling sound, like a buzzsaw...the jeep just turned over and the back is in flames...there it goes, oh, my god...the Guard troopers over here are opening up with everything they have! That big gun is spittin out brass, but the bullets aren't doing anything, and I know the big gun is fifty caliber. That oughta punch a hole through anything, so I'll bet those trucks are armored...there's that buzzsaw sound again, and bullets are coming through the trailers like they're made of paper! Metal, rubber, everything flying all over and...one of the jeeps wandered off to the side and hit a tree, I think they were hit, the big gun's still chattering and that buzzsaw down the road's still going and the road's getting chewed up now...oh, shit, my wife and kids! I gotta get them outta here before they move into town. Gotta call –"

At 9:15 PM, we received the final message:

"Hey, I'm back. I made it off the parkway and onto Irving Street. I've gotta get to the bomb shelter where my wife's taking the kids. The firing stopped down on the Parkway, and I don't know if the Guard got away or if they were killed. But as I was running up the ramp, I saw one of those black buggers coming up behind. Some were continuing up the Parkway too.

"Shit, I wish I'd jogged more, I'm totally gassed. Left on Alabama, okay, there it is. The shelter's at Alabama and 36th at the elementary school. Ten minutes max...hang on. *No, man, go the other way! They're coming up from the Parkway, I dunno, hide or something, that popgun's not gonna do any good...*

"Okay, I'm back. Damn fools running around waving those CheapShots like they could hit something with them.

"This is history happening. Here it is, everybody: At 9 o'clock on September 28th, the Nation's Capital was invaded, and not by the Soviet Bloc. I think it was the Army. I guess that'll end up in the history books. Hell, history's a lot messier than it sounds in the books, lemme say that.

"I hope Esteban knows about this. I hope everyone takes cover cuz this is bad, real bad. Okay, I hear helicopters to my left, so they must be coming off the river too. None over me. I guess the ground forces are working this area cuz I keep hearing that buzzsaw sound behind me. What are they shooting at? There's nothing but houses around here.

"People are standing around and looking, trying to figure out what's happening. Nobody's prepared for the Army marching in...*Hide, run! Don't just stand there, move!* ...Okay, I'm back...outta breath...coming up to Branch Avenue now, only two more blocks to the shelter. I wish I had the sense to vid that invasion down on the Suitland, shit, hang on a sec...*No, turn around! They're behind me, man, coming this way...they can't be behind you when they're behind me!* Oh, shit, okay, over to the church. C'mon, people, get offa the road, they're coming down Alabama too!

"Okay, I'm in the trees now with a bunch of other folks, corner of Branch and Alabama at the old Baptist Church. I can see the black buggers coming up Alabama, and yeah, they're coming down Alabama too...behind the buggers, I see soldiers, and as they come into the street lights...Hey folks, these guys ain't the Army, they look like...Holy shit! I'm gonna vid this, it's unbelievable.

"Did you get that? I sent it along as a separate mail. This is unbelievable! There's NSF Ironshirts walking down Alabama Avenue just like the old videos from Detroit! It's the same gray body armor and black helmets I saw at the museum! *Keep your head down and shut up, for chrissakes. You, put that gun away! You can't hit anything with that. All you'll do is give us away and they'll shoot...Fuck! What are you doing! Get down!*

"Hang on, I got to get outta here before they blast the –"

We haven't received another message. We have been calling back but have received no answer yet. There is no answer on his wife's tablet, either, and we hope that's because she and her children are safe in the bomb shelter.

The video he took can be accessed via the link on the sidebar. It's only twenty-two seconds long, but it shows the NSF Collateral Tactics Unit, popularly known as the Ironshirts, marching down a street in southeastern Washington, DC tonight.

At this moment, religious Americans should pray for their safety, for the safety of their children, and for their country, since perhaps only God can stop this madness from spreading.

MURDER IS UNDERRATED

Day 41
Monday night, September 28, 2043
11 Stony Bluff Road, Graysonville, Maryland

Victoria parked the pickup truck at Graysonville Marina beside a dozen others and walked under the road to a bayfront neighborhood. After a few minutes and a few turns, she found Stony Bluff Road and started walking north. The Chesapeake Bay lapped gently below, now placid in the wake of the latest storms, and broken branches and overturned furniture were scattered across the sandy lawns. Seagulls wheeled in the night sky and bickered over morsels of food.

She stopped at a small cottage, the only house on the street with lights on. With her hand on the pistol in her pocket, she walked up the flagstone path and knocked on the door.

It opened a crack, and a fleshy pink face topped by thinning gray hair peered out. When he saw who was outside, he tried to shove the door closed, but she threw her weight against it and forced it open.

Tommy Talbott backed away from her and the black pistol in her hand. "Such a cold welcome, lover," she said, closing the door with her foot. "You were always happy to see me here."

"Tori, let me explain, please."

"You betrayed me and my daughter to the NSF. You think I want to hear you rationalize that?"

"I was supposed to bring you in and make you part of the Working Group. I was supposed to save your life, but that night at St. E's, you just wouldn't listen." He shook his head slowly as he inched back to a wall. "You never listen. You were on a crusade, and you were going to do what you wanted no matter what. I tried to save your life, Tori! All you had to do was listen, and none of this would've happened! Don't blame me for –"

"Shut up. I didn't come here to shoot the shit." She aimed the pistol at his breastbone. "I take that back. That's exactly my plan."

"No, Tori, please, please, remember all we had and all we did and all the good times...I did it because I love you, Tori, I love –" The pistol cracked and bucked in her hand, and Talbott staggered back to the wall with his hands over his chest and blood dripping through his fingers. He looked down at his hands and then up at Victoria and the smoking pistol. His face slackened and he slid to the floor, his eyes asking the questions his mouth couldn't.

She knelt beside him. "I never forgive betrayal. It's one of my little rules." She felt his wrist for a pulse; it was thin and irregular, and it would stop once his heart pumped the rest of his blood into his abdominal cavity. "But since you love me so much, would you do me one last favor? Would you hurry up and die? I need to get moving."

Tommy's mouth twisted into a sneer, and then he whispered, *"Hicktoria Twa –"* She rammed the pistol into his mouth and blasted the back of his skull into the wall. His body fell to the side, smearing blood and gray matter across the delicate jacquard wallpaper, and he thudded to the floor with his eyes wide open but seeing nothing.

She dipped her index finger in his blood and wrote IT's DR. LANG TO YOU on the wallpaper, punctuating it with a clear, bloody fingerprint. After wiping her fingers with an antiseptic towelette, she stuffed it into Tommy's gaping mouth and sat back on her haunches to appreciate her still life's composition.

Bright red blood trickled across the floor to her shoe. As she watched it meander along the wood's joints, the ever-present weight of madness lifted from her mind. Pursing her lips, she contemplated the surprising sense of contentment and serenity within. *As a therapeutic tool, murder is underrated,* she thought. *Maybe someday I'll write a paper on homicide as a treatment modality.*

She reached into his trousers, found a ring of keys, and dangled them before his unseeing eyes. "I guess a nasty break-up letter would have done the job, but I really needed these. Thanks, lover."

HER FEET RATTLED THE METAL BRIDGE leading to the community dock, and the air's salty tang tickled her nostrils. The smell was clean and honest, and she couldn't wait to be back at sea where the rules of survival were harsh but predictable, unlike life on the maddening land.

Her journey would be long and arduous: to Mexico by sea and then overland to Sacramento. Once she reunited with Ada, they'd drive to Canada or back to Mexico, where they'd build a new life.

Once on the dock, she turned and walked to the long boat berths. The outline of a long white yacht sharpened in the mist – Whiskey Tango Foxtrot, Tommy's baby. At almost sixty feet, she was seaworthy even through a Category Five hurricane, which she might encounter if Hurricane Zoe veered west.

She grabbed the rope holding the boat to the dock, whipped her arm a few times and unwound it from the binnacle, and then tossed it onto the deck with a flick of her wrist. It landed in a neat spiral.

After a last look at the lifeless fug, and all the mysteries and horrors it concealed, she jumped onto the deck and climbed to the bridge.

DISPATCHES

Midnight Sun
News Post of September 29, 2043

CITY OF PHILADELPHIA SECEDES

Our Witness in Philadelphia reports that the City of Philadelphia has seceded – but from what is unclear:

"The city is unsettled by the Anacostia news and Warner's talk about the government being behind this epidemic. At first, folks were calling Warner's accusations just another crackpot conspiracy theory, but the Anacostia smackdown just kinda validates all that, y'know? So now people are saying she's right.

"We didn't need to hear this Anacostia shit cuz all our gumption's tapped out after the virus burned through here. Even though we were all offered the vaccine as part of the Containment Ring, everybody knows somebody that died from the bug. Everybody's frustrated that they can't do anything about Cheyn and Anacostia, and there's a lot of fear walking the streets waiting for those damned Ironshirts to show up here too.

"There have been a few riots, but they were small, more like street fights. They petered out fast, and we haven't had an incident since Mayor Ubintu closed all the roads into the city. Now there's something to do, even though we know the Ironshirts would just blast away the barricades we're building, but it makes people feel good. Everyone still visits Warner's Freedom Clock too, and it's still running, which helps raise our confidence. If Warner can beat them, maybe we can too.

"We already finished the barriers on all the western and southern approaches to the city, and we have crews working on the north end now. We haven't bothered with the bridges to Jersey cuz nobody's come across them since the virus hit. It's dead over there. Philly lost about twelve thousand folks to the virus, but across the river – I'd guess nobody made it in Jersey.

"That's the way things have been in Philadelphia – unsettled and unsure – but that changed a few hours ago. The 109th Cavalry, from the National Guard armory out near Schuylkill, clopped into town on their horses and made a ring around City Hall. This attracted a lot of attention – maybe to find out if they were imposing martial law, but I also think it might be that we're city folk and we don't see horses often.

"The crowd got huge, fast. In an hour, a million people were crowding around City Hall and down Market and Broad, and it got violent. The soldiers wouldn't say why they were there, and some hooligans started throwing trash at them, but they just sat on their horses like statues and took it. When the mob started pressing up against the horses and pushing them back into Penn Square, though, a National Guard major came out through the line. He didn't say a word. He just rode over to one of the light poles and hung a piece of chain from it. I guess I should say he *hanged* a piece of chain cuz we all know what that means. Everybody wants to hang Cheyn.

"That calmed the mob down a bit, knowing that the Guard wasn't there to take over.

"Forty-five minutes later, Mayor Ubintu came out with the Council and addressed the crowd. He didn't have a microphone, so he stood on a car and yelled as loud as he could. Most people didn't hear it, but I was close and I did. He said, 'The City of Philadelphia is now Free City Philadelphia!' After that, I couldn't hear a thing because it got noisy.

"I sneaked into City Hall and found a councilman I work with, and I asked him what was going on – have we seceded? Are we our own country now? He said he wasn't sure what Philadelphia was, but it wasn't under the control of Washington anymore, or maybe even Harrisburg. I asked how you could secede from one without the other, and he just gave me a tired shrug. He said he wasn't sure what was going on, just like the men who signed the Declaration of Independence."

Molle: Thank you for coming again today, Mr. Speaker. I didn't know you were such an early riser!

Hayborn: I didn't sleep all night, Arista. I was getting a handle on the Anacostia event.

Molle: I've heard rumors. Some say it was an accident, and others say it was terrorism.

Hayborn: In a sense, they were both right. I was just there, and central Anacostia has burned to the ground. Destruction is widespread throughout Southeast. I'll be flying over there later this afternoon to interview the survivors and survey the damage again.

Molle: What happened? I heard noises from Southeast last night, but no one knows anything.

Hayborn: I'm sure the president has directed the Media Regulatory Corporation to suppress the news, and with good reason. From what I gather, President Gibbon reconstituted the National Security Forces Ironshirts and sent them into Anacostia to end their insurrection. I felt that their rebellion needed to end, but never would I have imagined or supported sending the Ironshirts to punish them.

Molle: Astounding news, Mr. Speaker. Thank you for bringing this to me and my audience today. It's hard to believe.

Hayborn: Just step outside and look down South Capitol Street. You can see the smoke from here. I share your disbelief, and I share the anger of all Americans that our own president would unleash destruction on our fellow citizens. It's uncalled for, but more than that, it's an impeachable act.

Molle: Doesn't the president have the authority to direct the National Security Forces?

Hayborn: Yes, but the Domestic Tranquility Act that formed the NSF requires the president to obtain House Domestic Tranquility Subcommittee consent before initiating suppressive action on Americans. He didn't do that.

Molle: But that committee hasn't met for years, Mr. Speaker.

Hayborn: It was no longer needed once the Ironshirts were disbanded. President Gibbon has apparently reformed and deployed them without congressional approval, which is contempt of Congress.

Molle: On those grounds, do you believe that you could impeach the president, Mr. Speaker? We were discussing this just the other day.

Hayborn: Yes. The Judiciary Committee is preparing Articles of Impeachment that I'll bring to the House floor today. It's my duty to do so before this president destroys his own nation...Arista, what's wrong?

Molle: I'm receiving a news report...this is so tragic. Oh, I don't believe this.

Hayborn: What is it? Has Gibbon wrecked something else?

Molle: No, sir, he hasn't. President Gibbon is dead.

A FEW FOR THE ROAD

Day 42
Tuesday morning, September 29, 2043
Seven Up, Colorado

Krista checked on Ken after breakfast, but his condition hadn't changed. His cheeks were rosier and his breathing was normal, though, so she left him alone.

She walked out to the garage with Ada. They sat by the concrete wall and talked for a while, but neither was in the mood for a long heart-to-heart like yesterday's. Krista unfolded her tablet and checked the news, and Ada opened her packet of diagrams and rested her head on Krista's lap.

She read the packet for a few minutes and then flipped another page. "I've been thinking about this bioreactor design. This doohickey is more complicated than it needs to be. I could rig a tabletop bioreactor to do the same thing with some simple glass tubing and insulation. Look, here's what I mean." She held the diagram for Krista to see and noticed her glaring at her tablet. "What's the matter?"

Krista dropped it into a pocket. "Feckin battery died again. But I had enough time to read *Midnight Sun*, and the world's gotten all spastic out there."

"What happened?"

She rubbed the back of her neck and looked through the garage door. "A White House steward found President Gibbon dead in the shower this morning. The coroner says he had a cerebral embolism and bashed his head on the edge of the tub, but his physician says that's bollocks. He gave Gibbon an MRI yesterday, and he was healthy as a horse."

"A dying horse?"

"He didn't die naturally, kiddo," she said. "It was an assassination. The security people say that somebody hacked the perimeter intrusion system.

And the steward says Gibbon only took baths. He hasn't taken a shower for decades."

Ada cocked an eyebrow. "He was definitely offed. But who'd do it?"

"Everybody but his mom and dad, I think," Krista said. "I don't know who did it, but I think I know why. It was a reprisal because of Anacostia."

"Anacostia?"

"Anacostia." She lit a cigarette and exhaled a shaky cloud. "It was flattened last night by those goddamn Ironshirts."

Ada sat up and whirled around. "Are you kidding me?"

"I wish. A *Midnight Sun* Witness sent a live report that he saw columns of them marching into Southeast last night, and this morning the town's not there anymore. Nothing's confirmed, but it won't be. The MRC will spike the story." She rested her head against the wall and closed her eyes, her lower lip trembling slightly. "That's my worst feckin nightmare," she said almost to herself. "I see those Ironshirts on the really bad nights, like when I eat Thai food just before I go to bed."

"I thought they were long gone."

"So did I, sister, so did I. This is the worst news ever. I thought that was all over."

"But why would they attack Anacostia? I go there a lot, and the folks are pretty harmless. Except when they're shooting at each other, but that happens everywhere. It doesn't make sense."

"Probably because they weren't dying off quietly enough. I read that they were squawking about not getting the vaccine, and Gibbon probably squashed them for it. And then somebody squashed Gibbon." Krista shook her head and glared through the garage door. "It doesn't make sense, and I don't want to talk about it."

"All right. This might be good, though. If the NSF is playing flyswatter on the East Coast, they might be too busy to hunt us down. Maybe things have changed."

"Things have changed, but they've changed for the worse, Ada. They'll keep looking for us, and I can tell you why in two words: President Cheyn."

"That sounds bad."

"It's terrible. This guy shouldn't be anywhere near the nuclear button." She blew another shaky plume through the door. "Well, it's not

A Few for the Road

my fault. I didn't vote for him. I literally woulda voted for a bottle of hot piss in a Texas truck stop trashcan before I voted for Cheyn."

"Literally?"

"Literally. Woulda done a write-in."

"Maybe Bottle O'Piss will be on next year's ballot. After all, the Democrats nominated a retard last time. Piss isn't much of a stretch."

"She wasn't retarded. She was differently gifted, and she had a homespun wisdom and such an earthy anima – *and* she wasn't clever enough to screw things up, which looks really attractive in hindsight. It was good that the Democrats nominated a neurodivergent candidate for once instead of those bloody megabrain types like Cheyn. Dude's so smart, he doesn't realize he's gone stone stupid."

"Right. Call it what you want, but she had an IQ of eighty-nine, Krista."

"IQ didn't count in that election. Gibbon wasn't channeling Einstein either."

"Okay, so he was a retard too. Why did anybody vote for anybody back in '40?"

"The political system doesn't work if you don't vote, Ada dear."

"If you *do* vote, the political system doesn't work, Krista dear. That's measurable, that's repeatable, that's a fact. End of inquiry."

"Very true. I'm not sure it ever worked, to be honest." She stubbed out the cigarette and lit another. "President Cheyn. He puts the 'dick' in 'dictator,' and he just got the feckin nuclear codes. I'm tempted to close this bloody door and stay here till everybody works this insanity out of their bones, or they blow up the world, or whatever comes first."

Ada shook her head. "We can't. Cheyn's president now, and you know what he's capable of. It's more important than ever that you get your videos to Sacramento. Somebody's gotta stop this guy. This isn't the time to run and hide."

"I'm not planning to run, just hide. It's the perfect compromise."

"Krista –"

"I know, I know. We've got to go because I'm some feckin awesome hero. Believe me, I hear it all the time."

"You oughta play your role in this shitshow flick, Krista. You're the strong female lead. You can't change that now."

"I'm not playing the lead. I'm playing Monica Mitten's role in *We Serve Man*, the hapless, schizophrenic basket case who ends up as stringy stuff in some zombie's teeth."

"Or maybe you're playing the strong but quirkalicious type like Kaci Wilkins in *Diner of the Undead*. Crazy was her superpower."

"That was just some screenwriter wanking off. People like her don't exist in real life." She flicked her cigarette onto the driveway and pulled out another. "I've spent my whole life striving for respectable mediocrity, but I won't even get that. Nuh-uh, I get to do the deadly hero's journey, complete with all the feckin scary monsters and dumbass hero challenges. What's next? Have I got to divert some river or something and clean out all the shitty stables?" She lit her cigarette and glared out at the cactuses. "I don't want that role. I haven't got to do it, either. It's not like I've got a bloody contract or anything."

Ada walked into the bunker and returned a minute later with two cold beers. "We'll leave as soon as Ken wakes up. Let's have a few for the road."

Krista grabbed a bottle and twisted off the cap. "That's the only way I'm getting through this day."

BUOYS WILL BE BUOYS

Day 42
Tuesday morning, September 29, 2043
Bering Sea, fifty miles east of St. George Island, Alaska

"Two million in technology just ripped out of the hull," Quinn said, buttoning his parka to keep the below-zero wind out. "And the fisherman will want another million for that net."

Under low gray clouds a quarter mile away, three seamen butchered a rope-and-cable net with bolt cutters and knives, trying to free their severed communications buoy while an appalled Russian fisherman watched. He turned to Bricker and waved his arms.

"He's going in the drink if he keeps that up," Quinn said. "She has her hands on her hips now. The last guy who saw that never lived to talk about it."

"He'd be dead meat if it wasn't for the *Sovetskaya Pobyeda* watching," Ripley said, looking through her binoculars at the Russian fast frigate floating two hundred meters off their port side. The sailors on deck were photographing every inch of the rarely seen missile boat. They'd entered American waters purportedly to provide assistance to the fishing vessel, but they'd done nothing except ogle the *Henry*.

"Blow me, Ivan," she muttered, raising a gloved middle finger to her counterpart on the Soviet ship.

"Mister Ripley, stow that finger," Quinn said.

She closed both hands around the binoculars and chuckled. "Hey, they understand Navy Sign Language, bless their commie hearts!"

They stood tethered to the deck just aft of the Vertical Launch System hatches and a few feet away from two seamen working beneath a nylon tent. Ripley blew a few bubbles, but they froze instantly, so she picked up the binoculars again and scanned the horizon. "Here comes the whirly from the *Carnegie*."

"They'll do a hazing," Quinn said. "It doesn't do much good, but they don't care. The Arctic Fleet runs on pure testosterone. Watch this."

The helicopter stopped near the *Pobyeda* and hovered just above the surface. The downdraft from the blades pummeled the seawater and threw up a thin haze of mist. Crewmen on the *Pobyeda* scrambled for cover.

"That's the first time I've seen that," Ripley said. "Pretty cool."

"I did that more times than I could count when I was skipper of the *Astor*," Quinn said. "It's fun except when they do it to you. The whole deck freezes over from the spray. You need torches to get the ice off."

The electrician's mate called out, and Quinn walked aft and leaned into the shelter. "The flanges are bent," the mate said. "When the comm buoy's tether got yanked out of the mount, it twisted the flanges here and here. There's no way to get a new mount in, not at sea. We need to be dockside for that."

"You can't rig something?" Quinn asked.

"I could, but it won't hold, not with the drag forces we get from the buoy. Not at thirty-five knots, at least. Maybe if we kept it to ten knots maximum."

"Forget it. Make this as clean as you can and leave the shelter in place. I don't want the *Pobyeda* to see any more than they already have. We'll leave it on the surface when we submerge."

"Aye aye." The mate went back to work with a heavy hammer and tried to pound the bent metal below the deck.

"Our high-frequency communications are going to be limited for the rest of the patrol," Quinn said to Ripley. "We've done this before, though. We'll spool out the towed antenna and rise to mast depth if we get a signal, but mail, news, and entertainment are gone. We'll be cut off." Quinn stamped his feet and looked across the water at the Soviet fishing boat. "That's not so bad. I think the news from the shore is affecting crew morale."

"I know," Ripley said. "I was walking through the Mushroom Farm yesterday. At the entrance to one of the crew berths, I saw a piece of chain hanging from the bulkhead."

"As a political statement? This is a small boat, Tala. There's no room for opinions."

"That's for sure. I talked to the six men in the berth, and they all denied putting it there, but that's what I think it was. I marched them to the machine shop and made them put it back where it belonged, and then I sent them to Chief Izu for career counseling."

"I didn't see that in the report," Quinn said.

"I didn't want to report them. I thought it'd damage morale to spread that kind of news through the boat."

Quinn patted her on the back. "That's a good compromise, Tala. You're getting the hang of the leadership game." He watched the seamen pull the buoy out of the net and throw it into their inflatable boat. "Tala, with all the bad news we've been getting, losing this buoy will turn out to be a blessing in disguise. I'm sure of it."

CHEYN SMOKING

Day 43
Wednesday morning, September 30, 2043
National Tranquility Center, Fort Belvoir, Virginia

"It was an assassination," Raphael said, looking at his tablet. "I have Gibbon's medical history here, and I agree with his physician. There's no way he had a natural cerebral embolism."

"I agree," Downs said. He leaned back in his chair and looked at the ceiling of his office. "They should look for a puncture wound in the carotid artery near the collarbone. I'll bet he had a venous gas embolism – like we studied in sophomore year at MMU, remember? A syringe full of air that dissipates after death and leaves no evidence behind – an elementary technique, and not something a professional would employ. It's a completely unbelievable way for Bill Gibbon to die. He jogged for ten miles every morning, ate only vegetables and free-range chicken, and played tennis for two hours every afternoon. His dad runs five miles a day, and he's ninety. And he had a well-known phobia about showers."

Raphael nodded and rested his feet on the desk. "Cheyn did it. He needed to get rid of Gibbon before Noah took them both down, so he sacrificed the president and put himself in power."

"Not to mention that Cheyn also fired all the Elders on his staff after taking the oath of office. He's gone rogue. He's a risk to us."

"I know," Raphael said with a frown. "We'll have to smoke the dude now."

"Right. You need to talk to Noah, and it can't wait for the Elder's Synod on Sunday. It has to be now. Redacting a sitting president isn't easy, and we'll need time to get the right assets mobilized. If he agrees to it, we need to know right now."

"I have a call in to him," Raphael said, rubbing his eyes. "Look, you might be all bright-eyed and bushy-tailed, but it's the middle of the night for me. Give me some time to catch up."

"You don't have to do it all yourself. You just work the political side and get the approval. I'll handle the execution."

"What? And let you have all the fun?" Raphael sat up in his seat. "I'm just tired right now, Bob, but I'm not stepping aside on this one. No frickin way, my friend. Most of my friends wanted to grow up to be president, but I wanted to grow up to *shoot* the president. Good thing none of my buds made it to the Oval Office, huh? That woulda been a bummer." He scratched his head. "My favorite movie when I was a kid was the Zapruder film. I'd play it back and forth all the time."

"I did too. The Kennedy assassination was a work of art." Downs laced his fingers behind his head and smiled. "I still haven't figured out how they did it."

"They were true craftsmen."

"You don't see that anymore these days," Downs said.

"It's sad. Once people cared about quality, but now…"

"I know, I know. There's something wrong with this world, Raf. Nobody wants to work for anything anymore. They just want instant gratification, and they don't care about pride of accomplishment. I blame the Internet."

"True dat. Anyway, the wonder of the whole operation is that we'll never know. They were that good. I hope we can come close to that, but I don't expect to reach the level the Kennedy team did."

"Oh, I don't either," Downs said. "We don't need to because there'll be a transition of power right after, but I'd like to run a respectable op for the sake of pride. We should start by following their model – a world-class sniper and a clueless fall guy. Do you still keep in touch with Carlos?"

"From time to time," Raphael said. "He lives outside Flagstaff now. He married one of those Catholic Revival Latinas down there, and they have twenty kids or something, but I know he still shoots. Last year, he said he hit the ten-ring on a target from three thousand yards out."

"He was always the best. Do you think you can tempt him out of retirement if you dangle enough gold in front of his face? After all, he has a lot of mouths to feed."

"Maybe. If Noah greenlights the project, that is." Raphael pursed his lips and tapped his finger on them. "I need to take the right approach with Noah, but in the end, he'll have to approve it. Cheyn's too dangerous, and he's nowhere near as stupid as Gibbon."

"Yeah, Noah really nailed Gibbon on that consent-of-committee breach. I think everyone forgot that Congress had to approve major domestic operations, even me."

"He's clever, that's for sure, but Cheyn's no fool either." Raphael gazed through the window and then snapped his fingers. "Hey, you know what – if we can promote Cheyn to glory before he nominates a vice president, Noah's next in line to become president! Then the succession will be constitutional, and there'd be no need for a coup. And the loyalty of the strategic forces would be guaranteed."

Downs reached across the desk and bumped fists with Raphael. "I'll bet that'll be the clincher for Noah. Cheyn handed him a gift by snuffing Gibbon, didn't he?" Downs smiled again. "It's good to have it all going our way again."

IN SATAN'S SADDLE

Day 43
Wednesday morning, September 30, 2043
Castle Herrera, Seven Up, Colorado

The desert sunrise rose to its final, glorious crescendo: The brown earth lightened slowly to tan, and then sunlight flashed across the cactuses and set their pink flowers aglow.

When Krista was a child in New York, dawn sneaked through the canyons of buildings as if daunted by the land of men and skyscrapers. In Washington, dawn was when the fuggy smudge of streetlight gave way to the smudge of sunlight. However, the sun trumpeted its arrival here in the desert.

She leaned against Ken's truck, and then something thumped inside the bunker. Running into the radio room, she saw Ken sitting on the floor with a dazed expression. Krista knelt beside him. "You're up at last. Good."

He looked down at his lap, hissed, and reached for a blanket. "Wet myself," he said.

"You've been out for two days and we couldn't get you up, so we couldn't do anything but keep you dry."

"Hungry," he said.

"That's good," Ada replied. "That means you still have a stomach. We got the virophage into you in time."

Krista turned around. "Where'd you come from? I thought you were asleep."

"I was." Ada handed him a glass of water. "Here. Sip, don't drink."

He emptied the glass and set it down on the floor. "It really *is* you. That wasn't a hallucination."

"It wasn't," Krista said. "We found you here just outside the door."

"I remember that much. You gave me the vaccine."

She nodded, and Ada knelt on the other side of him and felt his forehead.

"Will I be all right?" he asked.

"Yeah," Ada said. "How do you feel?"

"My ass hurts and I'm a little weak."

"You've been through a lot, so that's normal," Ada said. "I saw protein drinks in the fridge. That'll perk you up." She edged around them and ran downstairs to the kitchen.

"You're really Krista Warner," he said. "What are you still doing here? You have more important things to do than hang around with me."

"We needed a break in the worst way. We've had missiles shot at us, bullets, death rays…I won't be going into all of it. Just trust me that the rest was welcome. On top of that, we didn't want to leave you alone."

"You can leave me," he said. "I'm used to caring for myself. I'll be all right as long as I can get up and move around."

She helped him back onto the bed and sat next to him. "Ken, can I buy your car? I've got money–"

"You saved my life. It's yours. Anything I have is yours."

"Thanks. We'll drive you to the next big city and drop you off at a hospital."

He laid his hand over hers. "No, I'll stay here. I have enough food and water to last two years, and the place is off-grid. Besides, I'd like to finally use this place the way it was intended. If I need anything, I'll just ride my ATV into Seven Up."

Ada returned with the protein drink and handed it to him. "Seven Up's empty. We came through it on the way here."

"Empty? Did the virus hit there? Are they dead?"

"We just saw one dead guy. I think the rest took off," Krista said. "You're the last living man in Seven Up."

He gazed at the wall of radio equipment for a few moments and then shook his head. "I don't know why I was so determined to be the last man on Earth," he said. "I thought I'd feel special or something, being the one that survived."

"You sure don't want to watch everybody else die," Krista said. "You don't feel special. You feel sick to your stomach and wonder why you were cursed to witness it."

"And it's lonely," Ada said. "You feel lonelier than you ever did. We were lucky we had each other to keep us sane."

"I know what you mean. When I was laying here dozing a few minutes ago, I felt that awful loneliness, and I just wanted to go back to sleep to get away from it. Truth is, I wasn't expecting to face the end of the world all by myself, but Cherilynn..." He frowned and handed the empty drink box to Ada. "Anyway, I built this three years ago because I was sure there'd be a nuclear war, and we were gonna ride it out and repopulate the world with sane people. We live next to Cheyenne Mountain, right near NORAD, so we would've been the first ones incinerated. And I figured I'd feel great being the last man standing." He laughed bitterly. "What a fool I was."

They walked him down to the bathroom. When he returned to the radio room, he sat on the cot and rubbed his face. "I'm exhausted already," he said. "I need some sleep, but I don't want you sticking around for me. Go. Take anything you need, but go. Get to California."

Krista nodded. "We'll leave tonight."

"Where are we?" Ada asked. "We just know that we're in Colorado, that's all."

"You're out on the plains, thirty-five miles from Colorado Springs and fifty miles from Denver," he said. "Which way are you going?"

"North, and that's all we know," Ada said. "We don't plan ahead. It keeps the Federals guessing."

"Okay, if you want to head north from here, avoid I-25 and Denver." He coughed and reached for a glass of water. "The virus hit there a few days ago. People were dying behind the wheel and making fifty-car pileups on the highways. If I were you, I'd go straight over the mountains, pick up Route 24, and go north from there. The roads should be clear. The virus doesn't spread to cold places, and it can get mighty cold up at those altitudes."

Ada nodded. "All right. We'll aim for Route 24."

"But I wouldn't get there by way of the Springs, either, because the virus was just starting to hit when I left. If it's been two days, it might be as bad as Denver. I'd take one of the forest roads over the mountains and pick up Route 24 in Gunbelt Valley on the other side. Don't worry, my K2 can handle the Colorado upcountry."

"Okay," Krista said. "Thanks."

"You're welcome," he said. "I'm going to take a nap now, and then I'll help you get ready to go if I can." He lay down and pulled the sheet up to his shoulders.

KRISTA AND ADA LEFT THE BUNKER AT DUSK and drove southwest toward Colorado Springs. After passing through a few vacant towns, Ada turned on the satnav monitor and pulled up the map showing Route 24. "Okay, after this, we go over the mountains and then down into the valley. This road here," she said as she tapped the monitor, "takes us to a little town called Gunbelt, which intersects Route 50 and Route 24. We'll turn there and go north, and we'll be in Bumfuck Wyoming by sunrise."

"Sounds easy. We might have a nice relaxing drive for once."

"And a safe drive too." Ada pulled at the five-point harness that held her in the seat and then thumped the ceiling. "This thing has a roll cage built into the roof. This is a tough truck." She sighed and stretched. "I don't want to jinx things by saying this, but I think we'll be okay now. The Federals aren't looking for this truck, so as long as you don't insist on giving me driving lessons, it might take us all the way to California."

They drove down a two-lane highway through fields high with brown grass. After a few more miles, walls appeared on both sides of the road with the roofs of houses peeking over them.

"Okay," Ada said. "We're in Colorado Springs. Three more miles and we go under I-25. We turn after that."

A few minutes later, she pointed at an overpass ahead. "There's the Interstate. I think Ken was right. I see black lumps on the road up there that look like stalled cars."

"They look like cars, but why are they –" Krista heard a yell from behind the truck. In the rearview mirror, she saw two young men running after them in the middle of the road. "Oh, it's just another crowd of knackers. I'm growing tired of the thugs, believe you me."

Ada turned around and looked. "They've gone savage like in Columbus. But they don't have guns. I'm not worried."

"As long as they're not shooting at us, I couldn't care less," Krista said. "Wow, that's a real pileup over there."

As they passed under the road, the shapes became clearer: Cars and trucks were scattered along the highway's shoulder. Some lay on their roofs, and others looked burned.

"I'm glad we're not going that way," Ada said. "That'd be a mess to drive through, and it's probably like that all the way to Denver. Turn here."

Krista wheeled the truck hard to the right. "Tell me *before* I've got to turn, wouldja?"

"I thought you knew. The satnav says to turn right."

"Just navigate. Pretend it's an atlas. I need to focus on driving."

In another minute, Ada told her to slow and look for a road on the left. Krista rolled the truck to a stop at the intersection with a dirt road, looking at the road sign. "Vulture Canyon Road? Now that's a portentous name."

"It's just a colorful name," Ada said. "A Wild West kinda name, that's all. It doesn't mean anything."

"Sure it does. It means this road goes through a canyon of vultures."

"Or maybe it was named after a guy who owned a ranch here a long time ago. Like Joe Vulture or something like that."

"Joe Vulture," Krista said. "Sounds like the lead singer in some bloody British punk band, not the kind with a ranch in the middle of nowhere. Nuh-uh. This is a canyon where feckin black birds eat gross dead things."

"Where did the Brave New Krista go? Are you going all weenie again?"

"I said I was feeling better, that's all. I didn't say I became fearless." She looked through the windshield. "Okay, I don't see any vultures circling up there."

"Relax. They don't eat live animals anyway," Ada said. "Well, most of the time, that is. I read that sometimes they'll attack a live –"

"Shut up or I'll make you drive." Krista peered around the truck for carrion-eaters on the wing and spotted the two men running around the corner. "God, there they are again. They just won't give up." She pressed the gas pedal and turned onto the dirt road. "I hope it's just a name, that I do."

THE DIRT ROAD MEANDERED ALONGSIDE A DRY DITCH. Beyond a fence on each side, brown grass stretched for hundreds of yards and ended at a thick forest of pine trees.

"This isn't so bad," Krista said. "A little bumpy, but not bad. I wish we had a truck like this in Maryville."

Ada sat back in her seat and pointed at the dashboard. "It must be made for serious duty. Did you notice it has an altimeter and an inclinometer?"

She peered over the steering wheel. "Well, look at that. What's it for?"

"This truck's made for climbing mountains. The inclinometer shows how steep an angle you're driving up. Right now, it's five percent."

"Huh. Well, it's good to have, but I'm not planning to test the thing."

"Yeah." Ada looked through the side window. "The trees are getting closer, so the valley's getting narrower. We should be getting into the canyon soon, y'know, the one with the big scary vultures?"

"Oh, you can't scare me," Krista said, looking outside with worried eyes.

The trees crowded the road more with every mile until they thickened into a dense wall. The road twisted and climbed for a few minutes, and then the trees thinned on each side, revealing steep granite walls that soared a hundred feet up. At the top of the cliff, a mountain goat stared down at them. Krista stopped the truck at a bend in the road. "This is so beautiful," she said.

"Majestic," Ada agreed. "Let's get out and look. I need a potty break anyway." She opened the door, cursed, and slammed it shut.

"What's the matter?" Krista asked.

"It's freezing! We shoulda asked Ken for coats."

Krista opened her door, stuck one foot out, and instantly pulled it back inside. "Jaysus! My breath froze and shattered on the ground!"

"I'm not dropping my drawers in that. I'd make little peecicles." Ada looked at the altimeter. "Eight thousand feet. It gets colder as you go higher." She checked for a thermometer, but it was the one instrument the truck lacked.

"It's brass monkeys out there, and I'm just wearing sweats," Krista said, hugging herself. "I can hold it till we cross the mountains. When will we be over them?"

"No clue. The satnav just says the next turn is in fifty-four miles. That's at Route 24."

She pulled the truck onto the road. "I'll make it quick, then. That should only take an hour or so."

The road climbed steeply around a series of gentle bends. The dirt surface had washed away in spots, and especially at the curves, it became a field of small round boulders that jiggled their bladders.

"I wish I took that potty break before," Ada said. "We're at ten thousand feet now. I'll bet it's even colder."

"Oh, grand, thanks for reminding me. Look around in back and see if there's a bowl or something. We might need to make our own potty soon."

Ada unbuckled her harness and twisted to reach behind her seat. As she did, they ran over a boulder that launched the truck into the air. She bumped her head on the ceiling and then fell into Krista's lap, and both of them swore.

Krista pulled the truck to the side. "We've got to do it eventually," she said. "Let's just jump out now. We won't freeze solid, not in a few seconds."

Ada shook her head. "I'll wait. I'm not so sure I can pee anyway. You're jiggling me so much, I think my bladder's just one big bruise."

"What? I'm driving over feckin boulders here, Ada darling. There's no gentle way to do it."

"Just keep the bouncing to a minimum, Krista darling," Ada grumbled.

Krista pulled back onto the road. At the next curve, they saw a sign by the roadside:

SATAN'S SADDLE 6 MI
12,103 FT
LEVEL 10 DIFFICULTY

"Twelve thousand feet?" Ada groaned.

"Satan's Saddle?" Krista asked. "It says Satan's Saddle, Ada. I'd prefer the vultures."

"All right, I'm gonna pee now. You stay here in case you need to recover my body." Ada opened the door and ran to the side. Thirty seconds later, she hopped back in and turned the heat control to high.

"Cold?" Krista asked, but Ada just smiled. "All right. If you can do it, I can." She opened the door to a blast of arctic air and was back in her seat less than a minute later, her teeth chattering. "I think I sprained my nipples. Is global warming ending?"

"I hope it stays around for one more night," Ada said. "We really need coats."

"Right. What if the truck broke down, and we had to walk?" They looked at each other in panic.

"Okay, let's not do that," Ada said. "Make nice-nice to the little truck so it doesn't break, please?"

"I'll be gentle." She pulled onto the road carefully. "But Satan's Saddle is a bad name no matter how much lipstick you glop on it. And what does Level Ten Difficulty mean?"

"You'll find out in six miles," Ada said.

"I don't care about my eternal soul!" Krista said. "There's no way I'm driving down that road! I'll sit here and swear till Satan himself comes up from Hell and gives me a fucking medal for all my fucking cursing!"

"Talking like a potty mouth won't make the problem go away."

"After all, it's his bleedin saddle, isn't it? *Isn't it?*"

"C'mon, try to keep a grip –"

"Big, fat-arsed sonofabitch, he must be. Look at the size of this bloody saddle! He must have a mahoosive pair of cheeks."

"Krista –"

"Gotta have a bunghole the size of the Lincoln Tunnel. I bet he blows some serious ass jazz with that thing. It must be absolute murder up here on Pot Luck Night."

"You need to focus –"

"I don't! I really don't! I need to get seriously dissociated right now, that's what I need!" Krista glared through the windows at the rocky landscape. "Where are those bloody fairies when you need them? Huh? Where'd the little bastards go?"

"Please try to calm down and pay attention, okay?"

She pressed her palms to her temples and rubbed. "I'd rather not, if it's no trouble."

"Well, it's a lot of trouble for me, all right? If you lose it, we're stuck up here. You're my only way off this mountain."

"I never had 'it,' whatever that is, so don't go on about me losing something." She sagged back into the seat and closed her eyes. "I can't do this, Ada. I just can't."

"C'mon, it can't be that bad." She looked out past the hood but only saw open sky.

"Well then, look for yourself and tell me what you think!" Krista pointed through the windshield. "Go on!"

"Is it cold out there?"

"Absolutely not! It's like a feckin summer day! Go on, give it a try!"

Ada climbed out and instantly broke into uncontrollable shivers. The truck idled in a windy, boulder-strewn clearing between two stony mountains rising thousands of feet. She walked to the front of the truck and stopped short – the front wheels rested inches from the edge of a cliff, and a narrow curl of a road twisted and hairpinned down into a dark valley, nothing more than shelves of dirt and rock dumped against the nearly vertical cliff face. She leaned over a little more to see if it had guardrails, but when she saw the valley's bottom a few thousand feet below, her stomach lurched and a wave of dizziness nearly knocked her over. Holding onto the truck, she walked carefully back to her door and climbed in.

"Okay," she said, checking the heat control. "That's what they mean by Level Ten Difficulty."

"Fucking impossible is what it means." Krista thumped the steering wheel.

"Could you stop with the swearing? We can either go forward or go back. You're the driver. It's your choice."

"It's almost ten o'clock already," Krista muttered, holding her head in her hands. "If we turn around, it'll be dawn when we get back to Colorado Springs. We've got to take the Road to Hell. That's why I'm swearing."

"Well, thank god I can't drive. That looks gruesome."

"Thanks. You're splendid emotional support. How could I do this without you?"

"If it's any help, this truck is built for this." Ada thumped the ceiling. "It has a roll cage and everything built right in."

"To roll a mile downhill? So the truck won't be dented, but we'll be sister soup when it gets to the bottom?"

"Try not to get yourself all tense. That'll just make it harder."

"I know," Krista grumbled. She folded her arms across the steering wheel and laid her head on them. "Everything I do goes wrong. I get on a train and it blows up. I get on a road and it goes off a cliff. I always end up on the Jersey side of the deal."

"And despite that, we're still alive."

"I've just been lucky up till now," Krista grumbled.

"Right, and I'm starting to see a pattern. Whenever things get tough, you get weirdly lucky. Something bigger is going on, maybe even something like your Life Force."

She sat up with a half-smile and blinked away her tears. "You believe in the Life Force now?"

Ada frowned and looked through the windshield, shaking her head. "No. I'm starting to think that your Life Force might be a sub-nucleonic particle action of the Unicon. Maybe a neutrino swarmfocus or something."

"Hunh? Your Unicorn is farting sparkly luck particles all over me?"

"Unicon. Universal consciousness. Can you try to get it right?"

"Unicorn works better for me."

"Okay, fine, I give up. You're hopeless. Listen, whatever you want to call it, it's there, and you'll make it down this road. I know it."

Krista wiped her eyes and dabbed her nose with a tissue. "Are you saying this because you believe it, or just because you don't want me to flake on you?"

Ada tilted her head and smiled. "Trust me."

"The numbers on this inclinometer thingie are blinking and the red line is flashing. What's that mean?" Krista asked.

"It means to go slow cuz the truck is tilted forward too much, I think. Blinking things are usually warnings. I learned that in Driver's Ed."

The truck tilted down at a forty-five-degree angle, and Krista pushed against the steering wheel to keep her weight off the harness. "How much longer till this is over?"

"We're about halfway there," said Ada, holding onto a handle above the door with one foot propped against the dash. "There's another turn coming up."

The truck was barely crawling, but Krista slowed it even more. "It's too small, just like the last one."

"And the one before that. Just do what you did last time."

She turned the truck as much as she could around the hairpin and pulled forward to the edge. The right front wheel started to dip, and she slammed the shifter into reverse and rammed the truck back into the hill. "The side keeps caving in. I can't get close to it."

"Right. The soil's soft on the edge. Just stay away from it."

"That's easier said than done, darling. The whole feckin road is an edge," Krista grumbled. After inching forward and back a dozen times, though, she turned the truck to face down the next slope. She let off the brakes, and they were thrown against their harnesses again. "I hate driving on this side. I can see all the way to the bottom. I can even see the lights of Hell down there now. We're driving into the pits of Hell, right into some flaming, brimstony pit of suffering, I just know it."

"You see lights?"

Krista nodded. "Way down at the bottom. How much more of this have I got to endure?"

"You asked me that two minutes ago, so we're two minutes closer, all right? Relax."

"I'm trying to relax!" Krista yelled. "I'm mellow, goddamnit, so stop lecturing me about it or I'll kill you!"

"Ohh-kay," Ada said slowly.

She jinked the truck around another hairpin. It was Ada's turn to gaze down the cliff, and she spotted lights under the trees. "Those are house lights, I think. I see windows down there, and I can make out a roof. There's twinkling lights down there too, like flashbulbs or something going off."

KRISTA HAD BEEN MAKING A SOUND that was part whale song and part whistling teakettle for the last ten minutes.

"Would you please stop that and talk?" Ada asked. "You're scaring me."

"You wanna talk? Okay! I hate this car and I hate this state and I hate this trip! My feckin ass is numb and I haven't felt my fingers for two hours! And I need a cigarette and I need to tinkle and I've got a window seat over the Yawning Void of Death and I wish I was back in Columbus so I could drive over that shaky footbridge backwards because I'd like an easy drive for a change!"

"Could you go back to that steam whistle sound again?"

"How much longer?" Krista snapped.

"Dunno. It looks like we're mostly down, but I'm not sure," Ada said. "Wait – there's a sign up ahead. Maybe it'll tell us something."

They stopped beside a weathered wood sign on a post stabbed into the hillside. It said:

THE WITCH'S TIT
AN OFF-GRID B&B
2 MI AHEAD
IF YOU CAN READ THIS SIGN
YOUR STAY IS FREE

"That must be the place with the lights on," Ada said. "It's almost over now. Just a few more turns and we're done."

The next hairpin was the worst so far – when Krista inched the truck to the edge, the entire side collapsed, and they nearly slid over. She backed the truck so hard into the rocky hill that small boulders shook loose and cracked the back window. "Ken's going to be pissed when he finds out I broke his truck."

"He gave it to you, Krista. He's not expecting it back."

"Still, I'm hoping we can get it down in one piece. I don't want to break down all the way up here." She pushed the truck forward onto the path and stopped.

"What's wrong?" Ada asked.

"The road's out ahead." She pointed through the windshield to where the road had washed out and left a deep gully in their path.

Ada sat up in her seat and looked at the hole. "That sucks, doesn't it? Well, you have to go over it. You're not backing this truck all the way up this mountain, are you?"

She shook her head and released the brake. The front of the truck dipped into the gully and then rose slowly out.

"See? I told you, this truck's built to do this –" Rocks clattered outside, and the rear of the truck began to slide sideways into the deepening gully. "Go, go, go!" Ada screamed, and Krista stomped the gas pedal. The truck hopped out of the landslide, and they bounced down the rocky road until they slammed into the dirt wall at the end of the next hairpin.

"I know what you mean about Columbus now," Ada said, rubbing her shoulders where the straps had pinched her. "This is torture."

"I want this over," Krista said, rubbing the tension from her neck. "I know, I know, the only way to get down is to keep moving."

"We're not far from the bottom now. We're at the top of the trees, so we're dropping below the timberline. It can't be much longer."

"Good." Krista backed the truck up and shimmied it around the turn. She lined it up with the next leg of the road and then stopped: The landslide had fallen onto the road ahead, leaving a mound of dirt and rocks as high as the truck. "Oh, hell. How do we get over that?"

"We'll have to," Ada said, eyeing the mound. "But if we try to drive over it like that, the soil will slide out and the truck will go off the edge." She grabbed her cigarettes from the console and offered one to Krista, all the time glaring at the mound of dirt.

"I'd really like to avoid going off the edge," Krista said. "Come up with a brilliant idea."

"I will, I will. Just gimme a minute to spock this, okay?" She sucked fiercely on her cigarette with her eyebrows knitted. "The problem is the angle of repose of the soil combined with all the shear planes the rocks create. The soil will behave like a fluid. We have to mitigate that." She tapped her fingers against her leg for a minute, and then she opened the door and ran to the back of the truck.

"What's going on?" Krista asked when she opened the tailgate.

"I have the answer," Ada said. She unclipped an entrenching tool from the trunk and unfolded the small shovel. "We just have to field-engineer a new road. If we get rid of the rocks, we can trim that pile down and drive over it."

"*That* ginormous mound of rocks?" Krista's shoulders sagged and she looked up at the cliff. "I envy cowards. They have someplace safe to run away to when the going gets rough, but me? I've got to play dodgeball with missiles or move bloody mountains –"

"Stop whining. It's mostly dirt. An hour or two and we'll be done."

"I'm allowed to whine," Krista muttered. "That's in the Bill of Rights somewhere."

"Focus on getting off this mountain first." Ada handed her the shovel. "Time to sister up and get this done."

They walked downhill to the landslide, and Krista climbed atop the pile and began shoveling dirt to the sides. Ada started pulling rocks from the soil and piling them at the base of the wall.

As she picked up a large stone, a frigid wind swept along the mountainside. She shivered, feeling the emptiness of the dark valley, and wondered again where her mother was.

Wherever she was, she hoped that she was okay.

At THAT MOMENT, VICTORIA WAS SIPPING CHAMPAGNE in a lounge chair and watching fireworks burst over Miami Key.

The party had already been in full swing when she anchored in Biscayne Bay beside dozens of other yachts. Lights were pulsing beyond Miami's fabled Forever Seawall, and drums and guitars were throbbing; lasers played across the skyscrapers and changed colors in time to the music. She had no idea what they were celebrating, but she'd opened a bottle of Tommy's 1996 Perignon to toast the occasion.

A timer rang, and she set her glass down and walked into the galley to drain her pasta. Thanks to Tommy Talbott, she'd be dining on creamy penne Alfredo with soft, warm breadsticks and a zippy Italian white wine.

The yacht had been ready for a long journey when she stole it, with its fuel tanks brimming and the galley fully stocked. When she turned on the navigation computer, she understood why: Tommy had already plotted a course from Maryland to Grand Cayman Island, and he'd been planning to depart around the time she had. From the pile of skin magazines in the bedroom, she figured he'd also planned to leave his wife behind.

She drowned the pasta with sauce, grabbed a fork and a handful of breadsticks, and returned outside to see the fireworks. Rockets shot into the air, so many firing off that they could barely be seen through the dense yellow smoke. The mortars boomed a final, shirt-shaking salvo, and the partygoers on the levees cheered.

The pasta went down easy, and she opened the wine bottle and poured a tall glassful. Now that the fireworks had ended, the lights on Miami Key had dimmed, and she could see up Biscayne Bay.

A long bridge spanned from Miami Key to the fortification of Miami Beach Key. In the middle, a Mal-Mart squatted on pilings beside the roadway, where the Venetian Islands had been before Hurricane Ivanka

In Satan's Saddle

scoured them away back in '37. She spotted a brightly lit object in front of the entrance that looked much like the Rialto Bridge in Venice.

After a second, she realized it *was* the Rialto. She recalled reading that Mal-Mart had promised to place public art on the bridge in return for access to it, and they'd actually imported the Rialto from drowned Venice and plopped it in their parking lot.

She raised her glass and toasted the Rialto. "Irony, I hardly knew ye," she whispered, and then she looked at Miami Beach Key, which was now surrounded by sandy levees and not beaches. She'd swum on those beaches during her first Spring Break, and now they'd been dredged and mounded around the island to protect it from the rising waters.

She upended the glass and emptied it in one gulp. If she didn't think of something else, she'd slit her wrists, so she closed her eyes and concentrated on the next day's trip.

The highest tides would come just after dawn. She'd leave an hour before then, head south to Homestead and then sail west through the shallow waters covering the city's ruins. That route would cut five hours off her trip, and saving time was crucial because Hurricane Zoe would start lashing southern Florida with Category Five winds by early afternoon.

However, the journey would be tricky – Miami's inundated suburbs weren't shown on her charts, and she risked hitting underwater debris and damaging the hull. Once she reached the site of Homestead, all she could do was find a row of light poles that had withstood Hurricane Ivanka, motor alongside them at a crawl, and hope she didn't hit any submerged obstacles.

That would be the only white-knuckle part of the trip, though. After entering the Everglades, she could open the throttles and cruise northwest across Everglades Bay to Marco Island on Florida's Gulf coast. After topping off the fuel tanks there, she'd drop anchor in a remote cove to get some sleep before the cross-Gulf sprint to Tampico, Mexico.

Unlike Florida's Key Cities, Marco Island wasn't protected by a seawall and connected to the mainland with a bridge; when sea levels began rising, Florida calculated that it would be cheaper to abandon the island and relocate the residents to nearby Naples Key. Most of the islanders had refused to go, believing that the rising waters were only a temporary phenomenon sensationalized by a media trying to crash the oceanfront real estate market. They expected to have the last laugh when the Gulf finally receded from their doorsteps.

The telecom providers accepted the climate science, though, and refused to spend millions laying undersea fiber-optic to a future sandbar. That was why Victoria was heading there: If the islanders didn't have Internet access, they might not know that the Federals were hunting her. She couldn't say the same about Naples Key. Nevertheless, she planned to keep her pistol handy as she refueled the yacht.

She yawned and sat back in the chair. She hadn't slept for sixty hours straight and had been sailing at full throttle for the last forty-two, powered entirely by fear and caffeine as she tried to get as far from Washington as possible. But now that the stimulants had worn off, the pasta and wine were putting her to sleep.

With another yawn, she stood and then stumbled through the door to Tommy's stateroom.

AFTER AN HOUR OF WORK, Krista and Ada were sweating and exhausted. "I'm not cold anymore," Krista said, leaning on the shovel.

Ada dropped another rock on the wall she was building near the edge. "I know I'll be sore when this is over. The good thing is that we're almost done." She stood, pressing her thumbs into the small of her back, and then walked across the earthen bridge. It was solid beneath her feet. When she jumped up and down near the wall, the rocks didn't move. "I say we give it a go."

"Are you sure this will work?"

Ada snorted. "Stop fretting over every little thing."

ADA TAPPED THE MONITOR a few times and checked the schematics. "It's a Bicep interface, so it was easy to reconfigure. I transferred all your torque to the inboard wheels so your outboard wheels won't tear up the edge of the road. But you absolutely can't stop or we'll get stuck."

Krista threw her cigarette away, took a sip of water, and gripped the wheel. "Ready?"

Ada nodded, and Krista pressed gently on the accelerator.

"Get closer on my side. Scrape the door against the mountain if you have to. Keep the wheel turned this way, c'mon."

"I'm trying," Krista said, and she gave the truck more gas. The inside wheel spun for a second, and then the truck climbed the soft hill of dirt. Ada's door screeched across the rocky wall beside her. After what seemed like an eternity, the front end rolled down the other side of the mound and back onto the rocky road.

AFTER TWO MORE HAIRPINS, Ada said, "That was the last turn. The road levels out ahead." She took Krista's hand and squeezed it. "You did it! We made it in one piece."

Krista looked up at the cliff face and the narrow shelves of dirt piled against it. "I can't believe we did that."

"Yeah, we did." Ada pointed to a pile of metal by the side of the road. "But a lot of people didn't."

Krista stopped at the metal mound, a pile of overturned and dented jeeps. A sign painted on the side of one said SHORT WAY MEMORIAL, and a row of dusty white crosses stood in the ground in front of it. "I'm glad I didn't know about that before coming down."

"Sometimes ignorance is bliss." Ada looked at the clock. "It's three in the morning, so why don't we call it a day? That B&B promised a free stay if we made it."

"Definitely. I'm so ready to get out of this feckin truck, I could scream."

The road curved into a dense forest. After a few hundred yards, they stopped at a lighted wooden sign that said THE WITCH'S TIT, which was surrounded by a half-dozen smiling people.

"What's this?" Krista asked as the crowd surged toward the truck. A man opened Krista's door and plucked her out, and lights flashed in the night.

"It's a girl!" a woman's voice cried. "And she's not even wearing a crash helmet!"

More lights flashed, and someone tugged the hem of her hoodie. Krista looked down at the small twin boys standing in front of her.

"You got big balls, lady," the first one said.

"Hairy, clinky ones, lady," the second one said.

"Ever'body back!" somebody bellowed, and a beefy arm wrapped around her shoulder. More lights flashed.

"Your eyes were closed, Kurt!" a woman yelled, and then the flashes twinkled again.

"Forty-three years since sumbody took the long way down," someone said next to her, and she blinked away the stars in her eyes to see a tall, barrel-chested, bald man. "And at night! Ain't nobody's rode the Saddle at night! Kyle, c'mon over and get yer pitcher with – what you called, daredevil?"

"Umm...Sue. Sue McConnell."

"C'mon over and get yer pitcher with Sue!"

A younger man, nearly as bald as the first, wrapped his arm around her as the cameras flashed again. A girl yelled, "Hey, look Pa, she even brought her kid!"

Kurt looked from Krista to Ada. "Now *that* takes some Simon-pure nerve, don't it? Bringin yer own kid over the Saddle!" Someone shoved Ada next to Krista, and the arms wrapped around them again.

"She's my sister, not my daughter," Krista mumbled.

"Even better!" The camera flashed again, and then something popped like a gunshot. Krista and Ada dove for the ground, but big hands reached down and pulled them up. "Hell, I'd be a little tetchy too, after all that!" Kurt pressed a glass filled with sparkling amber liquid into Krista's hand. "To Sue!" he bellowed.

"To Sue!" the crowd yelled back, and they emptied their glasses and looked at her expectantly. She raised her glass in a weak salute and downed the champagne. As soon as it left her lips, a woman refilled it.

"Let's get a pitcher over here! Right where we're gonna put the statue!" Kurt lifted her off the ground with one arm and carried her to the lighted sign, champagne dribbling from her glass the entire way.

"Statue?" Krista asked after Kurt planted her on the ground.

"Yer the first woman in history to ride the Saddle!" he said. "Damn right I'm puttin up a statue to the Queen of Witch's Tit!"

DISPATCHES

Molle's Hill
NewsHub Political Affairs Channel
Broadcast Transcript of September 30, 2043

Molle: Thank you for taking the time to visit today, Mr. Speaker.

Hayborn: I like to keep an open channel of communication with the public, Arista. Transparency is a virtue for public servants.

Molle: It's certainly an admirable quality, and one that's so rare in the brave men that lead us in these troubled times, Admiral.

Hayborn: I've never been in the Navy, although I revere our warriors at sea as much as anyone else.

Molle: I'm sorry. I just interviewed an admiral, and I'm a little mixed up. It's these lights, Mr. Speaker. Sitting under them all day long does things to me.

Hayborn: It's quite all right, Arista. I understand. In this time of distress, I find it hard to keep things straight myself.

Molle: Thank you. I *am* distressed by the great man's passing.

Hayborn: Yes, President William Gibbon is destined for the history books. Yesterday was a sad and tragic day for the American people. Unfortunately, the nation's problems don't wait, and they've only worsened since his passing. I just heard that our credit rating has been lowered again.

Molle: That's a relief! I had a financial guru on the show a few days ago who said they were going up.

Hayborn: Our borrowing rate will go *up* if our credit rating goes *down*, Arista.

Molle: I'm sorry. It must be the lights again.

Hayborn: Our credit rating has been lowered from B to C. B is better than C, just like when you were in grade school. To borrow money, we'll now pay more interest.

Molle: That sounds bad.

Hayborn: It is, and so I urge President Cheyn to control the economic wildfire that California has set. He needs to do it now, or there's a risk the United States will default on its bond payments. That would be bad, Arista.

Molle: I understand. Will you be attending President Gibbon's funeral?

Hayborn: Of course.

Molle: Will they use a horse-drawn carriage?

Hayborn: I'll check into it. Before the funeral, though, President Cheyn has other challenges to tackle, such as the spread of this virus, the sliding value of the dollar, and the dangerous intransigence of California. This president must grow to handle the crises this nation faces, and he must grow quickly.

Molle: Our new president will be burning the midnight oil for the next few days, then. And I recommend Black's Midnight Oil –

Hayborn: Arista.

Molle: Yes?

Hayborn: I think you have this product placement wrong.

Molle: I do?

Hayborn: Let's just say most people wouldn't burn a pleasure product like Black's Midnight Oil. Certainly not at a hundred dollars an ounce.

Molle: Oh. I must be confused again.

Hayborn: I'm sure it's these lights.

A MOLE UNMASKED

Day 44
Thursday morning, October 1, 2043
National Tranquility Center, Fort Belvoir, Virginia

"'Nother day, 'nother dollar," Raphael said. "It was a quiet night, all in all. Philly's been sedate since the mayor founded his own banana republic. We got some breaks in the fug, and we watched the locals building barricades."

"They won't matter," Downs said as he stepped onto the podium. "We won't see a repeat of Anacostia."

Raphael snapped his fingers. "Oh, I almost forgot – we have a bead on who's blackwalling Ada Lang's file. We traced a tag on one of her latest texts, and guess where it came from?"

"Where?"

Raphael gave him a cross look. "Be a sport, man. Take a guess."

"Scranton?"

"Nope." He crossed his arms and grinned. "It comes from a little shop down in New Mexico. You might've heard of it – Los Alamos National Laboratory?"

"Are you joking?"

Raphael shook his head. "I wish. The Activity must have some reach if they can place a mole in there."

"There must be moles everywhere, Raf. Where does this end? How far have they infiltrated us?"

"I have no clue, my friend. Even we can't crack Los Alamos security, though, so we can't trace that mole. It's a dead end unless we can get a human asset in there."

"Into the most secure nuclear weapons lab in the world?" Downs asked. "You're right. It's a dead end. I'll contact the FBI and get them to investigate. They can get access." He cast a sideways glance in Hogue's direction. She'd already donned her headphones, making it impossible to hear conversations on the podium, and he motioned for Raphael to come closer. "Forget about that. Did you talk to Noah yet?"

At the Tactical desk, Sara Hogue switched her headphones to play the signal from a directional microphone sewn into the back of her collar, and then she focused the mike until the two men's words were clear.

"He green-lighted us," Raphael said. "It wasn't a hard sell, but he wants us to keep lots of daylight between him and the operation."

"Understood. We've been doing that anyway. We're the only two who know about this, and neither of us will talk."

"I know, but he's skittish," Raphael said. "The Transition's changing too fast, and I think he doesn't know how to work all the angles. He's exhausted too, so he's getting risk-averse."

"The cure for that is to get this done," Downs said. "If we can pull off the op, we won't have to wait eight more weeks. It can be over next week. One clean shot and he can take a nice soak in that big White House bathtub."

"Bet he never takes a shower in *that* tub," Raphael said with a smirk.

Hogue stiffened, but she quickly regained her composure and pretended to review the Tactical asset deployments.

"Did you talk to Carlos?" Downs asked.

"Yep," Raphael said. "I'm flying out there now for a man-to-man with him. I don't want to discuss details even on a sat phone. We'll meet in the hills north of Flagstaff and take a walk in the woods. I'll make the deal, go over the specifics, and bring him back."

"He already agreed?"

"In principle, although he doesn't know the target. But he'll do it. His family's living below the poverty line already."

"What family life does to a man," Downs said. "Well, when he gets here, I want to talk to him. I have a sector of fire in mind for the shot already. By the way, I've been going through the files, and I have candidates for the Oswald role. You can read them on the flight."

Raphael stepped off the podium. "Will do, Kemosabe. The Watch is yours."

A FISTFUL OF DONUTS

Day 44
Thursday afternoon, October 1, 2043
US Route 50, one mile east of Gunbelt, Colorado

The lowly donut had never played a role in the fate of nations until one sunny Thursday afternoon in Colorado. Nobody could have known that the future of the United States hinged on whether the sugary delights would lure a man from his post.

When Mark Mason pulled the last donut from the box, it seemed as if the Stars and Stripes would need a makeover. "These are delectable. The lightest I ever ate, and not only that, they're real fresh. I usually only get donuts with an expiration date of ten years or something."

"They were still hot when I picked them up," Dani said. She opened a white cardboard box on her lap with O'D TO JOY – YOUR NEIGHBORHOOD BAKERY! printed on the lid. "Who woulda thought you'd find a bakery like that in this one-horse town?"

He wiped his lips, settled back in his seat, and watched the faces flit by on the monitor. "I've gotta taste the hot ones. They sound like they were, what's the word," he snapped his fingers, "toothsome, piquant, maybe even sapid."

"I should get hazard pay." She threw the box into the backseat and pulled out her tablet. "Seriously, nobody talks like that."

"Well, they oughta. Ignorance is just for people committed to stupidity."

"Instead of evolving from it, like you?"

"Yeah." He whipped his head around. "Hey, that was a low blow!"

She grinned and scanned the news on her tablet while Mark returned to watching the monitor. Faces flickered across it, but none were Warner's.

"What if she has one of her bodyguards driving, and she's hiding in the back or something?" Mark asked.

"Then we're screwed. This was always a long shot anyway."

"Yeah, I guess." Mark yawned and rubbed his eyes, and then he turned his attention back to the monitor. "So you read about that Anacostia thing?"

"What a mess. It sounds like everybody screwed up," Dani said. "The whole East is falling apart. That's what I read on *Midnight Sun*."

"Yeah. Glad I'm not there. The place is fissiparous."

"Mason, shut the fuck up already."

After another hour, they moved east on Route 50 and parked in the shade of some tall desert chaparral. They resumed scanning the highway for Warner, but the tedium set in again soon.

"Why on Earth do you love me?" she asked.

"I told you why plenty of times."

"Because I'm a redhead? That's not it. That's just a dodge to cover up the real reason," she said. "What is it?"

"Would it change things between us?"

"Not sexually."

"So why should I tell you?"

"I'd like to know," she said. "That's the kind of thing a person's curious about, y'know, why people love them."

"Okay, I'll tell you, if you tell me."

"Tell you what?"

"Why you love me."

"I never said that, Mason. Don't start putting words in my mouth."

"So how come you didn't transfer out last month?" he asked. "More pay, closer to Jennifer, better hours, and yet you said no. Why?"

She turned to look at the chaparral and sipped her water. "We have the same taste in donuts, that's all. That's important to some women."

He grinned and laid his head back against the headrest.

"You musta done something real foul in church to deserve this biblical kind of torture," she said. "I don't like being somebody else's affliction, and I wonder why God did this. What on Earth did you do?"

"Well, my mom says I peed on the priest when I was baptized, so I got a bad start with the whole piety thing."

"It has to be more than that."

A Fistful of Donuts

"Could be, could be," he said. "I don't know, Dani, and I don't think about it a lot. It might be easier to become an Arkie and just start out clean with a god that doesn't hold grudges. You just pay the coin and you're saved."

"Sounds like a washing machine. A coin-operated religion." She stretched and yawned. "I'm getting bleary-eyed. How long do we have to do this?"

MARK SAT BACK IN THE SEAT and groaned. "Nah, that's not her."

"It was close, though."

"Not even close."

Dani called up Krista's graduation picture on her tablet. "Yeah, you're right. How come you know her face so well? You just saw her picture once, and that was days ago."

"It's kinda weird, but her face just clicked with me."

"Clicked?"

"It's like I know it by heart. I've been thinking about that, but I don't know why. It's ineffable."

"Hmm – or maybe it's kismet."

He looked at her with furrowed eyebrows. "Stan Kismet? He's not even in our division. How could he –"

"Not the *guy* Kismet, you dingdong. The *concept* kismet, where...oh, forget it. That's too profound for you." She looked at the picture on her tablet. "She's gorgeous. Look at those eyes, big and vulnerable and soft and blue like a baby fawn's."

"Fawns have brown eyes."

"And those lips. I could kiss them all night long and into the morning and never come up for air."

"What would Jennifer say?"

Dani smiled. "She might go for a threesome."

"You're assuming Warner's lesbo, and I read that she was dating a guy when she was in Washington. You're barking up the wrong tree here."

"Oh, no, she's a lipstick lesbian. I can tell."

"That's bullshit! How can you tell?"

"It's a girl-to-girl message you channel after a while, Mason. You wouldn't understand."

"No way this chick's anything but straight. She was custom-built for man-on-girl action, Dani. You picked up the wrong channel."

"I don't think so. I'd bet a box of donuts that I'm right."

"Yeah? O'd to Joy donuts?"

She nodded.

"All right, Frye, you're on. First one to get her in the sack gets the dozen, right?"

"You got it."

He pointed to the empty box laying on the backseat. "Those suckers go fast. Well, screw it, I'm hungry, and I can't wait till I win. Wanna go into town and see if they have any hot ones?"

THE QUEEN OF WITCH'S TIT

Day 44
Thursday afternoon, October 1, 2043
The Witch's Tit, Witch's Bosom, Colorado

Sunlight crept through Krista's eyelids. She turned over and covered her head with a pillow, but she couldn't get back to sleep. With a grumble, she sat up in bed and saw a stone-and-timber room that looked like a ski lodge.

Her back muscles were tight from shoveling, and she stretched for a few minutes. When she was done, she pulled a curtain aside and looked down a long valley ending in cloud-scraping purple peaks.

After a hot shower, she sat on the bed to slip on her clothes. Ada sat up and blinked at the sharp light leaking through the curtains. "Someone left that damn sun on again," she grumbled. "I hate the sun. Maybe my dad was a vampire."

"I thought he was an iguana."

"Coulda been a vampire iguana. I dunno."

"Whatever. It's almost four o'clock. You should be getting a shower on you soon," Krista said. "We can get some grub and then blast off around dusk."

Ada pushed the sheets off and rubbed the welts the harness had left on her shoulders. "I thought I had a nightmare, but nightmares don't leave bruises."

KRISTA AND ADA WALKED DOWNSTAIRS to the dining room. Through a window, Krista saw Ken's truck parked beneath a tree beside a gravel driveway. It had been washed and waxed, and the chrome gleamed.

A slim, short woman walked from the kitchen. "Well, good afternoon! I'll bet you're famished. I made some turkey, lettuce, and tomato sandwiches in case you got up. Sit, sit." She ushered them to a table by the window and scurried to the kitchen. A minute later, she set two plates in front of them filled with immense sandwiches that hung over the sides of the dish.

"That's the biggest sandwich I've ever seen," Ada said.

"It's a meal." The woman took a seat next to them. "Name's Dot Donner. Kurt's wife. Pleasure to meetcha."

Krista and Ada both nodded, smiling with their mouths full.

"We all thought you was goners last night," Dot said. "That washout at the bottom's a killer. Ever'body gets cocky when they get near the end and then –" She drew her finger across her throat and stuck her tongue out. "Figgered you was just more fodder for the bone orchard, I did. Was gettin ready to cut y'all a new cross."

Krista nodded and took another bite.

"Kyle recorded the whole thing, top to bottom if'n you wanna see it." She pointed at a large monitor in the corner. "Got it all lined up for the party tonight."

"I'd rather not relive it," Krista mumbled.

"Awright. We'll just make it a world premiere tonight, then."

"What's happening tonight? Who's having a party?" Krista asked.

The Queen of Witch's Tit

"Oh, we gotta celebrate, so we're throwin a big ole hog-snortin fandango. You're the biggest thing to blow into this burg for years, and it'll be good for business. Kurt and Kyle are downtown now gettin a few cases of who-hit-John." Dot looked around the empty dining room. "Things been slow 'round here, and it'll be nice to get back on the map again. We didn't get no guests most part of the summer, and even the flatlanders skeedlin away from the virus don't come here. Dunno why. The Witch's Tit is so beautiful. Maybe we're too far from the highway." She sighed and walked back into the kitchen.

Ada watched her leave. "They're throwing a party for us."

"Right. A Donner Party. Who's on the menu?"

"This isn't exactly low profile," Ada said. "We need to blast outta here."

"Let's get the bags, and we'll slip out as soon as it gets dark."

THEY'D JUST SLID THE BAGS INTO THE BACKSEAT of Ken's truck when Kurt's shiny black pickup crunched into the gravel driveway.

"Hey, there! Yer finally up!" He walked to the back of the pickup and hoisted a case of beer on his shoulder, and Kyle did the same. "We got summa Witch's Tit's finest here. It's par'ful stuff, I'm warnin ya – gave a swig to my horse, and he fell right over!"

Kyle smirked. "Couldn't walk straight fer three days."

"It sounds like it'll be some party," Krista said with a shaky smile.

"Oh, yeah," Kurt said. "Ever'body'll be here, the whole kit and caboodle. The mayor hisself is gonna give ya the key to the city."

"There's a city around here?" Krista asked.

"Witch's Bosom. Damn guv'mint made us change the name when we got us a post office, few years back."

"Guv'mint messes up ever'thin," Kyle said, and he carried the case of beer into the kitchen. A few more people had walked up the driveway and eyed her and Ada from a distance.

"Guv'mint." Kurt spat into the gravel. "Ya can't live with it, and ya can't live with it. So yeah, it'll be a big blowout tonight, lotsa boot-scootin and all. I might even shake my shins too, I drink enough. Even got a NewsPulse crew comin up from Cortez to cover…well, damn, they're early."

A white van with a rooftop satellite dish pulled into the driveway and stopped behind Krista's truck. A middle-aged man climbed from the driver's seat and cranked the dish up, and a young man with a long black ponytail clambered from the back carrying tripods and lights. A perky blonde with perfect hair and skin, dressed in an immaculate blue skirtsuit and white blouse, bounced around the rear of the van and shined Kurt a thousand-watt smile. "You must be Mr. Donner!"

"That's me," Kurt said. "And this here's Sue McConnell and her sister…" He snapped his fingers and looked at Ada.

"Amy," Ada said.

"It's a pleasure to meet you both. My name's Tiara King." She handed Krista a business card and then studied her face. "You look so much like that fugitive Warner. It's uncanny! I guess it's the ponytail, but you're a dead ringer!" She beamed the smile at them again and turned to Kurt. "We have to set up right now. The producer's slotted us into a seven o'clock live national feed. With all the sad news about Gibbon and Anacostia, they want to broadcast an upbeat story about perseverance and surmounting the odds."

"A national feed? That's great! Do anythin ya need," Kurt said. "Just lemme pop the beer in the fridge, then I'll help out."

"Her color came out of a bottle," Ada whispered in Krista's ear. "A stylist did it, but I don't get why she'd bother –"

"I don't care about her hair. Downs will vaporize this place while we're still on camera. We've got to get outta here *now*," she whispered back.

The driver turned from a control panel on the side of the van. "We have a satellite uplink. We can be live in ten if Timmie can get his gear plugged in and running."

"Wonderful!" Tiara hugged Krista. "In two hours, you'll be a star!"

"I can't wait," she said. "But I don't want America to see me like this. I look like a bum in these sweats."

"Oh, nonsense. You look like you just conquered the most dangerous mountain pass in North America."

"All the same, it's my fifteen minutes of fame. I want to look good," Krista said. "I'll go into town and get new clothes."

The Queen of Witch's Tit

Tiara stroked her chin. "Something Western. A shirt with plenty of fringes and plackets and pearl buttons. And a long skirt that doesn't show ankle. Our audience is old-fashioned."

"I know just the place," Kurt said. "Danzig's Western Wear, just downtown." He hugged Krista and her feet left the ground. "C'mon, you two! I'll take y'all down right now. Hop in the truck! It's my treat!"

"I'd rather drive and explore this wonderful city of yours," Krista said. "It's just downtown?"

"Yep. Make a left at the end of the driveway and go a mile. Can't miss it, it's right on Henderson just past Family Ammo," Kurt said. "Doncha get yerself in an accident down there, y'hear? Y'all are the stars of the show tonight!"

KRISTA AND ADA ROLLED DOWN a cracked main street lined with lovingly preserved wooden buildings. A brick town hall sat behind a small park with an old cannon painted red, white, and blue parked in the center. On the street, a man laid a gold papier-mâché key into the back of a pickup truck.

"I'm a heel," Krista said. "They're going to be disappointed when I don't come back."

"So you blew your chance to be the Queen of Witch's Tit," Ada said. "No big loss. Besides, later on tonight, they'll realize that Sue McConnell was really a wanted fugitive. Then they'll get all the attention they want."

"We'll be long gone before they realize that, I hope. How long till we turn?"

Ada looked at the satnav display. "Eight miles."

They drove through more fields of brown grass dotted with cows. After a few minutes, they found a city with brick buildings lining the streets. A sign on a corner bank displayed the date, and Ada pointed at it and whooped. "Hey, it's October first! My birthday was yesterday!"

"Really? Congratulations! You're a big sixteen-year-old now!"

"Almost seventeen," Ada said.

"One day closer. Well, Federals or no, we've got to celebrate."

Ada shook her head. "We oughta keep moving. You never know when they'll figure out we were in Witch's Bosom."

"I insist. Just a quick stop to get something sweet. It's your Sweet Sixteen, and it'd be wrong if we didn't celebrate. Besides, I've got a chocolate jones or something. If I don't stop at a bakery this very minute, I'll go mad."

"*Go* mad?" Ada squinted and pointed through the windshield. "Well, there you go. There's a bakery up there on the corner."

"Got any hot ones, Lorna?" Mark asked.

"Was a time guys never asked that," she said with a twinkle. "They just took a gander."

Mark blushed and stammered, "I, I was actually –"

"Asking 'bout donuts, I know. Got some fryin right now," the white-haired woman said. "But you'll burn yourself on 'em, you ain't careful."

"I'll have a dozen of those, please."

Lorna leaned back and yelled through an open door at the end of the counter. "Bring out a sizzlin dozen, Jimmy!" She turned back and leaned on the counter. "Anythin else?"

"Nah." He handed over some bills and saw a small monitor on the back wall running a newsfeed. "Any autopsy results yet?"

Lorna rearranged a display of cookies on the counter. "Ain't heard nuthin. Truth be told, I don't pay much attention to what them flannel-mouth liars do down in Washington. Those folk are all nuts, you ask me."

"That's for sure." He leaned over the counter. "You think somebody offed him?"

She nodded. "Hell, yeah. They do that all the time. And they call *us* the Wild West." She laughed and laid another cookie tray on the counter. "Anyway, not like I care if they offed another politician. No shortage of them in Washington. Like cocka-roaches behind the wall, those people."

"They'll always find another sucker to do the job."

"Yep. And it's 'bout time the gummint types finally started killin each other. They been tryin to kill *us* for years."

"They have?"

"Yep. Every few hours, they send one of them chemical planes over us, droppin poison all over the upcountry. And the bastards don't even try to hide it – you can go outside and see it yerself, them fat white stripes crossin the sky."

The Queen of Witch's Tit

"Oh, you mean the contrails?"

"No, I mean the *chemtrails*. God knows what all that shit's doing. But I always wear a gas mask outside, so I'm safe."

Mark rubbed his mouth, trying to contain a rising snort. Once the laugh was safely stifled, he slapped his hand on the counter. "So, hey, I know you got things to do. I'll just go hold up that column there while I'm waiting."

"Awright. I'll letcha know when your dozen's out," she said.

He wandered away from the counter and leaned against a column near the door. Antique vending machines filled the room, and old posters papered the walls, but he decided to rest his weary eyes instead of checking them out.

The bell over the door jingled, and a small blonde and a curvy redhead in a sweatsuit walked through, vaporizing Mark's boredom. The redhead was a looker, at least from the back, with the most spectacular rear end he'd ever seen – plump but firm, curvy but lean, the perfect hips of a thoroughbred All-American girl.

The redhead bent over to look at an old soda machine, and her pants tightened. He crossed his hands over his crotch, trying to cover his throbbing erection and appear casual at the same time, but the heat still rose to his face.

The little blonde pointed at something. The redhead turned to see, and he glimpsed a pair of mountain majesties that any man would kill to explore. She told the little blonde her back was killing her, and then she lifted her hoodie and worked her fingers into the skin just above her hips – skin covered in black lace. As if that wasn't enough to turn him on, she slipped her pants lower and he glimpsed lace-clad cleavage.

His erection went supercritical and threatened to blow, and his head spun as every blood cell reported to his groin for duty. Leaning against the column, he willed his heart to slow down before it leaped from his chest.

Her left hand slid across the keys of an old jukebox, and he saw no ring on the finger that counted, not even a tan line. Those fingers caressed the handle of an antique slot machine – up and down, so sensuously that he found himself breathing in time to her strokes.

"We oughta just get something and go," Ada said. "Let's get moving."

"Just a minute," Krista said. "I love these antique machines. Look, here's an old ATM. Back in the days before paytabs, people used these all the time." She glanced into the mirror above the keypad.

"Naw, that still works, honey," Lorna said. "We got a lot of people up here that won't use them paytabs. They say the gummint can track you if you carry them, so they spend cash."

"I'm not sure paytabs work like that," Krista said, fingering the one in her pocket.

"Don't matter none to me. I only take cash," Lorna said. "Whatcha in the mood for today?"

"What have you got for a Sweet Sixteen?" Krista asked.

"Acquisition, Warner!" Buta called out. "Confidence 95 percent. ATM camera, Gunbelt, Colorado, corner of Harrison and Spencer. A bakery called O'd to Joy." An aerial image of the building flickered onto the Wall.

"Zoom in," Downs said.

"Sir, this is an archived image. The Blackeyes are temporarily blocked by cloud cover," Buta said. "Meteorology says it should pass in a few minutes and allow us live imaging."

Downs wheeled to Tactical. "Hogue?"

"We have three units in the area. I'm moving them in now. Two Executive Teams at the passes east and west of Gunbelt on Route 50, and a Special Activity Group at Wilson Pass north of town. I'll provide ETA's when I have them, sir."

"Excellent. Launch the Talon and get the helos in the air." Downs studied the enlarged map on the Wall. "How'd she get past our checkpoints and into Gunbelt? Buta, backtrack and see where she came from."

"I'll try, but I need a vehicle to track, sir."

LORNA TURNED TO WRAP THE CHOCOLATE CAKES they'd ordered, and Krista pulled her change off the counter. She glanced through the window and saw no gray Silverbacks racing up Harrison Street, but a man leaning against a column was watching her.

The Queen of Witch's Tit

His face was strong and angular, framed by longish brown hair, and his almond-shaped eyes were golden brown; he was tall and so broad-shouldered that his white polo shirt strained to cover him. His big hands were politely clasped in front of him, hands with a real man's girth and strength, hands that could comfortably swing a heavy mallet and pound hot iron all day long. She flashed him a shy smile, and he nodded back.

She looked down at the floor and blushed; the teddy felt like it had shrunk and tightened around her chest. Clearing her throat, she turned to watch Lorna wrap the cakes. Inappropriate thoughts flooded her mind.

"Is something wrong?" Ada asked. "Your face is flushed."

"I'm okay," Krista croaked.

"No, really, it's like you're having an anaphylactic reaction, like you were stung by a bee and your…" Ada stopped when she saw Krista's nipples pushing up the hoodie, and she turned and saw the man against the column. "Omigod!" She giggled into her hand. "You're getting a Category Five over *that* trog?"

"Shut up!" Krista hissed.

THE REDHEAD TURNED TO LOOK OUT at Harrison Street. Unbelievably, her face outmatched the body – a perfect nose, plump lips that demanded kissing, and deep-blue eyes – and then she looked at him. She blushed and smiled like a schoolgirl, and he fell in love instantly.

She was gorgeous, with a sprinkle of girl-next-door freckles across that perfect nose, and those lips…suddenly, he remembered where he'd seen them before, and the realization froze him into place.

He was looking at the fugitive Krista Warner.

A white-haired man in an apron walked through a side door and handed Lorna a box. "Here ya go," she said, "and remember, they're still hot."

He cleared his throat. "Thanks, Lorna." He left with his mind dazed and his body aching.

"Sir, we've regained visuals," Buta said. "The vehicle they're driving is a K2 all-terrain crossover registered to a Kenneth Herrera of Colorado Springs. He doesn't appear to be in it."

"Excellent," Downs said. "Hogue, find Herrera and bring him here for cognitive mapping. Buta, how'd that truck get there?"

"The furthest we can backtrack the vehicle is to a hotel in Witch's Bosom, eight miles northeast of Gunbelt."

"Hogue, we need firepower in that town. How long till you can get more units there without using the teams pursuing Warner?"

She scanned a map on her monitor. "I can have eight Collateral units from Fort Carbon there in approximately ninety minutes, sir. We can use them in an area this remote."

"Agreed. Send them in and find the Activist collaborators. No, belay that. Just tell the Collaterals to sanitize the place. That's something they can do." He pursed his lips and watched as Warner climbed into a white truck. "She doesn't seem to be in a hurry, so she's unaware of the pursuit. When will the Talon be over the target?"

"Twenty-seven minutes over target, twenty-four minutes to launch range, sir," Hogue said.

"Good. When that drone's in range, launch two missiles and destroy that truck. I don't care where she is or what's around her. Take her out even if there's collateral damage."

"The pursuit teams might be nearby. What should I tell them, sir?" Hogue asked.

"Nothing. If they're around that truck when the missiles hit, then their fate's in God's hands. I'm not taking any chances. Warner won't get away this time."

MARK SLID INTO THE DRIVER'S SEAT. "I just saw Warner!"

"Where?" Dani asked.

"In the bakery. She's with a girl." He picked up his binoculars and focused on the bakery entrance.

"Are you sure? Did she look like this?" She held up her tablet with Warner's picture on the screen.

"Exactly like that. I'm sure it's her. Here, see for yourself when she comes out."

She took the binoculars just as the door to the bakery opened. A tall redhead holding a box and a paper cup looked up and down the street, and

Dani clicked the capture button on the binoculars. The picture appeared on her tablet and she zoomed in. "Holy shit. You're right."

He thumbed the truck on and watched Warner walk to a white car. "Call it in. She's driving a white K2 with Colorado tags."

Dani tapped a button on her tablet as Mark pulled out of the space. "Three, this is Four, come in," she said. "Yeah, Hank, we spotted her...I'm not kidding, no, we just spotted her in Gunbelt...yeah, she is, a white K2 with Colorado tags. Get down here and notify everyone else. We'll be in pursuit. I'll contact you when we know more."

He pulled up to the traffic light. On the other side of the intersection, Warner turned right, and he flicked his left turn signal. "She's going north on Route 24," he said. "If she heads outta town, we'll pull her over out there. I don't want any attention."

Dani unclipped her shotgun from the rack.

"I want this to be a quiet operation, Dani. We're not going in with guns blazing."

"I know," she said. "I just want to be prepared in case things go wrong."

TERMS COMMONLY USED IN 2043

Aluminati: Pejorative slang for members of the Second Creation movement, an extremist group within the Archangelists. The term implies that they wore tin-foil hats, although there is no evidence this actually occurred.

Archangelist: a member of the Archangelic Church of the Son of Christ.

Arkie: Popular term for an Archangelist.

Base-M: A hallucinogenic street drug that was growing in popularity in the early 2040's. Due to eradication efforts, the drug disappeared by mid-century and is unknown today.

BoHo: Bohemian Homeless, itinerant urban artists of the working class.

Collateral Tactics Unit: The military arm of the National Security Forces, known popularly as the Ironshirts.

Corporate-Americans: Corporations. The 31st Amendment provided them all the rights and protections of human citizens, as well as exemption from taxation.

Elders: Leaders of the Second Creation movement. See *Aluminati*.

Ellesmere A4: An enteric retrovirus weaponized by the US Army to incapacitate enemy forces. It readily mutated into the deadly Ellesmere A7 variant and was deemed too unstable for combat use. See *Neovirus*.

Executives: Elite operatives of the National Security Forces, often used for assassinations and surveillance.

Federals: Popular term for the National Security Forces.

Fug: A mixture of acidic coal smoke and ground fog, primarily affecting the eastern two-thirds of the country. The word is believed to be a contraction of the F-word and Fog.

Great Correction, The: A prolonged recession that eliminated the American middle class and placed all economic power in the hands of corporations.

Joe Slick: Navy term for the Lancet Missile.

Lancet Missile: A hypersonic stealth missile. See *Joe Slick*.

MRC: The Media Regulatory Corporation, a public monopoly formed to control the dissemination of news and information on the Internet and other electronic media.

MRCS: Missile Release Control System, an automated targeting and launch system installed on Patriot class submarines. It was intended to reduce human error and the amount of manpower required to operate a missile boat.

Neovirus: Civilian term for the RVE viruses Ellesmere A4 and A7.

<u>NSF</u>: National Security Forces, whose primary mission is to uncover and suppress domestic dissent. See *Federals*.

<u>Patriot Class Boat</u>: A guided-missile submarine originally designed to carry Warhammer cruise missiles. The submarines were retrofitted in 2041 to carry the Lancet missile with the new W104 nuclear warhead. The Pacific Fleet boats in 2043 were:

SSGN 807 – USS *Patrick Henry*	SSGN 814 – USS *Ethan Allen*
SSGN 808 – USS *Paul Revere*	SSGN 815 – USS *Nathaniel Greene*
SSGN 809 – USS *Thomas Paine*	SSGN 816 – USS *John Paul Jones*
SSGN 811 – USS *Nathan Hale*	SSGN 817 – USS *Seth Warner*
SSGN 812 – USS *John Adams*	SSGN 818 – USS *James Otis*
SSGN 813 – USS *John Hancock*	

<u>PRC</u>: The Persian Regional Conflict, a naval and aerial war in which the United States sought to prevent the unification of Persian and Arab populations into one nation. It ended in a stalemate and an embargo on the shipment of Persian Gulf oil to the United States.

<u>Ranks:</u> The rank and file, or the lower class. This group once comprised skilled laborers but after the Great Correction came to include most of the surviving middle class as well. Also known as Breeders, Naggers, Mullets or Working Class.

<u>Recombin:</u> A virophage engineered to attack Neovirus.

<u>SAG (Special Activity Group):</u> Action squads of the National Security Forces, often used for pursuit, capture, and localized suppression efforts.

<u>Soviet Bloc:</u> Also known as the Group of Sixteen, those nations allied with Russia to achieve nuclear parity with the United States.

<u>Stiffer:</u> A person who has died on the street from an untreated illness.

<u>Tenpez:</u> A coin containing ten grams of gold issued by the State of California in the 2020's. In 2043, its value was approximately one thousand dollars. The name is believed to be inspired by a candy popular in the mid-20's.

<u>Transition, The:</u> Archangelist euphemism for a hostile takeover of the United States government.

<u>Transportation, The:</u> The forced resettlement of the urban poor from Detroit and Cleveland after a period of rioting and urban warfare in those cities. See *The Troubles*.

<u>Troubles, The:</u> A period marked by the broad repeal of civil liberties and repression of public dissent, spanning from early 2024 to late 2027. See *The Transportation*.

www.ingramcontent.com/pod-product-compliance
Lightning Source LLC
Chambersburg PA
CBHW020244150626
46552CB00020B/143